CLAIMING HIS BOUGHT BRIDE

BY

RACHEL BAILEY

AND

SEDUCING THE ENEMY'S DAUGHTER

BY

JULES BENNETT

MILLS & BOON

"No point hiding your reaction to me, Lily."

Her eyes narrowed in contradiction, but her chest moved in rapid, shallow breaths.

A smile of victory threatened, but he let only one corner of his mouth curve up. "Don't worry, there will be time for that. A lifetime of opportunities."

Gasping, Lily stepped back, rubbing her palms over the skin he had held. "No, Damon. I agreed to marry you. I agreed to have your baby, which it so happens I'm already carrying. But I did *not* agree to share your bed. It won't be that type of marriage."

The smile playing on his lips extended into a full-blown version. A challenge. He loved a challenge if the prize was worth winning. And this woman in front of him was worth bedding— he knew that well.

CLAIMING HIS BOUGHT BRIDE

BY
RACHEL BAILEY

Published in Great Britain 2011
Harlequin Mills & Boon Limited,
Eton House, 18-24 Paradise Road, Richmond, Surrey TW9 1SR

© Rachel Robinson 2010

ISBN: 978 0 263 88090 8

51-0111

Harlequin Mills & Boon policy is to use papers that are natural, renewable and recyclable products and made from wood grown in sustainable forests. The logging and manufacturing processes conform to the legal environmental regulations of the country of origin.

Printed and bound in Spain
by Litografia Rosés S.A., Barcelona

To my own personal hero, John.
For everything.

Thanks to
Diana Ventimiglia for believing in this book
and for her continued guidance.

Jennifer Schober for her faith in me.

Robyn Grady, Barbara Jeffcott Geris, Melissa James
and Sharon Archer for their brilliant critiquing.

Rachel Bailey developed a serious book addiction at a young age (via Peter Rabbit and Jemima Puddleduck) and has never recovered. Just how she likes it. She went on to gain degrees in psychology and social work, but is now living her dream—writing romance for a living.

She lives on a piece of paradise on Australia's Sunshine Coast with her hero and four dogs, and loves to sit with a dog or two, overlooking the trees and reading books from her ever-growing to-be-read pile.

Rachel would love to hear from you and can be contacted through her website, www.rachelbailey.com.

Dear Reader,

I love a reunion story—especially with a couple where the passion still runs deep. So it was such a pleasure to sink into Lily Grayson's life when she meets with her ex-lover, the rich and gorgeous Damon Blakely.

Having been brought up around art and galleries, it was natural for me to infuse Lily's life with touches of the art world through her job as a gallery curator. Monet's series of water lilies have always spoken to me, and Lily shares my appreciation (though Damon prefers a different series by Monet—one that more reflects his personality!).

As an avid reader of Desire™ books, I'm thrilled my own first Desire™ novel is finally here. Lily and Damon's story will always hold that special "firstborn" place in my heart and I hope you enjoy reading it.

Best wishes,

Rachel

One

Lily Grayson placed a hand on her still-slender waist and searched the familiar ballroom. Shimmering silver and gold streamers hung from the expansive twenty-foot ceiling; a string quartet provided presupper music, which blended with the chatter of two hundred black-tie guests. A high-society birthday party was in full swing, but enjoying the festivities could play no part in Lily's plan.

Lips dry and her breathing shallow, her gaze flew from face to face, looking for the man she needed to speak with urgently. The man she'd once loved, but could never trust with her heart…or their unborn baby's emotional well-being.

Damon Blakely.

The multimillionaire corporate raider whom men feared and women coveted.

A waiter paused, tray covered with flutes of crystalline champagne and fine-stemmed glasses of wine, but she shook her head and continued her circuit of Travis Blakely's sixtieth birthday party. In the six months she'd been with Damon, she'd visited his uncle's Melbourne home several times, but not once since their breakup almost three months ago. Since Damon had let her down when she'd needed him most.

The thought led back to her gran, home alone tonight, recovering from another bout of pneumonia, part of the ill health that had incapacitated her recently. If only Gran would accept more help, but she refused to move in with Lily or let Lily live with her. Gran valued her independence and Lily couldn't help but feel powerless. But she wouldn't be sidetracked with thoughts of her beloved grandmother now. She'd see Gran taken care of, one way or another.

Tonight she needed to find Damon.

Lily continued searching from guest to guest as she wove through the crowd. The women in evening gowns of satins and sequins reminded her of peacocks parading for attention, and the sounds of clinking glasses and a hundred indistinct conversations culminated in an assault on her ears. She'd rather be anywhere than here—this was not her world. But it was *his* world and she needed to find him.

Searching still, she swung around. Her heartbeat stalled before exploding in her chest as her gaze collided with his.

Dead ahead, suave in a tux, red wine in one hand, the other free to shake the hands of acquaintances who stepped into his path, Damon smiled and passed comments with those who waylaid him. The charming lord of all he surveyed. But his distinctive eyes, with the black ring circling the ice-blue iris, were focused on her.

An exquisite shiver passed down her spine at the intensity of his gaze and her body reacted with predictable awareness. Lily closed her eyes to tamp down the response but her lids immediately fluttered open. He stirred within her an overwhelming hunger. Even now, she couldn't keep her eyes from devouring him.

Damon towered over the other guests, and she realized that instead of searching for him, she should have stood on the entrance stairs to spot his characteristic waves of midnight-dark hair. Or closed her eyes and let her body find his with the magnetic link that still drew her to him.

He finished talking to a rotund man, who laughed heartily at Damon's parting comment, then took several strides toward her before being tapped on the shoulder by an elderly statesman Lily recognized from the newspapers.

She eased out a breath—it seemed she wouldn't need to approach him. He was coming to her. As her blood heated and skin tightened at the thought, she took an involuntary step back. Amazing. Even after all his neglect and the utter anguish he'd caused, the force of her attraction was still overpowering.

Leaning against a cool pillar, she waited, taking in the scene of Melbourne's elite at play. At odds with those around her, she'd never wanted a life of extravagance. Growing up with Gran, who'd struggled to keep a roof over their heads after her son—Lily's father—had gambled the family home away, she'd wished only for security. Financial stability, no more.

The cloying scent of too many expensive perfumes and colognes mingling in the enclosed space made her head spin, and she looked longingly toward the exit. She needed to get this over with. The stress of trying to anticipate Damon's reaction to her news was pushing her to breaking point. She was still coming to grips with it herself.

Finished with the statesman, Damon took the last few strides to reach her, his broad shoulders and long legs showcased by the tuxedo.

He didn't say a word, just seemed to drink her in, his sensuous mouth parted slightly before he downed the rest of his wine and discarded the glass on the tray of a passing waiter. Then he clasped her elbow and slowly reached down to press a kiss to her cheek, a little too close to the corner of her mouth for propriety, but then Damon had never worried about convention when it clashed with his interests.

"Hello, Lily." He seemed to roll her name around his mouth before delivering it in his deep voice, something that had always sent her pulse erratic. "You look gorgeous."

His compliment hummed through her blood, even as she told herself not to listen. She'd learned long ago that people said what they wanted you to hear. A lesson she'd relearned recently thanks to the man still holding her arm.

She swallowed and found her voice. "Hello, Damon. You look good, too. You always did in a tuxedo," she conceded.

His mouth curved and pale blue eyes gleamed. "I'd rather hoped you preferred me out of my tuxedo."

An unbidden image of them entwined on his bed rose in her mind. The memory of his tanned, muscled body contrasted against crisp fine cotton sheets made her inwardly groan. When an ache deep and low in her stomach began to throb, Lily gritted her teeth and withdrew her elbow in a move others in the room wouldn't notice, but which sent a clear message to Damon—touching was a right he no longer possessed.

A raised eyebrow told her he'd taken her meaning and wasn't offended. He sank his hands into his front trouser pockets. Confident and sexy to the core.

She needed to tell him now, before his lethal sexuality scrambled her brain further. Needed to get him somewhere private so she could tell him about their baby as well as her plans to move on with her life.

He leaned close and whispered in her ear, his warm breath tickling sensuously. "There's something I'd like to talk to you about in private."

Lily froze. Had he guessed? No, he couldn't have—she wasn't showing yet and at fourteen weeks, her morning sickness had passed. There were no clues and no one else knew, she'd made certain of it. Her secret was safe, until she told Damon in her own words.

And now he wanted to speak to her in private—it seemed fate had cut her a break for once. She would grab the opportunity. "When?"

He gave a self-satisfied grin. "How does now suit?"

Her legs felt weak but she maintained the cool facade. "Where?"

For reply he took her hand and led her away. As firecrackers shot through her veins, Lily shook her head.

Obviously she needed to make clearer her position on the no-touching rule. However, for expediency's sake, this one last time she would allow the contact.

Though perhaps she shouldn't take his acts of entitlement and their effects on her so personally; all women seemed to succumb to Damon Blakely's innate sensuality when they were in his orbit. Far more important to her were other qualities—traits Damon seemed incapable of understanding or displaying. Emotional reliability. Prioritizing others' needs before his own. Worse, she knew that would never change.

He drew her down a quiet hallway toward the rear of the stark mansion where he'd grown up, until she recognized the heavy double sliding doors of Travis Blakely's private gallery.

Damon flicked on the lights and her art-gallery curator's eye was drawn to the priceless artwork hanging on the walls and enclosed in glass on podiums.

She drifted forward and ran a finger along the edge of one glass cabinet, not turning to him, even when he spoke.

"We haven't been alone in, how long?" A wall of heat moved behind her and for one crazy moment she let herself simply absorb his warmth in hope of soothing her chilled heart.

"Almost three months." She turned, bringing her within a foot of him. Her heart skipped a beat to find him so close.

"How have you been? Your gran?" He casually reached to toy with a strand of her long silver-blond hair, sending a frisson of heat across her skin.

"I've been fine," she whispered, wishing her voice had been stronger but unable to help his effect on her.

"Gran's been under the weather, but she's coming out of it now."

At least physically. Her medical bills had mounted up and, with no assets or income besides the old age pension, Lily was worried for the woman who'd raised her since the age of twelve. Gran had already lost so much, her son, her health, her house, her nest egg…

Damon released the lock of hair and grazed his knuckles down the side of her cheek in a touch as light as butterfly wings. "That must have been hard for you."

Lily nodded, torn between her body's reaction to Damon's touch and the thoughts his words evoked. She owed Gran everything, loved her beyond measure.

"I suppose she still won't let you help." His voice was quiet, beguiling.

On the verge of slipping under his sensual thrall, she caught herself. She had to wrest back power over her own body.

She stepped away and moved to the other side of the glass cage, putting the artwork between them as a token symbol of protection. Only then did she trust herself to reply. "She says that after raising me to stand on my own two feet, the last thing she wants is for me to be financially behind the eight ball because of her."

Damon didn't appear to feel thwarted by her physical retreat, more like she'd thrown down the gauntlet and he'd accepted. He prowled the trail she'd followed, yet bypassed her position and leaned against a nearby column, ankles crossed, hands resting on narrow hips. The pose of a predator biding his time. "Have you come up with any options?"

She took a breath, held it, then admitted, "Not yet. But I will." Finding a way to look after Gran was a priority.

He pushed off the column, rolling his shoulders as he hunted the shadows of the room, before turning and ending squarely in front of her.

His eyes seemed to consume her whole. "You seem sure about that." His arched eyebrow told her that he didn't share her confidence.

Truth be told, she had no idea *how* she'd make sure Gran was taken care of, but she wouldn't consider failure.

"Don't worry about me, Damon, I'll find a way." The heat radiating from him, the raw sexual hunger in his gaze, made it difficult to think, to say anything, but she needed to change the subject. "It seems I should be more worried about you. I heard Travis disinherited you after we broke up."

"Ah, yes. The millions of tainted dollars, this loving family home." He swept an arm around, eyes filled with derision. "Everything."

"Including the one thing you've always coveted." *Had wanted more than he'd wanted her.* His late father's company, BlakeCorp.

Looking down at her hands, she blinked away any remnants of emotion that thought still evoked. She was over it. Over him.

Movement drew her attention back to his face. He was closer again. The barely visible tension in his features dissolved, replaced by his usual arrogant self-assurance.

Hands clasped behind his back, Damon leaned in to whisper in her ear. "I have an offer for you. To help your gran."

Undiluted shock surged through her entire body. Her neck snapped back and she sought his eyes. It was the last thing she'd expected. "What offer?"

"I'll buy her a house. One with all modern safety features for someone her age, but where she still has her independence. I'll pay off all her outstanding medical expenses. And I'll employ a private nurse to help until she's back on her feet. Longer, if she'll allow it." He smiled, assured his offer was too good to refuse. "You know she'll accept. She knows I can afford it and she always had a soft spot for me."

"Why would you do that?"

He shrugged and took her hand, drawing her still closer, pressing his advantage. "Travis invited me here tonight to make me an offer. I want to extend the offer to include you. And your Gran."

Lily narrowed her eyes. "I thought you'd both sworn never to lay eyes on the other again." In fact, she'd been astonished when Travis's secretary had rung to follow up on Lily's RSVP tonight, and had revealed that Damon was expected. But she'd immediately seen her chance to speak with him—Damon had been out of the country and, unsure of when he'd jet off again, she'd grabbed the first opportunity to see him she could.

But she had to stay on guard. Game playing came as naturally to the Blakelys as making money. "Why would Travis come to you now and make an offer?"

"Been keeping up on the family goings-on, Lily?" His thumb ran up and down on the wrist he held. "Perhaps you still have my best interests at heart."

Lily blew out a dismissive breath and withdrew her hand. Her stomach churned. How much more of this game could she take? "Damon, for pity's sake, cut the theatrics and answer my question."

He smiled—the slow smile of a panther assured of catching its prey. Though, just who he thought his prey was this time—her or Travis—she wasn't certain.

"Travis received some tragic news from his doctor today." Damon didn't even try to pretend that any news that was tragic for Travis would adversely affect him. There had been no love lost between the two long before she'd met either of them.

She knew Travis had raised Damon with more than an iron rod—he'd also used emotional abuse and deliberate neglect as tools to rear his older brother's son. Damon had never wanted to talk much about it, but it'd been easy enough to put two and two together—and the answer had broken her heart. Perhaps she'd given Damon one chance too many when they'd been together, knowing how he'd never really escaped the torment of his childhood. But she couldn't go on giving him chances now. Things had changed.

One thing she knew, Damon would never forgive Travis. What surprised her was that they'd lasted so long without either one destroying the line of inheritance.

She tried to gauge Damon's feelings from his expression but failed. "If he's talking to you again, the news is obviously something that's made him confront his mortality."

Damon nodded. "Despite retaining the services of the best cardiovascular surgeon in the country, last month's operation to repair his heart was unsuccessful. Test results that came in today confirmed it. And he's apparently not a good candidate for a heart transplant—lack of donors, his age and the mistreatment he's given the rest of his body have seen to that. He pressed them for a prognosis. They've given him twelve months to live."

Despite Travis's mistreatment of Damon as a child, she couldn't help feeling a pang of sympathy.

And sympathy for Damon, faced with losing the only family he had left, albeit an estranged and loathed family member. Impulsively she reached out and laid her hand on his forearm, stroking the material covering his golden-brown skin.

"Damon, I'm sorry."

He made a dismissive sound and clamped down on her hand with his free one—not allowing her sympathy, but not permitting her to break the contact, either. "Actually, there's good news come from this. He's prepared to revise his will."

Lily blinked several times. "He'll give you your father's company back?" Was that why Damon was at this party tonight?

A glint appeared in his eye. "That was my price."

She hesitated, holding off congratulating him on achieving his longtime ambition until she'd heard the cost.

"It seems Travis has become sentimental. He wants to leave a legacy to his family." Damon's scornful smile clearly showed his opinion of his uncle's change of heart.

Lily frowned in confusion. "He's leaving you everything?"

"No, he's still determined I'll never touch a penny of his money. But he offered to leave his entire portfolio of assets and cash to my child. He said my child will be rich." Damon's smile didn't reach his eyes. "He failed to take into account that any child of mine would be rich without his *generous* offer." He moved away, restless, tension radiating from him in waves she could almost feel, but the emotion was tightly leashed.

Any child of his? He was seriously thinking about children? She'd hoped that, despite his incredibly busy life, he'd want to play some role in their baby's upbringing—though not a role that could allow him to repeat the cycle of the Blakely's cold, emotionally harsh parenting style. Perhaps something more like a big brother. She'd assumed he wouldn't want more than that—he'd told her more than once he didn't want children.

He stopped before a portrait of a Victorian woman surrounded by children dressed as small adults, gazing at the figures as if they held secret wisdom.

"Your child?" Instinctively her hand went to her belly as she watched his broad, tense back. And then another thought struck—had she missed a vital piece of Damon's history where he already had a child?

He turned in a cold, almost casual way and faced her again, this time with several feet distance between them. "*If* I conceive a child before he dies."

Lily nodded, with a streak of intense, perverse joy that Damon had no other children before the one she carried.

No. She gritted her teeth. She had to stop letting possessive thoughts like these sneak through her defenses. They were counterproductive to her goals. She needed to tell him her news, ask his cooperation and keep both her baby and heart protected in the process.

Stray possessive thoughts could play no part in her future relationship with him. She needed her wits about her. She was prepared to provide for this baby if Damon rejected fatherhood or denied paternity; she earned a good wage as assistant curator at the gallery. But she'd hoped with all her heart he'd want to make sure his child had every advantage. It seemed from his comments he would.

Rich was another story though. She didn't want Damon's fortune. The Blakely family was a stellar example of how excessive wealth corrupted morals.

Her hand found the silver heart pendant at her throat. "What did you tell him?"

He looked at her, down his long, proud nose. "I said no."

The vision of the two Blakely lions squaring off earlier in the night was strangely compelling. "So that's when he offered you your father's company?"

"He dangled BlakeCorp as a bribe and then threw in a touch of blackmail. Told me he'd leave all his worldly goods to his cousin's son, Mark, if I refused. And Mark would break it up and sell everything to the highest bidder—as long as that bidder wasn't me, as per my dear uncle's directions."

Lily had met Mark once at a family dinner. He had the Blakely ruthless, money-hungry gaze and it had chilled her from across the table. "So how will you produce this baby?"

Curiosity made her ask. She knew she should tell him now about her pregnancy, but first she desperately wanted to know what plan he'd devised.

"Ah, good question. And it's not just *any* baby. He wants a legitimate heir." Damon lifted a sardonic brow.

She drew in one long breath. "You'll marry?"

"Which is where you come in." Suddenly he was close again, so close she could feel the heat from his body, smell the rich red wine on his breath. "I want to marry *you*." He clasped both her hands and smiled in a good imitation of reasonableness.

Lily's head swam and her throat felt thick. His complete disinterest in having children in the past had allowed a hope he'd let her raise their baby on her own. But things had changed.

The room around her began a slow spin. If she told him now about her pregnancy, nothing would stop his pursuit of her. He'd made a decision that he wanted a child. Her child. For the sake of BlakeCorp, not because of love or commitment.

Damon always got what he wanted.

She bit down on the rising panic—everything had veered out of control within short minutes. Her simple plan of doing the right thing and telling him about the baby, asking him for financial support, and looking for a mutually agreeable role he could play in the child's life was now a complicated tangle.

"Lily?" He lifted her chin with a finger. "If you marry me, you and your gran would both be taken care of beyond your wildest dreams."

Still she couldn't speak. Couldn't think.

"I know it's a lot to take in, but this will work very well for us." He leaned in to feather a kiss along her jawline.

Damon was a man others regarded as beyond powerful, but she'd known from the start that his greatest power was his ability to enthrall. To mesmerize her with negligible effort. The knowledge, however, was little protection. She felt herself falling…. His lips brushed the sensitive skin of her throat, leaving a decadently moist trail.

"There were things left—" he paused and nipped her earlobe "—unfinished between us last time. I'm not fond of unfinished business, Lily."

She swallowed hard. "You mean I left you and you hate losing."

She felt his mouth curve into a smile against her skin. "We were good together before," he said between smooth kisses along her throat. "A marriage between us could work."

Would it? Her knees felt boneless from the ministrations he was paying her neck. It was obvious sexual compatibility would never be a problem. But now she couldn't play *make a decent go of it* or just *try* it. Breaking up over him letting her down that last day might seem an overreaction to some, but that had merely been the last straw for their relationship. She remembered the disillusionment when he dropped her home on her birthday, halfway through a romantic dinner, because work had called. Another time, he'd become so immersed in a stock market fluctuation, he'd totally forgotten to meet her. It was a day she'd really needed him—the tenth anniversary of her parents' deaths. Both times he'd promised to make it up to her, and she supposed he had, but she'd learned Damon wasn't a person she could rely on to be there when she needed him most. And her obligation now was first and foremost to the tiny life dependent on her.

Her own mother had put her husband's needs ahead of her child's. As a professional gambler, Lily's father had needed to travel, mostly in poverty, and Lily had been dragged from place to place, craving stability, routine, reliability. Until the age of twelve, when she'd moved in with her grandmother, she'd known none.

This baby's needs came before hers or Damon's.

She needed to find a way to make this new development work for her.

"If I were to agree," she croaked out through her dry throat. She swallowed, willing her voice to work. "I have some conditions of my own."

His eyes widened slightly but he nodded. "Tell me."

"I'd marry you if it meant Gran would be taken care of." Lily stepped back and wrapped her arms around herself. She'd walk over broken glass for that sweet woman.

"I sense a 'but' coming." His mouth curved.

"But bringing a baby into the equation is a different matter entirely." She took a deep breath and stepped farther away, outside his aura. "I'd want to bring this baby up on my own. One thing I learned from living with my parents and then Gran is it's not the number of people in the family that matters, it's the capacity to love, and prioritize each other. To be emotionally reliable for each other." Gran would be there for her now, too, and that was all she needed.

She braced herself to explain, to tell him the truth. As their baby's father, he deserved it, and she needed him to understand. "I'd never cut you off from your own child, but you have to know already that your version of commitment isn't what a child needs. Your priorities…" She trailed off, not sure how to word it without causing offence. Not sure how to tell him she didn't want the cycle of the Blakely men's frozen hearts thrust upon her innocent baby.

Uncertain, she clasped her hands together in front of her belly. "We would work out beforehand what role you'd want to play. Visitation rights that don't interfere too much with your work."

Damon thrust his hands into his trouser pockets. "Visitation rights?" The look in his eyes said he had no intention of being that far removed from his child, but she pressed on.

"I also want to be financially stable enough to know that my child will always have a home and things he or she needs. You'll make an account for the baby, in my name. I need to be secure." Her own wage was enough if push came to shove, but this was a way to ensure her baby would never go without.

He nodded, eyes calculating as she spoke. "Go on."

"And lastly, I want a contract ensuring these conditions are met." She raised her chin, hoping he didn't argue this point because it was an absolute bluff—she was in too far to walk away. Her baby's needs were paramount.

"You don't trust me, Lily?" A rare emotion passed across his face, but she wasn't sure it was hurt. Far more likely he was mocking her.

"I'll marry you and have the baby you need, Damon, but I'll raise it on my own with money from both of us.

Sign a contract to that effect or you'll have to find someone else."

He rocked back on his heels, a smile playing around his mouth. "You drive a hard bargain. Good for you." The smile that had threatened finally broke free and this time it reached his eyes. "These are precisely the qualities I want in the mother of my child."

He stepped forward but she moved sideways, evading him. She was shaking inside and, knowing the negotiations were at a critical point, needed all the distance from his masculine solidness she could manage. "You haven't answered. Will you sign a contract with my conditions?"

He reached for her, playing to her weakness, but she again evaded and crossed her arms under her breasts. "Damon?"

His gaze rested on hers, intense and unwavering. "My child will grow up where he should—in my house with his mother and father."

She felt the blood drain from her face. Once Damon made up his mind, he was unwavering…and she had so little bargaining room. Her mind raced so fast she began to feel light-headed. She needed to find a way to give herself some emotional space in this arrangement.

But there was only one option, and she sent up a quick prayer that he agreed, because she couldn't back out of this deal now. "I'll concede to living in your home, but only on the condition that we have separate bedrooms. On opposite sides of the house."

One side of his mouth quirked. "Are you sure that's what you really want, Lily?"

Her body screamed *no,* even as her mind continued to fine-tune her position. "This will be a paper marriage—we'll live separate lives under one roof. I won't share your bed, Damon. Now or ever."

He chuckled with genuine amusement. "Ah, sweetheart, you're forgetting the child we need to make." He cast her a look that in the past would have made her come to him. "I'm looking forward to that part immensely."

Lily finally allowed herself to return the smile. She knew he'd try to change the parameters, turn the situation to his benefit, but at least if she could get him to sign a contract, she had a leg to stand on.

If only she felt as confident about resisting the invitation to his bed.

"As it happens, that won't be a problem," she said, laying her hands over her waist. "I'm already pregnant with your baby."

Two

Damon called up all his famed reserves of self-control to avoid swaying on his feet.

She was pregnant?

His head swam as if he'd been sucker punched. He supposed he had been. In all the preplanning and strategizing, he'd not once factored in this possibility. It had just never occurred to him that she already nurtured his baby inside her body.

His gaze fixed on her stomach, searching for answers. He found none, just her flawless pale fingers stretched across the narrow expanse of her waist.

Heart beating slower than usual with shock, mind trying to make sense of the new information, he lifted his eyes to meet hers. She stood very still; a serene mask covered her features. How could she be so calm after delivering news this momentous?

Then it came—the crack in Lily's veneer. She pulled one side of her full bottom lip between her straight white teeth and bit delicately down. He'd lost count of the number of people he'd played in his line of work, the number of meetings where he'd wrested control from unwilling board members. The key was always to wait until that small sign of unease appeared—to be able to recognize it—then to act without mercy.

Yet he remained unmoving, emotions frozen.

She was carrying his child?

Then, as if time caught up with crashing reality, his body came back to life. Heart pumped hard, mind cleared, adrenaline flowed.

He had a child. That baby in her womb *belonged to him.* He'd never considered children in his future, not until his uncle's ultimatum, but now that the reality presented itself, he knew he'd *never* let that child go.

Lily's condition of separate bedrooms be damned. He hadn't been prepared to sign his name to that idea even before her announcement, but now there was no way in hell he'd let her create distance between them. The baby and the woman carrying it were his and would stay that way no matter what he needed to do to ensure it.

He glanced over at her. She was exquisite with her forest-green eyes, her alabaster skin, her silver-blond hair glimmering under the soft light. He desired her like no other. Even since first meeting her at a gallery fund-raiser, she'd gotten under his skin. And now she'd be forever tied to him.

Unwilling to show her any of his innermost reactions, he spoke with little inflection to his words. "You played that card close to your chest, sweetheart."

"Not—" she cleared her throat "—not really. I suspected…thought I knew…but only had it confirmed by a doctor today. It's why I came here tonight. To find you and tell you." Her hands remained across her belly, almost protectively.

"So you were pregnant when you left me." His voice was flat, almost accusing, even to his own ears.

She grimaced. "I didn't know I was."

He raised a brow. The outcome was the same. And he had another question while they were on the topic. "Tell me honestly, Lily, why did you leave?"

With shaking hands, she pushed a strand of hair behind an ear. "Is there any purpose in dredging this up now?"

Maybe not, but the question had bothered him— pride had kept him from pursuing an answer. But now she was here in the flesh, he needed an answer. "We're getting married. I think a short analysis on the breakdown of our past relationship has relevance."

She lifted her chin, but ruined the effect by biting down again on her full bottom lip. "Because I was too low a priority in your life."

That again! He'd prioritized her above almost everything, higher than a woman had ever been, and she still wanted more?

Needing to move, to use some of the adrenaline hurtling through his veins, he strolled with controlled movements to look into a glass cage enclosing an ancient clay urn. Several museums had offered exorbitant amounts of money to buy the artifact, and yet here it'd stayed. Trapped by Travis in this mausoleum, the way Damon himself had been for many years.

Nothing mattered more to him than reclaiming his heritage. He'd been made to feel like a poor, pathetic relation, when his father's business savvy was the only reason Travis wasn't still working as a junior assistant somewhere. It was time to restore rightful order to the world.

He swiveled to face Lily, the only woman who'd ever sparked dreams that didn't include BlakeCorp. The innate sensuality in the way she moved; her mouth, made for such sweetness and such sin; her heart, so untainted by the blackness that consumed his.

But everything had changed. And he needed to be very clear about his priorities. This woman was the key to BlakeCorp…and his baby.

"We'll marry as soon as I can arrange it." He stepped forward and grasped her upper arms, ignoring his body's insistent response to her. His blood had heated the moment he saw her in the ballroom, and now his groin screamed for attention.

He heard her breath catch at the touch but she tried to smother it, to deny his power over her, simply nodding her answer.

He let his voice drop to the seductive timbre she always responded to. "No point hiding your reaction to me, Lily."

Her eyes narrowed in contradiction but her chest moved in rapid, shallow breaths.

A smile of victory threatened, but he only let one

corner of his mouth curve up. "Don't worry, there will be time for that. A lifetime of opportunities."

Gasping, Lily stepped back, rubbing her palms over the skin he had held. "No, Damon. I agreed to marry you. I agreed to have your baby, which it so happens I'm already carrying. But I did *not* agree to share your bed. It won't be that type of marriage."

The smile playing on his lips extended into a full-blown version. A challenge. He loved a challenge if the prize was worth winning. And this woman in front of him was worth bedding—he knew that well.

He let out a slow, easy breath and sank his hands into his trouser pockets. "Let's just see how things unfold."

"I know how things will unfold. We'll be married in name only. We might live under the same roof, but we will be living separate lives. I let you hurt me before when I relied on you, needed you. And every time you had to choose between your business and me, you chose it, no matter how high my needs were or how minor the work issue. Be warned, I won't be as naive this time."

He waved her claim away. "Ancient history. We're starting anew. Something I'm very much looking forward to." He brushed a kiss on her cheek and held out his arm to escort her back to the party. After a brief hesitation, she raised her chin and preceded him out the doors.

He watched her go, appreciating the shape of her back, the sway of her hips.

Nothing would stop him from claiming his child or his father's company—they rightfully belonged to him. And he had a burning need to have this woman under him again. Fate had conveniently wrapped all the things he wanted in one neat, sweet-smelling package.

All he must do was coax his bride-to-be back into his bed.

The following morning, Lily wandered through the crowd of art-lovers as they milled around the display of Impressionist paintings her gallery was showcasing.

This exhibition had been her special project—selecting the paintings she wanted to show together, arranging with interstate and international galleries to borrow artwork to complement their own examples of the style, organizing events with schools and the public to coincide with the opening week. And she'd loved every minute.

She continued her stroll. The sounds of a busy exhibition always pleased her—the muffled footsteps on the tiled floor, voices raised or lowered in wonder and awe, an occasional guide sharing their passion.

Blended with that was the knowledge that today was the second to last day, giving her a twinge of sadness that usually came with the end of an exhibition. From tomorrow night, they'd begin taking down the display, returning paintings, completing paperwork. In a few days' time, another exhibition would fill this room.

Lily paused to appreciate some of her last moments with her favorite Monet. One of his series of water lilies, it was incredibly popular with the crowds for its lavenders, greens, pinks and blues—its undeniable intensity and luminosity.

But she loved this series because it showed the multitude of ways there were to look at the same subject, depending on time of day, the season or the position of the observer.

Similarly, there were many ways to view marriage: a fairy tale come true with hearts and flowers; a deep commitment with a soul mate that transcended the mere institution…or a pragmatic contract used to secure an inheritance.

She'd never yearned for the trappings of a fairy tale, but, despite her parents' train-wreck of an example, she'd always secretly hoped that somewhere she had a soul mate and they'd eventually find each other.

Marriage to Damon was not such a union.

As the reality of her situation hit her again, the room around her rocked then swooped, leaving her feeling faint.

Oh, God, what had she done?

"The water lily collection always struck me as overly sentimental," a deep voice said close to her ear.

She turned quickly to see Damon staring at the Monet, hands on hips, bunching the sides of his dark gray suit jacket above them.

"I like his series of the French cathedral more," he said, gaze still on the artwork. "Same concept of capturing the subject in different lights, but a much more interesting outcome."

She inhaled an intoxicating breath of his spicy scent. He always smelled so damn good. She'd noticed his cologne on other men and it'd had nowhere near the bone-melting impact it did when blended with Damon's own scent.

With effort, she brought her attention back to the conversation on art. "Buildings are more interesting than flowers and nature?" Though, she knew the answer from Damon's point of view. The material, the concrete, the financially tangible were always more valuable than simple beauty. What *did* interest her was his apparent knowledge of the French Impressionist. When they'd met, he'd claimed to have little understanding of the art world.

He turned, taking in her expression, and raised a brow—a look made all the more devilish by the accompanying heavy-lidded gaze. "I like buildings. And don't look so shocked that I recognize the painting. If you date someone with a PhD in fine art for six months, something's bound to rub off."

Lily laughed softly, conceding the point. "So now you're a gallery regular?"

"No, I've come to see my fiancée." He cupped her chin and brushed a kiss across her lips. "I always did prefer snow lilies to their watery cousins."

Words of praise dripped so easily from his tongue—with or without sincerity—that she refused to respond. She'd fallen for his silver-tongued flattery before. It had led to heartache whenever he left her without looking back. She must not forget.

And yet a part of her she couldn't control craved his kiss, craved *him* beyond reason.

He released her chin and dropped his hand into his trouser pocket. "And to finalize some arrangements. How soon can you get time off work?"

Her mind clicked into gear, pushing aside any remnants of hurt that he could so easily, so clinically, switch topics of discussion. It was only what she'd expected. Men like Damon did not while away the time talking about paintings. They mentioned them as a lead-in to getting what they wanted. Another reminder not to let down her guard.

Instead, she began thinking through the question and implications. This exhibition was almost over and she'd be going into detailed planning of her next project—a good time to take a day or two off if necessary to organize legal documentation for their wedding. "What do you have in mind?"

He rocked back on his heels, all casual confidence. "We fly out to New Zealand in three days, exchange vows and fly back. You'll need a week off work to cover the flights and a couple of days there."

Her stomach lurched. She seemed to have missed a step. "New Zealand?"

He lifted his shoulders then dropped them in a confident gesture. "Much quicker than waiting for the paperwork to go through in Australia. I originally considered Las Vegas, but decided the shorter flights to and from Auckland will be better for the baby."

A group of gallery patrons gathered about the Monet so, feet on autopilot, Lily moved away toward the middle of the room. Damon followed.

Her mind whirred too fast for any one thought to be clear. She needed time; he was moving so fast. It hadn't even been twenty-four hours since she'd agreed to marry him, and now here he was, asking her to leave the country in three days.

Her lungs labored to draw in enough oxygen. "Can I think about it?"

"Sure." One corner of his mouth lifted in an incomparable show of self-satisfaction. "I've already booked the flights so there's no rush to secure seats."

The world stilled as a strong sense of déjà vu settled over her. This was what it'd been like to be involved with Damon Blakely the last time. She sometimes wondered why she hadn't seen these warning signs when they'd first met. The cavalier attitude to other people's plans and choices. The belief he knew better, that his decisions weighed more than those of mere mortals. The same warning signs her mother should have noticed in her father.

Defensive anger rose to fill her chest. "You booked tickets without checking with me first?"

The best seats, too, she knew without asking. The man had gall for an expensive gamble like that. But then he wouldn't have seen it as a gamble—he always got what he wanted.

He lowered his voice and his eyes darkened, the pupils expanding to almost meet the black ring around his ice-blue irises. "This is a priority for both of us. We need to make sure our baby is legitimate."

The anger dissolved as quickly as it'd arrived, leaving her deflated, empty. He was right. They did need to ensure the baby was legitimate for the terms of the will. She'd cede on this one point, but only because it made sense, not because of his tactics.

"I'll need to check with the gallery director." She shook her head and began heading for the staff offices, Damon almost a step ahead even when she led. "I'll let you know by tonight."

He dropped a casual arm around her shoulders, which she knew would be more to stop her walking in another direction than a gesture of affection. "Come to my place after work and tell me what you've arranged. You haven't seen my new house yet." His voice had deepened into black velvet.

He'd changed tactics, turned on the charm. Her mind could acknowledge the game plan in this move but her body reacted to the timbre of his voice with primal hunger down low in her belly.

The gleam in his eye told her he knew exactly the effect he was causing. He pressed his advantage, fingers caressing the exposed skin of her upper arm where his hand hung. She kept walking, trying desperately to control her rampant hormones that urged her to turn to him, to let him charm and seduce her, no matter the cost.

But no, the stakes were too high now. His agenda wouldn't have their baby as first priority and that was the *only* agenda she could approve at the moment.

She stiffened and pointedly tipped her chin to his hand as it lazily stroked her sensitized skin.

Never slow on the uptake, Damon dropped his arm— but let it trace a lazy path down her back as he did so.

Damon always held himself in such control she wondered for the hundredth time if he'd shown any genuine feeling—besides desire—in all their time together.

Dismissing the thought, she waited for the next tactic he'd pull out of the bag. The wait was short.

"Melissa is cooking pasta tonight." His tone was casual, as if he were doing her a favor. "She'd love to see you again."

Lily thought of Damon's housekeeper with her bush

of light brown curls and ready smile. "I'd like to see her again, too, but I'm pretty tired these days after work."

She was past the morning sickness stage and now the main side effect of her pregnancy seemed to be fatigue. Besides, she needed as much distance from Damon as she could get. Distance seemed to be the only effective strategy in resisting him, and even then its value was questionable. "I'd rather ring and have an early night."

Immediately, his expression morphed into concern and he swung around in front of her, blocking her path. "Are you getting enough rest?" He clasped her elbow. "Perhaps this job is too much for you in your condition."

Resisting the urge to roll her eyes, she hooked the sides of her hair behind her ears and took a deep breath before answering. "Damon, I'm fine. I'm a little tired from the pregnancy, but nothing to be alarmed about. I'm more than capable of doing my job."

Though the thought *had* crossed her mind that if she was this tired at three and a half months, how would she cope at eight months? Or after the birth when she'd be struggling with disrupted sleep? She had no experience of babies, of motherhood, and that deficiency scared her.

He considered a moment then nodded with deceptive slowness. "Fair enough. I'll bring Melissa's pasta to you. What time will you get home?"

Her heart pinched tight. Despite his high-handed manner, it was nice to have someone other than her grand-mother worry about her—even if it was only to guard an investment. So she smiled her gratitude even as she rejected his offer. "I'll be fine. I made a big pot of soup last night and there's some still in the fridge. I'll heat that."

She sidestepped him and continued toward the restricted access area.

Without missing a beat, he was beside her, matching her strides. "Soup? Does that have everything a baby needs?"

A gallery staff member walked past and waved. Damon watched Lily wave back but felt her tense beside him and instinctively knew her reaction was about his question not the colleague. He frowned. She didn't like him helping?

She kept walking. "I appreciate your concern, but I can look after myself." Her voice was calm and only a tinge of exasperation laced her words. "And now I have to go back to work." They'd arrived at the doors to staff offices. "So if you'll excuse me, I'll call you tonight."

He nodded, watched her swipe her security badge and walk through the door.

She was wrong. Someone needed to look after both her and his baby. And he knew just the person for the task.

But for now he had to get back to work. There were many loose strings to be tied before he could leave for a week.

Striding from the gallery, he headed for his Lexus, then drove the inner-city streets back to his company's headquarters.

His second-in-charge, Macy, greeted him outside his office door, her long brown hair drawn back, starkly emphasizing her sleek features. "Mr. Blakely, I have some good news."

"Come through." Damon had first employed Macy for her outstanding business skills. But he'd since discovered her thinking and strategizing was eerily similar to his, making her indispensable.

They walked through and Macy closed the door behind them. Damon rounded the desk, taking off his jacket and letting it hang on the back of his executive chair before sitting.

Macy stepped forward and handed him a report. "We've secured another of Travis Blakely's companies, Melbourne Brewing Limited."

Damon allowed himself a self-satisfied smile as he skimmed the report. "Good. He doesn't know about this one, either?"

"No, I bought the loan he'd taken out using MBL as collateral. Another one he'd taken without informing his attorneys."

Damon let his eyes drift closed to savor the rush. Revenge was oh, so sweet. He couldn't wait for the day he told his evil excuse for an uncle that he'd bought all his assets out from under him. He'd vowed as a thirteen-year-old—black, blue and bleeding from being "disciplined" by his uncle's fists—that this would come.

Damon already held the deeds to the old man's house—again Travis had used it as collateral on a loan to cover a business deal gone wrong. Damon simply bought the company that had given the loan.

Travis's main mistake had been in growing arrogant, in letting his ego make business moves his bank balance couldn't match. And Damon had been more than willing to cash in on that slip.

Though, Damon had used other tactics where needed. He'd acquired the mansion's private gallery in a deal brokered by his man on the inside. Travis thought he was selling two paintings but instead had signed over the entire gallery for a song—all because he'd assigned the task to an employee whose loyalty Damon had bought for an absurdly high price.

He knew Travis was only aware of losing two companies, ones where hostile takeovers had been necessary. And even with those, Damon had covered his tracks well enough by using companies within companies, so the only people who knew he was at the top of the chain were the two people in his office.

He spared his 2IC an approving nod. "Good work. You'll be getting a bonus."

Macy barely acknowledged the boon as she slid gracefully into the chair across from his. "That makes twenty-three companies you've acquired from Travis."

He threw the papers onto his desk and loosened his tie, righteous victory filling his chest. "Only five to go." So close now.

Macy retrieved the report, running a finger down a table of figures as if committing them to memory. "The most well-protected five, including—"

"Including BlakeCorp." He finished her sentence, stomach clenched. "I have a backup plan. You got my memo that I'll be out of the office next week?"

Macy nodded. "Do you need me to accompany you?"

"Not this time. I need you here, running things. I'll be unavailable some of the time—it's not strictly company business." A vision with silver-blond hair rose unbidden and he allowed himself a moment of appreciation before tamping down on it.

Macy arched a brow and he knew what she was thinking. He was never away from the office for anything but work.

He smiled. "Oh, I'll be working on our objectives— I'll be putting plan B into place in case we don't get the last five companies in time."

Macy's eyebrows drew together creating a tiny frown line between them. "I know I've said this before, but I'm not confident we'll be able to get those last five. Especially BlakeCorp."

Deep down, neither was Damon. In fact, the task was close to impossible. But he wouldn't stop before he owned it all. His pride demanded he take everything away from the uncle who'd treated a small child so shamefully, who hadn't honored his dead brother's wishes. That included Travis Blakely's portfolio of assets, every last coin of his cash reserves, his home, his reputation…everything. He didn't want to merely win, he wanted to see Travis destroyed, utterly and completely.

He sank back into his chair, seeing Lily's delicate beauty again in his mind. Her pure heart could never understand his black motives in his campaign against Travis. Wouldn't understand the darkness that lived inside him every waking moment.

But now that Lily was pregnant with his child, by God he'd make it a real marriage.

Everyone wore masks of one type or another. He just had to ensure his stayed firmly in place.

Three

Three days later, Lily watched from her kitchen window, a bowl of fruit salad in her hand, as Damon pulled his Lexus to the curb in front of her rented house.

He slid out and her breath caught. His khaki pants and moss-green polo shirt should have looked casual, but with the pants' crisp crease down the front and the shirt tucked in above a simple belt that had probably cost the equivalent to a month of her wages, he somehow appeared ready to lead a board meeting. Or seduce a woman.

She almost choked on her strawberry as the thought took hold and irresistible desire stole over her. The familiar luscious heat started low in her belly.

Determined not to lose control of her body, she carefully set down the bowl and gripped the edges of the sink. She would not get distracted by something as counterproductive as sexual attraction. To do the best for her baby she needed to be focused—and she would be.

She glanced out the window again and watched as Damon, folded papers in one hand, set his keyless lock and strode to her front door.

Lily took a deep breath and dried her hands to let him in. But instead of pressing the buzzer, he took out the key she'd given him while they'd dated and let himself in. Her heart twisted at the familiarity of the action, for the memories of naive happiness it evoked.

She'd asked for that key back; he'd told her he'd get around to it, but she'd known he had no intention. She guessed his reasons had something to do with a bruised sense of entitlement. She'd had every intention of changing the lock. Then she'd suspected she was pregnant, one of her assistants on the Impressionist exhibition was reassigned, and then… Well, then Travis had fallen ill and Damon had asked her to marry him.

"Lily, it's me," he called from the hall.

"I'm in the kitchen," she called back, picking up her bowl again and perching on a kitchen stool, elbows resting on the polished wood counter. He could see himself through the house—she didn't want to seem too eager and reinforce his view of their relationship.

Damon appeared in the doorway and propped one shoulder against the frame, his casual pose belying the heat in his eyes. Every cell and molecule in her body went on instant alert and every drop of hormone screamed her need for him. For all the heat and pleasure that his gaze promised.

Focus. Her chin kicked up. There were more important priorities than physical want. Like her future. And her baby's future.

He chuckled, slow and deep. "They'll feed us on the plane."

Her grasp on self-control almost wavered as his sensual rumble resonated through her, but she staved off the threat by concentrating on his words alone. "I know, but I'm pregnant and I'm hungry. This will tide me over until we board."

Broad shoulders straightened as his amusement evaporated. "Lily, you're not on your own in this. If you're hungry anytime, anywhere, tell me and I'll get what you need."

Her breathing hitched, but she wouldn't be swept away by his words. She was more than capable of feeding herself. "Thanks, but I've got some cookies in my bag. I'll be fine."

He took a step closer, his voice deepening. "I don't just mean now. I'm serious. You're carrying my baby, so you tell me whatever it is you want and I'll find it. I don't care if we're in the middle of a traffic jam or on a snowbound mountain. I'll arrange it."

His gaze was unwavering, resolute. He meant it. Well, for now. His promises only lasted until work called, but her pulse fluttered nevertheless. In this moment, he was here, looking after her, and he'd never been more attractive.

"Thank you," she whispered. She took a piece of cantaloupe and chewed carefully, desperate to do something to shield her overwhelming yearning for the man before her. She forced her gaze down to her fruit.

A silence followed and the tension escalated despite her resolve not to look up. She could feel his eyes on her—her skin prickled with heat wherever they landed. Still, she would not look.

She knew she'd have to eventually—they were getting married. At some point she'd have to face what he did to her and find a way to handle it. But for the life of her, right this minute, she couldn't think how.

Then, from the corner of her eye, she saw him open the folded papers and lay them out flat on the counter beside her.

"The bank account for the baby in your name, as requested. I've deposited an amount my lawyers tell me should be enough to support a child until he's eighteen. I didn't want you to be worried that I'll stop payments. I'll still add more at regular intervals."

Lily stopped chewing as her eyes rested on the very generous value of the account. Her mind stilled, then clicked into gear. She hadn't expected this move precisely but, knowing Damon, she had been waiting for a counteroffensive ever since she laid out her conditions. And here it was.

He'd arranged the lump sum in the bank account so there would be no need for a contract to ensure his payments. Money in the bank equaled no contract to get money. His first step in a plan to avoid signing anything pertaining to her other condition—separate bedrooms, separate lives.

Her shoulders slumped. She should have guessed he'd fight on that one. Damon always held tight to what was his.

She rubbed little circles on her temples, attempting to relieve the building pressure.

The very fact that he was manipulating her now reinforced her decision that their child couldn't grow up in the mold of the Blakelys. It would be too cruel to let an innocent baby learn the Blakely cynicism and how to bow down at the altar of the almighty dollar.

Damon played to win. At any cost. Their relationship had already been chalked up as one of those costs and she'd vowed to never give him the chance to treat her heart as expendable again. Or her baby's precious heart.

She opened her mouth to speak again, but he cut her off. "Are your bags packed? I'll take them out."

She folded her hands on the counter and squeezed them until her knuckles turned white. She needed to be strong or he'd walk all over her. She'd told him her conditions; she just had to stick to her guns and not let him manipulate her. "Damon, you haven't given me a contract yet."

He didn't flicker an eyelash. "Contract? I've already given you the money. It's the independence you wanted."

Attempting to put herself in a less submissive position, she stood. It wasn't much of an improvement, given his massive presence, but she could only work with what she had. He stood on the other side of the counter, leaning against it with one hip as if there was nothing she could say that would worry him.

She lifted her chin. "I want separate bedrooms on opposite sides of the house. I'm not saying the vows without a contract ensuring that."

Damon smiled. Her threat appeared to amuse him. He prowled around the counter and came to a stop mere inches from her.

"Sweetheart," he drawled, voice low and hypnotic, "I'm not signing my marital rights away. If you're so sure we can't live together, perhaps you should consider a different contract. Leave me sole custody."

Her hands instinctively flew to her waist. His eyes held hers. He may have been amused but he wasn't joking. She felt sick to the pit of her stomach and struggled to make her voice work. "The courts won't be swayed by your money, Damon. Or by a man who can't keep his word—you promised you'd sign the contract."

His gaze roamed to her hair and his hand reached up to run down its length, from crown to where the ends lay on her shoulder. She flinched and yet still felt compelled to lean into him. She hated herself for that weakness.

He didn't retract his hand, instead lingering over the exposed skin at the curve of her neck. "Actually, I didn't agree to sign anything."

His hands began to work their magic, sending ripples of heat and pleasure out from the spot his fingers caressed, along each and every nerve ending, all the way to her toes. As a distraction, it was effective—she paused instead of responding.

Pressing his advantage, Damon closed the last gap between them and used his other hand to press the small of her back so she leaned into him.

"Now we need to be reasonable," he breathed into her ear. "I've given you more money than most people see in their lifetime. You need this marriage as much as I do. I'm assuming you've already told your grandmother about the new house?"

Lily swallowed with difficulty and nodded.

Without her noticing, he'd maneuvered her around so her back was against the counter and she was trapped between it and the muscled wall of his chest. She could feel him against her skin, feel him *under* her skin. He'd invaded her blood and it pumped for him through her body, powerful, dark, spellbinding. As if every strong beat in her chest was his name.

He brushed his lips along her earlobe and she felt the words on his breath as much as heard them. "And yet you're willing to risk that over an unwinnable point."

She dropped her chin, only barely stifling a moan. She couldn't think. Couldn't make a thought form that didn't involve his body.

It had always been this way between them, simmering passion that ignited with a simple touch from their first kiss. Before, even—from the first time their gazes had connected at the gallery fund-raiser. Damon had prowled over, offered her a champagne flute he'd acquired on the way and asked, "How high a donation for a private tour of the gallery with—" he checked her name badge "—an assistant curator?" He'd kissed her before they made it halfway through the Australian Colonial Art exhibit.

And now he was doing it again—skipping preliminaries and rushing straight to the passion she could barely resist. If only he'd stop crowding her! She needed to step away, but there was nowhere to go. She placed her hands firmly on his shirt and pushed. He stepped back several inches, that same amused smile on his perfect mouth.

She had to focus. He was trying to take all her bargaining power away, but she wouldn't let him forget…he needed her. "You won't get BlakeCorp without me."

He raised his brows in innocent surprise. "You think I'd choose a business over a child of my own flesh and blood?" He ran a knuckle lightly down her cheek. "Lily, why make this harder than it needs to be? No one gets everything they want at a negotiation table. That's why it's called negotiation. You played your hand well and you're getting a good outcome—the bank account and your gran taken care of for the rest of her life. And me."

Him? Her whole body flushed, but she needed to stay on her game or he'd outplay her. "Damon, whether you sign a contract or not, I won't be the kind of wife you want."

"And what kind is that?" He turned slightly to lean back against the counter, ankles crossed, and thrust his hands deep into his pockets. His earlier amusement had returned.

She narrowed her eyes, wanting him to understand how serious she was about this. "I won't sleep with you."

Gran always said, start as you mean to go on. This was a marriage on paper for the sake of a will. It was not now, nor would it ever be a real marriage. She couldn't let the lines blur—not even once. Her heart was having enough trouble resisting falling in love with him again as it was. Sleeping with him would court disaster.

"Let's just say the negotiations will be ongoing on that point." He raised one brow and her stomach fell. He still intended seducing her.

Then another thought struck. "You have booked separate bedrooms wherever we're staying, haven't you?"

It'd be just like Damon to expect her to share his bed despite the boundaries she'd laid. He probably had some ridiculous excuse ready like, just because they shared a bed didn't mean they had to make love.

Though separate bedrooms might not be much of a defense when it came down to it….

He nodded, poker-faced. "As a matter of fact, I have."

"So you won't mind if I check that?" She knew how he worked and it wasn't necessarily honorable, not when he wanted something as badly as he wanted this.

A lazy grin spread across his face. "Not at all." He reached into his back pocket, withdrew his wallet and found a slip of paper that he handed her. It had a hotel name and phone number. Had he really done what she'd requested or was this another bluff?

She folded the note and stuffed it in her handbag on the bench. She'd ring to make sure when she got a private moment. When he wasn't breathing down her neck, making her lose her thoughts.

He looked around as if that was settled. "Where are your bags?"

She blinked, tried to get her bearings, and glanced down the hall. "At my bedroom door."

Lily watched him stride away, an edge of panic creeping up to clutch her chest. She had a strong feeling that she'd jumped out of the frying pan and into a bushfire.

Damon inserted the Auckland hotel room key card into the honeymoon suite's lock and turned to appraise his new wife. How would she react to being carried over the threshold? Not well, if her mood during their vows was any indication.

Her frame of mind notwithstanding, she'd looked like a vision from heaven in the Peace Chapel. And the sharp constriction of his chest had almost blindsided him. It was *right,* this union.

He'd bought her a small bouquet of lily of the valley and she'd clutched it tightly, her gaze resting on the blooms during most of the ceremony.

Her downcast eyes only added to her resemblance to the aged paintings of holy women housed in his child-hood home. She'd been ethereal.

She still was as she stood motionless, waiting for him to turn the door handle.

Normally he'd be willing to risk her wrath and just sweep her into his arms to enter the room, but he had a lot riding on her mood tonight. Plans they'd both enjoy if she'd only relax.

He presented his arms. "How would you like to enter, Mrs. Blakely?"

Lily's forest-green eyes flickered with pain before landing on contempt. "I've told you, we don't have that type of marriage, Damon."

He looked her lush frame up and down. Then why had she worn white? The cotton summer dress may not look much like a traditional wedding gown, but she couldn't fool him—her sentimental streak had chosen the color as intentionally as he'd chosen her bouquet.

She could deny it all she liked, but her selection proved that deep down she acknowledged the validity of their marriage. Which gave his libido hope that the wedding night would turn out to be as traditional as the color of her dress.

He smiled at his bride as she waited for him to open the door. No doubt about it, the sentimental streak that had chosen her white attire would like to be carried over the threshold. And damn if he didn't relish the prospect himself.

He reinserted the key card to activate the lock, then leaned down and scooped her up in one smooth motion, carrying her through the door into a room elegantly decorated in whites and creams, and kicked it closed behind him.

He was pleasantly surprised she didn't object. She'd probably convince herself later it was due to shock. No matter, for now he'd savor the moment.

The scent of wildflowers enveloped him, the pressure of her body against his consumed him and he paused to let his eyes drift closed and fully appreciate the feeling.

She was tall, yet so delicate he'd often thought of her as a snow lily come to life—willowy, as if seeking the sun. He raised his lids to look his fill. Her fairness—creamy skin and silver-blond hair—only enhanced the illusion. Her eyes, the color of untamed foliage, showed where she truly belonged. Her natural habitat wasn't the art galleries her work kept her in, but where the wild lilies grew.

"Very nice, Damon. Now put me down." One side of his mouth curved at her hundred-percent controlled tone, but he sensed she was close to breaking point. He released her legs first, then, holding her torso with both hands, let her slide the way down.

His blood heated both at the sensation and at the memories it evoked. Of them making love through the night. The slide of nakedness. Of the sound deep in her throat when he touched her the ways she liked. His groin flexed and reported for duty.

By the time her feet touched the plush cream carpet strewn with rose petals, her pupils had dilated. Her breathing held an edge of raggedness.

He didn't release her. "You thinking along the same lines as me, sweetheart?"

There was a certain satisfaction in being able to call her that again. It suited her so completely, as if the term had been created for her alone. And he was sure he saw a flash of approval in her features every time it passed his lips.

She arched a brow. "I'm hoping against hope this is still the suite with two bedrooms. How's that compare to your thoughts?" She pushed against his chest and moved away. "I rang ahead to check from the airport but I've learned to never assume anything with you."

He almost laughed, but caught himself in time. Smart girl. He'd changed the arrangements only as they waited outside the chapel, predicting she'd check the hotel number he gave her before then.

He adopted an innocent air. "In a honeymoon suite?" He looked pointedly from white walls and Austrian blinds, across to a table of palest pink marble with two white lacquered chairs, to the complimentary champagne waiting in an ice bucket. "Can't imagine how likely that option would be."

Her jaw dropped and her mouth formed a perfect

little O. Then her fists clenched at her sides. "This is *not* a honeymoon. It's a contractual agreement."

He grinned. "Language can be so confining. Let's just wait and see exactly what we have here."

She shook her head as if words failed her. Then he watched, enjoying her profile as she bent to unzip her suitcase, left neatly beside his on matching luggage stands by hotel staff. Her sweet upturned nose, lush pink lips, just begging…

"If you think I'm sharing a bed with you, then you haven't remembered me properly." She straightened, lemon silky robe and pajamas over one arm, the other planted firmly on her hip.

Oh, he remembered all right. Remembered she liked to think she was in control. And sometimes he let her. Then, when she'd stopped fighting, he'd convince her of his point in other ways. Oh, yes, he remembered some very pleasant convincing.

She rubbed a hand over her eyes and leaned a little unsteadily onto the wall beside her. "I need a long, hot shower. And when I come out I expect you'll have arranged separate beds." As she lowered her hand from her face, he was shocked to see her now-lackluster complexion.

His stomach fell and all thoughts of passion evaporated. "Something's wrong. Is it the baby?" Maybe he'd pushed her too fast in her condition? Despite getting the all clear from three doctors for the flights, had it been too much for her to fly while pregnant?

He moved to her side and encircled her in his arms. The health of the tiny life she carried was the one thing they were in complete agreement on. He needed this baby—his plan B. But it was more than that. Something personal between him and the child that he couldn't yet define. A connection, a link.

She twisted to move from his embrace. "Nothing's wrong with the baby. I'm just tired from the rush to pack and the flight."

This time he didn't let her go. Instead, he guided her to the cream, overstuffed couch. "Sit down for a few minutes."

When she opened her mouth to disagree, he laid a finger across her lips. "Just this once, do something I suggest without arguing. Rest before getting in the shower. I don't want you fainting in there." He arched an eyebrow.

Her eyes widened as she took his meaning—either sit with him for a moment or risk having him checking on her, naked and wet in the shower stall. A job so appealing his temperature nudged up a couple of degrees just thinking about it.

With innate grace, she sank into the luxurious couch and rested the side of her face on the high headrest. He had to remember she was almost four months pregnant. Easy to forget when she showed so few signs, but he'd thought about the situation a lot since the night she'd sprung the news on him.

And in a surprise to himself, he'd grown more fascinated by the idea she was carrying his child inside her. Moved, even. When he'd devised this plan after his uncle's offer, he hadn't stopped to think of the emotional bond he'd feel to the baby. After his disastrous childhood, he'd have been happy going through life never reproducing.

And yet…even now, there was a tiny version of him under Lily's hands as they rested on her belly. Where did the baby fit? Lily may be tall, but she was slim. In fact, she could use a bit more meat on her bones. He'd start working on that from today, too. This woman was carrying his child and he'd make damn sure both of them had everything they needed.

"Tell me what you know about the baby." He hadn't finished forming the thought before it was out of his mouth.

Her eyes opened slowly, lazily, and she smiled. "I don't know much yet. No gender. But everything is progressing as it should be for this far along."

Damon grabbed on to the small morsel of information, yet still needing more. "Can you…" He cleared his throat. "Can you feel him move?"

"Not yet. Sometime in the next couple of weeks, the experts say."

Sitting there on the couch, hands clasped over their child, lashes fluttering to rest on her cheeks, she was so damn beautiful, the epitome of what a mother should be—soft, protective, kind. Despite his threat in her kitchen about giving him sole custody, he'd never act on it. Having been deprived of a mother's love for most of his childhood, he knew its value.

His hand reached out, almost of its own volition, then retracted. It seemed an intimacy too far. Strange, when they were married and would be lovers again as soon as she stopped fighting it. And this was *his* baby.

Yet something still kept him from forcing this intrusion on her without invitation. Something about her now, perhaps the glow radiating from her skin, which made her look like the Madonna portrait that had hung in his childhood schoolroom.

She was high above him, he with his blackened heart. He was under no illusions about the darkness that consumed him inside, a consequence of being raised by an instrument of the devil. A man who had no boundaries on the methods he used—even on a child. Cruelty, humiliation, violence, thievery.

Damon had always prided himself that no matter how low he sank, he never stooped as low as Travis. But now, looking down on Lily, untainted by darkness, he could see his own true colors.

God knew, it was too late for him. The only way to save himself now was to have her purity beside him, part of him. She'd give him an heir, BlakeCorp and personal salvation.

He needed to have her, now more than ever.

Decision made beyond question, he smiled, using all his charm. "The color's returned to your cheeks. You look well enough for that shower now. I'll order up some food while you're in there."

Her eyes drifted open, a cool green gaze landed on his for a moment, lingered, then she turned away and nodded.

Unsettled but determined, he watched her go and made a vow to himself.

He would have her. Tonight.

Four

Lily lay across the bed in the dusk-darkened room. She stretched, feeling the slide of her satin pajamas on her skin, listening to the shower running, knowing Damon was in there, soapy, warm and beautiful. The open-plan room design only made things worse—no lock separated them, he stood just out of sight, literally around a white-tiled corner.

And he knew it, had planned it this way.

Being this close was playing havoc with her mind and body, and he knew that, too. Wherever she was, part of her focus always seemed to be reminiscing about their lovemaking, trying to block those memories, or wondering about making new memories....

She could walk into that bathroom now, drop her pajamas and robe and slip into the shower. He'd welcome her, pull her close under the spray, perhaps languidly soap her up, running a hand over her glistening skin, and she'd slide her tongue along his strong jaw, down his throat, then—

No. She groaned as she faced away from that side of the suite and dragged herself back from the brink. That would only increase her involvement—and more than instinct told her she was too deep already. She *couldn't* fall in love with him again. It almost destroyed her last time. Never again would she fall for a man as self-serving, morally bankrupt, and as much of a workaholic as Damon Blakely.

She sighed and slid a glance toward the bathroom. Of course, she had to admit she loved the way he looked at her as if she were a rare delicacy. Loved the way he walked into a room and his presence instantly dominated it. Loved his troubled heart that he kept so guarded and hidden, even from himself. Loved the way his skin felt under her hands, under her mouth.

But, regardless of whether her heart remained intact this time or not, she knew one thing for sure: contrary to popular wisdom, love was not nearly enough.

Her mother had loved her father and the results had been devastating, for both of them and for her, their only child. She'd been notified a week after her fifteenth birthday that they'd died in a road accident. They said her mother fell asleep at the wheel and ran off the road.

Lily's hand went to her mother's silver heart pendant hanging on a fine silver chain around her neck. It was the sum total of her inheritance from her parents—the only item of value in their possessions.

She gripped the silver heart tighter as she wondered again if her mother had reached breaking point and seen no other way out. She'd cried for them and herself, but had been grateful they'd sent her to live with Gran three years earlier.

Supposedly the change had been to give her a chance to stay in one place, but Lily had always known that her grandmother had demanded she be sent to her. Her parents, like two kids on an adventure, lacked the will to disobey Gran, whose own backbone was pure steel. Lily had been offered occasional sympathy over the years as the girl given up by her parents. But even at twelve Lily had seen the situation clearly—Gran had rescued her and Lily would be forever grateful.

The years with her parents had been unpredictable and confusing, and had left her craving stability. They said one thing but meant another. Their well-meaning inconsistency was one of the reasons she understood the way Damon's mind worked. He'd promise her the world, but he always ended up getting what he wanted.

Words were easy for her parents, for Damon. Actions told the real story. Damon's priorities were the only ones that mattered to him.

She would never live that way again—it was soul-destroying to feel valueless.

More important, she would save her baby from that environment. Already, she loved this tiny person too much to subject it to the emotional torment a life with Damon would surely bring.

The water stopped and she sat bolt upright, listening to the sounds of Damon moving about in the bathroom.

A cold sweat broke out over her skin. The man in the bathroom was her *husband*. The thought hit her with sickening force. She'd gone through with it. She'd married Damon Blakely. They'd exchanged vows of love, fidelity and commitment. Vows neither of them intended to honor.

Jitters all the way to her fingers and toes replaced her fatigue. She'd really done it.

A knock on the door interrupted her thoughts.

"Room service." The call made her stomach rumble. How long since she'd eaten? Too long. She stood and padded out to open the door.

Three men in maroon-and-gold uniforms stood waiting behind multilayered trolleys. Lily's jaw dropped. What in the name of heaven was this? There must be enough food here to feed the entire floor! She stood back to let them pass.

The first two men pushed their deliveries past her, parked their trolleys beside the pale pink marble table and began laying out linen and cutlery. The third man gave her a slight bow on the way past and left his trolley a little behind the others.

"Dessert," he said, looking at her and then at a spot over her shoulder.

Lily turned to see Damon coming through the bedroom doorway, tying the sash on the large white hotel bathrobe that draped his frame, midnight hair damp, feet bare on the thick carpet. She remembered how her hands followed the trail of hair down his chest, hard stomach and lower. Dizzy with lust, she could do no more than lick her dry lips.

How would she resist this man if, *when,* he made that inevitable concerted effort to seduce her? He would try and she must resist no matter how much she craved his touch. It would be difficult, if not impossible, to re-establish her ground rules after they made love even once. She had to remember that he had an ulterior motive. She was his ticket to BlakeCorp.

"Ah, the food's arrived." His voice was a low rumble that soaked in and touched her deep in her bones.

Damon reached into the robe's pocket and withdrew several folded notes, which he gave to the men in turn. The first two bowed and left the room; the third looked down at the tip and grinned. "Thanks, Mr. Blakely."

Damon closed the door behind them, then leaned back against it, a hungry smile stretching his features. But his eyes were on her, not the food.

An answering quiver raced through her body. She couldn't let the false intimacy created by their paper marriage alter her decision to not sleep with him. And from the look on his face, he would turn every inch she gave him into a mile and then some.

Trembling, she turned back to the food, fussing with the place settings with unmanageable fingers.

"No need to be scared of me, sweetheart." She imagined—*felt*—him walking up behind her. When he spoke next, he was right behind her, his breath lifting the sensitive hairs by her ear. "I'm not the big bad wolf."

Oh, how wrong he was.

The heat from his body seeped into hers, turning her bones to warm honey. If only their relationship was unfettered—as it'd been before the will, before her pregnancy, before he'd broken her heart—she would be free to lean back into him and take what he offered. The pleasures he could bestow went beyond anything she expected to experience again. She shuddered with the desire her body remembered too clearly. If only she could have just one more sample—

As if reading her thoughts, Damon placed a butterfly kiss behind her ear, sending a delicious shiver across her skin. Then another kiss and another shiver. She opened her mouth, knowing she should protest, but before she could speak, he nipped at her earlobe and sucked it into the decadent heat of his mouth.

Lily stifled a groan, almost lost, barely able to form the thought that she should move away, but his warm breath rippled sideward to her cheekbone, and she caught the fragrance of toothpaste—fresh mint mingling with his own scent.

"God, what you do to me," he whispered.

What she did to *him?* Within short minutes of his ministrations she was ready to fly to the moon with him. She leaned back against his body, desperate to learn he was as affected as her. Just for a moment, she told herself. And, oh, he was. His arousal pushed against the small of her back.

"Damon, I—"

He raised a finger and placed it over her lips but it did more than silence her. The pad of his finger traced a leisurely path across her bottom lip before dipping into her mouth. Breathing choppy, body aflame, she welcomed the finger, closed her lips around it, sucked ever so lightly, intensifying the mounting tension pulling at her core.

Light-headed, she grasped for his arm in an attempt to steady herself so as not to miss a single delicious moment.

He swore under his breath then slowly withdrew the finger and placed a chaste kiss on the top of her head. "First things first," he rasped before clearing his throat. "I need to feed you." He took her elbow and guided her to one of the ornate white lacquered chairs. "Sit."

The room slanted at his change of direction but she sank down and let Damon push her chair in, trying to counter her disorientation. How had that happened? She bit down on her lip. Thank heaven now she had time to rebuild her defenses—make them impenetrable.

He sat in his own chair, toweling robe displaying a proud V of solid chest dusted with hair, golden forearms peeking out his rolled-back sleeves letting her see their muscles contract and flex as he lifted the lid off the first dish. The spicy aroma filled her senses and she reluctantly dragged her gaze from Damon to the food, still a touch dizzy.

"I ordered a selection. This one's Asian stir-fry vegetables." He held out his hand for her plate. She complied, realizing how hungry she was, and not just for Damon, then took the plate back after he'd spooned a portion onto it.

After scooping vegetables onto his own plate, he lifted the second lid revealing a cheesy topping covering something enticing underneath.

Again he held his hand for her plate. "I ordered the three dishes on the menu with cheese—you need calcium. But I made sure there was none of the soft cheese you can't have while pregnant." He looked up, one corner of his mouth curved in a lazy grin when he saw her surprise. "I've done some research."

Touched that he'd given so much thought to the ordering, she watched as he lifted lid after lid, working through the dishes he'd ordered for her. A lump grew to fill her throat.

By the time he came to the sixth dish, her plate was piled so high it resembled more a small mountain than dinner.

She laughed and threw up her hands. "That's enough. I'll never be able to eat all of this."

He nodded and continued piling new dishes onto his plate. "Just eat what you can. You and the baby need sustenance."

She waited for him to finish serving himself before tasting. The food was divine, just like the other five-star places Damon had taken her when they'd dated. But more than the food affected her.

Watching Damon eat, dressed only in a bathrobe, kept her blood simmering and her senses on high alert. The robe's wide gap at his chest gave her an unobstructed view of his strong, cleanly shaven throat, Adam's apple bobbing as he swallowed.

He held out his fork to her. "Try this. It's one you don't have."

Lily hesitated, breath catching in her chest. He'd fed her from his fork before, and occasionally from his fingers, like the night he'd fed her mango slices in bed. The memory of the sensual delights that night had brought dropped her mouth open and she accepted his fork.

The light-as-air pumpkin soufflé melted on her tongue.

"Mmm, fabulous." Her eyes drifted closed to make the most of the flavor, licking her lips for any remnants.

"I'll tell you what's fabulous," Damon said in a husky voice. "That licking noise you're making. Here, try this one."

Her eyes flew open as she realized how it must look from his position. She felt the blush creep up her neck. "Ah, no thanks. I have enough here." It wasn't fair to tease him, lead him on, when she had no intention of sleeping with him. Heaven knew, she certainly shouldn't have let him kiss her ear earlier. Her guard had to stay in place.

Then again, a voice taunted in her mind, Damon never needed encouragement. He always knew what he wanted and right now he wanted her.

"Well, let me try some of yours. I didn't get any of that creamy cheese dish," he said, pointing to the side of her plate. "I left it in case you wanted seconds." His lips sat parted for a second before he added, "Just a taste."

The rasp in his voice called to her and without thinking, she lifted her fork to his mouth. She instantly regretted it when his lips clamped around her fork. He held it between his teeth, his eyes intense as they captured hers as surely as he'd captured the fork.

Then he let the clean fork slide free, chewed leisurely and swallowed. "I've dreamed of tasting you again. Your lips…your skin. Your essence."

Lily couldn't speak, could barely breathe. She was baking inside, melting, *needing* his touch. She'd never had so skilled a lover as Damon, one who so thoroughly reveled in her body and in her pleasure. What she wouldn't give to experience that again. Just for one night.

No! She flinched at the physical pain of breaking eye contact, as if she was being torn in two. It took everything she had to take another mouthful and chew, pretending she was unaffected when she was ready to combust. Damon knew her weakness for his body. She suspected he knew that any woman would have a weakness for his skills once they'd experienced them. And one thing she knew about her new husband—he wouldn't hesitate to use any means at his disposal to get what he wanted.

And what he wanted was his father's company…and that meant keeping her with him until their baby was born so it would be legitimate. He'd use any means at his disposal—including seduction—to keep her in the marriage until then. Her heart clutched tight. She must be strong. Not put one night's passion ahead of her baby's needs, or she'd risk her child's future, the chance for her baby to have a stable and secure childhood—something that meant more to her than anything.

On autopilot, she kept eating—food on her fork, chew, swallow, repeat. With nerves jangling, the taste of the dishes no longer registered; all she was aware of was the man across from her. Without looking, she knew he watched her, could feel his gaze as a physical touch.

"You seem tense." His voice was so low it was almost a growl.

She didn't answer. Instead, she focused on her food, the only hunger she could safely assuage.

With slow, deliberate movements, Damon stood and moved behind her chair. "I can help with that tension in your shoulders." His hands gently kneaded her shoulders, and his heat seeped through her satin pajamas and robe as if he'd touched her bare skin.

She twisted away. "Damon, we've talked about—"

He maneuvered her back against the chair and cut off her words. "It's not the time for talking."

His fingers massaged deeply, with wonderful pressure and sensuous movements, spreading heat across her tired muscles. The relaxing rhythm of his hands through the slippery material lulled her into a place of mindless, sensual bliss. No one had touched her this way since…Damon. Her body, starved for warmth, soaked up his attention.

His newly shaven jaw scraped deliciously over her ear. "Better?"

His voice flowed across her skin. Perhaps just a moment longer. She tilted her head forward. She was so tired, her muscles were in knots, and Damon's hands were oh, so skilled. Might as well enjoy the massage he offered. She sighed and relaxed back into the intoxicating familiarity of him.

"Better," she relented on a sigh.

He reached around and loosened her robe then, slipping his fingers beneath the collar, he let it fall from her shoulders. Consumed by his touch, she couldn't find the wherewithal to even protest; only a distant part of her mind warned that she was inviting trouble. Inviting bliss. He parted her silky top a little and dipped his hands inside to keep rubbing her shoulders, skin on skin.

"Your muscles are so tight. You need to relax." His voice was easy, as soothing as a friend advising a friend—a well-timed tactic, she knew. He confined his hands to her shoulders, but this was more than a platonic massage, it always was with his touch. Her breasts tightened, their tips aching for his caress, and a dull throb pulsated at her core. Against her better judgment, her body was responding to his.

"Let go of all that tension you're holding, Lily." This time his voice dropped to a seductive whisper. Totally absorbed in the exquisite sensations, she let her chin fall to her chest. A small moan escaped her throat.

"Just relax." She felt his hands joined by his hot, wet mouth. He used his tongue and teeth in conjunction with his hands, amplifying the effect, dragging her deeper under his thrall.

When his hands slipped farther under her top to her breasts and ran across their tips, she almost dissolved into a pool of desire, her last remnants of self-control hanging by a frayed thread.

Yet she somehow forced the whisper out. "Damon, I'm already pregnant. We don't need to have sex." He was using her, she knew it, but his hands on her felt so good, their touch scrambled her brain.

She gasped when he cupped each breast and feathered moist kisses down the back of her neck. "If we're talking about need, don't doubt that I need you," he ground out. "What I feel when I'm near you has always been beyond want."

Lily bit her lip, her mind slowly waking to find itself at war with her body. "I don't think it's a good idea."

"We're married. We want each other." He nipped at

the spot where her neck curved into her shoulders, continuing to use his knowledge of her body against her. "The question is, why wouldn't we make love?"

Despite *knowing* a reason existed, with his tongue tracing circles on her shoulder blade and his hands on her breasts, she struggled to come up with her name let alone an answer.

Then his hands reached around, loosened the sash of her satin robe and any last vestiges of her earlier resolve evaporated. A moan ripped from her throat. She turned in her chair and sought his lips; she'd deal with the fallout in the morning. Forget forever. This was about here, now, tonight.

Damon needed no urging. His mouth claimed hers with the same hunger threatening to consume her whole. Without breaking their kiss, he circled around and came to kneel in front of her, between her parted knees, his hands holding her face.

Pushing his thick toweling robe to the edge of his broad shoulders, she ran her fingers over his back, luxuriating in the feel of his skin. Smooth and warm under her hands. God above, how she'd missed the feel of his skin against her body. Starving for him, she pushed the robe farther down, leaving the vast expanse of his back and shoulders free to her touch. The smell of clean, naked man—and not just any man, *her* man—made her light-headed with desire.

"Lily," he groaned and pulled back a little so she could see the emotion in his ice-blue eyes. "It's never been like this with anyone else."

He sank back into her, the wall of his chest pressed

against her breasts, as he whispered against her mouth, "Only you."

Not wanting to waste a moment on analysis, she opened her mouth to him, needing him more than she'd ever needed anyone.

"One of us is overdressed," he murmured. Deftly, he removed her robe, pushing it down her arms to pool behind her on the chair, not breaking the kiss for a second.

"Layers." Damon grinned as his fingers worked the buttons of her pajama top free. "Like playing pass the parcel as a kid." Undoing the last one, he opened the sides. "Except I don't have to share the prize."

He dipped his head and took one nipple in his mouth. Her lips parted under his exacting persuasion and she melted, hands drawn to his head, repeating his name, "Damon."

She imagined his hardness twitching between his thighs, down too low for her to feel, and she wanted more, God help her, wanted everything all at once. Yet part of her had to make sure he understood her position. She dragged his face back to hers.

"Damon," she gasped between desperately snatched kisses. "This doesn't set a precedent."

He grinned around her lips. "I understand."

Was that agreement? He nipped at her bottom lip and her train of thought began to disappear, yet she clung to it. She needed to have this clear before giving herself permission to enjoy him fully. "It's just this once?"

His mouth trailed across her cheek then he whispered with heated breath in her ear. "Whatever you say."

For now that had to be enough. She let herself go,

turning to him and kissing him with everything she had. "Now, please," she begged.

He pulled away. "Not a chance. I've been dreaming about being here with you for months. I'm taking my time." He gave her a slow, sensual smile full of promise and dipped farther this time, to her stomach.

Lily closed her eyes, feeling his tongue flick out and scald just below a breast, then teeth nipping on her side. His mouth moved across her belly, kissing a spot then sucking the skin in through his teeth. She writhed below him, the pleasure-pain a beautiful torture. When he released the skin, he blew on the spot and somewhere in the back of her mind she understood he'd marked her stomach. Claimed her and their baby.

Then he moved lower still and her mind went utterly blank. He pulled her silken pajamas down with hands that moved an inch ahead of his mouth, then tossed them aside.

When he reached the juncture of her thighs, he kissed her reverently, then laid his cheek against her and wrapped his arms around her hips, hugging tightly. "God, I've missed you."

The gesture and words brought tears to her eyes, but before sentiment could carry her away, he turned his face and raised one of her knees then the other over his shoulders. She shivered with anticipation, knowing of his sixth sense for lovemaking—he understood her body and its needs better than she did herself.

He slid his hands underneath her and cupped a buttock in each—lifting her to his face.

As his tongue dipped into her, little arrows of

pleasure darted out from her core to the top of her head and tips of her toes.

He withdrew his tongue, teasing. "You've missed me, too?"

"Oh, yes." She writhed in his strong hands still holding her firmly and his tongue dipped again, this time stroking deeply, smoothly, in a rhythm that slowly drove her wild.

Needing to do something with the building energy, her feet slipped down his back to his sides and she pressed her toes into his waist, pulling him closer.

His tongue circled and flicked, raising the tension in her every muscle. She reached out to grab the back of the chair behind her, needing an anchor before she burst free of the world.

One hand moved from her hips and then there were fingers joining his mouth, caressing…probing…finding…pleasuring…

Her body tensed to the point of exquisite throbbing and she let go of the chair, searching for him, needing to touch him, finding his shoulders and digging her fingers into his solidness.

With a tidal wave of sensation, she climaxed against his mouth, calling his name, feeling their souls entwine. The rush of pure rapture touched every part of her body—an eternity of ecstasy in every moment. And even as the intensity began to ebb, the blissful pleasure remained unabated.

She came back to awareness slowly as Damon slid up her body and pulled her into his tender embrace. Ripples of paradise still spread through her body and she rested her face on the crisp hair of his chest, knowing he was right—it had never been like this with anyone else. And she couldn't imagine it ever would be.

When they made love, they made magic.

Strength seeped back into her muscles, letting her snake her arms around his torso and hug him tightly. Then, unable to resist, her hands drifted lower, over his firm buttocks, scraping her fingernails lightly there, the way he liked, then moving around to encircle him in her hand.

Ah, the feel of him. Burning hot, silky smooth.

Strong arms wrapped around her and lifted her from the chair, then laid her down on the plush carpet beside him. For a moment she hugged him tight, the sensation of his naked length against her skin feeling so *right*.

Then, unable to wait any longer, she moved down his body, just to see him again, to wrap both hands around him, to claim him with her mouth the way he'd claimed her. Her mind may have chosen to break up with Damon, but her heart and body held a different opinion on the matter. Now they were in control, she leaned in, as possessive as any bear guarding what was hers.

Holding him before her, she closed her eyes and tasted him. He groaned, then rasped, "Lily, wait."

He edged his way back the short distance to the wall and leaned his shoulders against it, sitting with his legs extended on the soft cream carpet. His golden body smattered with dark hair was posed like an erotic portrait that the artist in her appreciated as much as the wanton woman who'd emerged. She followed on all fours, unwilling to let him out of her reach.

"That's better," he said, voice slightly slurred in satisfaction as he caressed her back, then around to cup a breast. "I can reach you better."

Her pulse picked up again, from the erotic view before her and the attentions of his fingers. He stroked the pad of his thumb across a taut nipple, sending shock waves down to the flesh he'd so recently pleasured, and she took him deeper over and over again.

He was hers.

"Lily, come here." His voice was strained, perched on the brink of release.

Reluctant to leave, she waited until he called again. "Sweetheart, bring those lips up here."

Smiling recklessly, she made her way back to his decadent mouth before he slid the two of them sideways down to the floor. She could feel the length of him against her and finally, *finally,* she knew he'd soon be inside her. Spiraling out of control, unable to wait any longer, she reached to pull him on top.

He didn't budge. "Can I hurt the baby?"

"No." She pulled at him again.

He brought her closer on her side, flush against him. "Even so—" looping a hand under her knee, he pulled her leg up and around him, locking it into place "—I'll feel better this way."

Hips squared against each other as they lay on their sides, she arched back to feel him closer still. Then in one even stroke, he entered her, filling her as only he could.

She gripped his shoulders, this time knowing she was leaving marks, and tightened around him, eyes drifting closed, just reveling in this *completeness* he gave her. Warm, full lips moved on hers and she opened her mouth, welcoming the twofold connection of their bodies, the dual intimacy.

He thrust again, her name on his lips.

She met each stroke with her own push, their synchronized movements building momentum, taking her higher, back to paradise.

Her breasts felt the repeated rasp of his chest hair as his breathing became ragged and his lungs expanded to gasp more air.

She was close to the edge…hurtling toward the precipice…falling over…flying, free…floating…

And she felt Damon convulse and follow her and the feeling of completeness returned, filling every cell of her being.

Five

As he held her tightly, waiting for their breathing to return to normal, Damon felt Lily press a tender kiss to his damp chest. He allowed himself a self-satisfied smile—Lily was back in his arms, having just loved him with her body.

He'd thought he might need to work a little harder than this to claim her again. But he wouldn't look a gift horse in the mouth. They were together again. They'd soon be a family. He'd have everything he could ever want—all his uncle's assets including BlakeCorp, his baby, and pure-hearted Lily in his bed permanently. Something close to happiness filled his chest.

He held her a little tighter until she pushed him back, laughing. "I'm having enough trouble breathing as it is, Damon."

He smiled indulgently and turned onto his back, drawing her across his chest. "I'm having a little trouble getting my breath back, too."

She lifted her face and propped it onto fists resting on his chest. Her features formed a wistful expression, with what was perhaps a small cloud of doubt reflected in her eyes. "I'm glad I'm not the only one."

He met her gaze. "No question of that." He tucked her head under his chin. "It seems the question of separate bedrooms has become moot. You have the bank account but you won't be needing that room on the other side of the house anymore."

He felt her flinch then draw in a deep breath. "Yes, I do."

Her words hit him in the gut, hard and fast. What was she talking about? They'd just made love. Consummated their marriage. "You'll share my room, my bed. I'm your husband now." The father of their baby. He held her tighter. "I'll look after you."

"Damon, you're…" She shook her head and rolled off him onto her back on the soft deep carpet, looking up at the ceiling. "This can't be a proper relationship. I've already told you, I need people who are emotionally reliable." Her voice was soft, but underscored with an unswerving belief in what she'd said.

A monster swelled in his chest. He rolled on his side, needing to face this head-on. He pitched his voice low and kept absolute control over it. Rule one when threatened: control is your friend. "Whatever you thought before doesn't apply now." Hadn't he just shown her how committed he was? Hell, he'd just married her. Did she think he took that lightly?

She twisted to face him as well, biting the inside of her cheek before speaking. "Do you remember the day we broke up?"

He nodded, bringing the details to mind. "Of course."

She took a shuddering breath, then another and when she looked at him, a sheen covered her green eyes.

He reached for her, to offer comfort, to end this nowhere conversation, but she held up a hand and he dropped his arm to his side for the moment. He'd let her say her piece, then they would move on.

She spoke with quiet determination. "I rang and asked you to come out to Gran's place because I needed your financial advice. You'd said you'd help, that you'd think of a way to save her small nest egg after the market turned."

"And I came." He'd played that day over in his mind countless times and had a sinking feeling about where she was going with this. But he'd only done what needed to be done.

Her body seemed to curl in on itself, yet she held his gaze. "No, you made the journey, but as soon as you arrived you took a call and left." The anguish in her eyes was as fresh as if it'd happened yesterday.

He hated that he'd contributed to her pain, but he could only offer the truth. Surely anyone—particularly his bride—would understand. "It was a business emergency. I had no choice."

She nodded, resigned, her shoulders hunched as if defeated. "You seem to have a lot of business emergencies."

What did she want from him—blood? His options in situations like these were so limited that alternatives may as well be nonexistent. His company bought and sold other companies, specialized in hostile takeovers. Even before he'd started fleecing assets from beneath his uncle's nose, there weren't many quiet days on the job. He thought she'd understood that when he'd explained on their first date.

He exhaled. Fine. He'd take the time to explain again. He spoke gently, but firmly. "In my line of work, situations often require immediate crisis management." As it was, each twenty-four-hour period barely had space to fit in six hours of sleep and the hour at the gym he needed to keep his mind operating at the top of his game. Anything else was a luxury.

Lily wrapped her arms around herself. He frowned. Was that gooseflesh erupting over her skin? He reached for his robe and wrapped it around her like a blanket. She waited, allowing him, and didn't object when he left his hands resting on the thick terry toweling at her waist. It felt right. She obviously knew it as well as him.

She kept her eyes on his hands. "That's what it was like in my dad's so-called job. Work came first. He barely noticed anything else until he won or his money ran out." She met his gaze. "It's your choice to live that way, solely for your own needs and priorities. But it's no way to raise a child."

"Lily," he said, using his most soothing tone, "this is an overreaction about one event. I know it was less than good timing for you but—"

"It wasn't just *one* time," she interrupted, then bit

down so hard on her lip, he worried she might break the skin and draw blood. "A week before that, I rang because I needed you. We'd had news that Gran's leg required surgery."

He frowned, searching his memory. "I don't remember that."

"I know." She gave a weak smile that didn't reach her eyes. "I waited until after work hours then rang and said I needed to see you. All I wanted was your arms around me, you telling me everything would be all right. But you had a lead on stocks from a mining company you were after. You said you'd be there all night."

Irritation flared as he set his jaw, hardly able to believe she'd chosen that one night. "That was an extraordinary circumstance. That company was vitally important."

"We were only together six months, Damon, but I could give you at least five other examples. If that's how dependable and committed you are during a honeymoon phase, how would you act after five years? Or ten?"

She sat up, clutching his bathrobe tighter, letting his arm slide away. "At the beginning I thought I could handle it, but the more it happened…" She closed her eyes and shook her head as if chasing away a horrid image. Finally she took a deep breath and met his gaze again. "I couldn't live with the neglect or hurt of being dismissed as less important than work." She gulped in a mouth of air. "I'm sorry but the bottom line is…you're just not the kind of man I need."

His face burned as if she'd slapped him hard and for an instant he thought she might have. He felt his jaw clench but collected himself, waited a beat then spoke in a carefully controlled voice, barely moving a muscle. "And what kind is that?"

Her eyes filled with tears and one spilled over, creeping down her cheek. "The kind who's there for me. And my baby."

A stab of self-doubt penetrated the barrier he'd carefully built around himself over the years. But he deflected it and cleared his throat. He could handle this. Handle her. He needed to remind her of one crucial fact. "*Our* baby, Lily."

"Our baby," she conceded softly. She stood and secured the already snug-fitting robe around herself as she headed for the bathroom.

Damon scrubbed his hands through his hair. He could fix this setback. First and foremost he was a troubleshooter. A damn good one. He could gain control here with the same expertise he used in a takeover bid, ensuring he kept her and his baby. He needed a plan—a foolproof one.

A way to prove he was the *only* man she needed.

As the plane taxied down the runway two days later and leaped into the sky, Lily settled back, surrounded by her wide seat for the four-hour flight from Auckland to Melbourne.

She was so tired she could barely keep her eyes open. Was part of her fatigue from flying while pregnant? Not being a world traveler, she had no idea, but sleepless nights certainly hadn't helped.

Damon reached for her hand and interlaced their fingers. "You okay?"

Since the incredible lovemaking and the ensuing tense conversation on their wedding night, things had been exceedingly polite between them. He hadn't tried to seduce her again and for that she was grateful.

Well, mostly grateful. He'd slept on the couch both nights—including the first night after they'd made love—leaving her restless, in a heated tangle of sheets, *aching* for him. Several times she'd been at the bedroom door in a haze of need, heading for his sleeping form before she caught herself. The wrench of turning from him had been almost unbearable, but she couldn't afford to give in again—she might not have the strength to pull away as she'd already done.

So, yes, she was grateful. He was honoring her wishes; why would she undermine that? She'd created the distance between them, made her bed. Now she had to lie in it.

Though deep down she wondered if he was planning something. Damon wasn't the type to give in easily, particularly not now that he'd decided she was a necessity of life.

Perhaps politeness was his latest tactic? Lull her into a false sense of security before bringing out the heavy artillery.

She sighed. If so, there was nothing to do but wait for the show. She was simply too exhausted to even think about it now.

He was still looking at her, waiting for her reply about whether she was okay. She gave him a weary smile. "When I've had more sleep, I'll feel better."

With a conspiratorial gleam in his eye, he said,

"I've organized a few surprises to take the load off when we get back."

Heart sinking, she stifled a groan. Anything Damon thought would be a pleasant surprise was likely as not to cause more stress. She turned her head against the headrest and faced him. "What surprises?"

He squeezed her hand, still interlaced with his. "No need for concern, sweetheart. They're good things." His gaze slid over her body and he smiled. "To make your life easier."

As if cold fingers gripped her throat tightly, she couldn't speak. Had she just been thinking they had distance? And now he'd confirmed her dark suspicions—he'd been strategizing all this time. And whatever he had organized, it wasn't as innocent as he implied.

She swallowed and tried to make her throat work. "I'd rather know now." When he pressed his lips together and looked as if he wouldn't divulge any more, she added, "Don't make me worry all the way home, Damon. Please just tell me what you've organized."

He considered a moment then smiled indulgently. "I've had your furniture and belongings moved into my new house. I used an outfit my company's called in before. They go in, pack everything, move it and unpack at the other end. Your things will be exactly as you left them in your place, down to the position of your hair-brush on the dresser in our room."

Lily shook her head and tried to clear her fuzzy mind. Did he just say that strangers had handled everything she owned, including the private and personal? That, whether she'd wanted to move every last thing or not, all her belongings were now in his new house, which she'd never seen and had absolutely no links with. And that her personal belongings would be in *their* room!

A dull throb began behind her eyes and she spoke through flattened lips. "You moved my things. Without asking or even telling me?"

His brows drew together in a confused frown. "I didn't want you lifting boxes while you're pregnant, or worrying about the move. I read that stress can cause miscarriage." His eyelids dropped to half-mast, ice-blue irises determined. "I plan to make your life one hundred percent hassle-free."

She almost laughed at the irony. After all the neglect in their earlier dating life, *now* he'd decided to go to the other extreme.

The dull throb drummed and pounded. She lifted a free hand to shield her sensitive gaze from the window's light. And he wanted to reduce her worry because she was pregnant. Right. He didn't think moving her things would cause stress? Was he blind?

No—she sighed—he was just being Damon.

She shook her head and kept her voice calm. "I told you I won't share your bedroom. I've said it over and over, in fact."

He looked at her as if she needed a gentle reminder. "You were with me all the way the other night on the carpet. Whether you say the words or not, it's obvious— you want this as much as I do."

She flushed. "That was once."

"It was twice for you, if I remember correctly." Heat flared in his gaze as it roamed her face, landing on her mouth. "Even if you count it as once, it was still the best *once* of our lives. Surely you won't throw that away."

Her body tingled as he lifted their joined hands and kissed her fingertips, then her eyes were drawn as he casually shifted his long legs, the muscles of his strong thigh outlined by the fabric. An answering flame to the one she'd seen in his eyes lit inside her. She closed her eyes to douse the sensation before she lost sight of her anger at his easy dismissal of her viewpoint. Had he listened at all to what she said after they'd made love?

Suddenly she understood. He'd listened too well. Maybe this was Damon proving he could be there for her. If so, he'd missed the point. And as soon as he thought he'd convinced her, he'd return to his workaholic ways.

He stroked his thumb along the back of her hand—meant to be soothing, it was anything but to her taut nerves. "It's not complicated, Lily. We're married, expecting a baby, and we need each other—I need you to get what Travis stole from me, and you need me for the financial security you've always wanted. Besides, even if none of that existed, I'd still want you with me." His mouth curved into a charismatic smile. "Relax, you don't have to fight me. I'm not the enemy."

Lily closed her eyes against the window light and Damon, and knew there was no point arguing now. She'd have to work it out when they got back. When she wasn't so bone-tired.

But first, though she might not like the answer, she pushed the question out. "What else have you done?"

His thumb traced a circle on the pulse of her wrist.

"I've told Melissa to hire some extra help for the house. With two of us and soon a baby, there will be more housework, and I don't want you to lift a finger."

His smile morphed into one of tender arrogance that only he could pull off. "I'll look after you and the baby—" his voice lowered "—no matter what."

Easing out an exasperated sigh, she opened her eyes and fixed them on his. To anyone listening, it might sound like a dream offer—and no doubt it would be if they had a real marriage, based on mutual respect and love, a marriage that had a chance of survival. Then she'd have gratefully welcomed his offer—and everything else that went with it, including a physical relationship.

Or if he'd made the arrangements from consideration rather than his real motive: to keep her close, to keep his baby under his roof. Her body iced over at the thought of being trapped again where she didn't count as a real person. If she wasn't careful, her baby could end up with that fate in his or her own home.

"It's the only solution." He stroked her cheek with a crooked finger. "I plan to spoil you rotten. You'll never want to leave."

Her cheek tingled from the brush of his finger.

And therein lay the problem. Even frustrated at him and *knowing* they had no future, she feared he was right. If history repeated itself, she *might* never want to leave.

The man she wanted with every beat of her heart had promised to spoil her rotten. If only she didn't know better. If only he hadn't chosen the exact words her father had used with her mother before each game of cards.

"I'll win big this time, Audrey. You just wait. I'll spoil you rotten when I do."

And sometimes he did. He'd score a windfall and then blow it all on her mother and buying a stake into the next game.

He'd buy Lily presents, too, dolls, dresses, toys. And then get a babysitter while he took his wife out to celebrate.

But a week later he'd pawn her new dolls and toys, deaf to her pleas and wrenching sobs as he ripped them from her arms.

By the time she was six, Lily had learned not to become attached to presents or material things—they could disappear as quickly as they came.

The plane hit an air pocket, jolting her out of the memory.

She surveyed Damon's arrogant face—the confident smile on his sensual mouth, his ice-blue eyes with their distinctive black ring, the proud nose. Then steeled herself to ask in a dull voice, "Is that all? Are there any more surprises?"

He arched an eyebrow, pleased with her question. "I plan to keep surprising you but there's one more for now. I asked Melissa to set up interviews for a nanny. The good ones are booked in advance, so it's not too early to start looking. She should have some appointments set up for when we get back."

A scream built in her throat but she swallowed it back. "You should have checked with me first," she said through gritted teeth. This was a step too far. In fact, he'd overstepped her line in the sand by about a mile.

He might have fathered this child, but the decision

on who cared for her child when she couldn't was hers, and hers alone.

He raised her hand to his mouth and kissed her palm. "We needed a nanny and I've organized for one."

Her blood simmered up into seething ire. He still didn't get it? "I don't want a nanny. I've checked with my boss and arranged maternity leave. *I'll* raise this baby."

And after that leave was over, she'd be the one to arrange care. There was talk about setting up a crèche at the gallery, which would be perfect, but whatever happened, she would *not* be coerced into choosing one form of care over another.

He nodded. "I'm glad you feel that way. I want our baby to have the best and that's you. But the nanny will help. She can take the baby while you nap and she can prepare his meals. A spare set of hands."

Her jaw fell open. How dare he supervise her life— her life with her baby—this way? There was no way she'd put up with his kind of dictatorship. "Damon—"

"Look—" his brow creased in sincerity "—maybe I've worded this badly, but I'm trying to help."

Still holding her hand, he squeezed gently. "I'm trying, Lily. I want us to work."

Brain weary, emotionally drained and too exhausted to fight, her body begged for nothing more than eight uninterrupted hours of sleep. She pressed her eyes shut and wondered if his attempt to help was genuine. A first step on the path to being the kind of man she and her baby needed?

She opened one eye and looked over his features, re-sentment ebbing away. Despite all the anguish and the worry and the doubt…*could* Damon become that man? Even doing it all the wrong way, was he actually getting something right?

Perhaps a leopard could change his spots.

As they stood waiting for the rest of their luggage, Damon switched on his phone, then grimaced.

"I have to make a call." His quick smile served as an apology. "Wait here with the trolley."

He strode away to the carousel, talking into his earpiece. A few minutes later, he reappeared with her suitcase, still talking a mile to the minute. As he left for the luggage collection, his expression was the epitome of a hassled CEO needed elsewhere.

When he returned, he'd finished his call and held his own suitcase. "There's an emergency at work. I have to go in."

Her heart sank. It had started already. It seemed leopards couldn't change their spots after all. "Of course you do," she said, not hiding the weariness in her voice.

He put the suitcase down and cupped her shoulders. "I wanted to be there when you walked into our place for the first time." It was as close to an apology as Damon came. His hands drifted down her arms, rubbing slightly. "I'll make this up to you, I promise."

He shook his head as if he had no choice. In his mind, he probably didn't. But there were always choices. Some of Damon's had been made long ago and were nonnegotiable. Such as, business and money-accumulation came before personal concerns. Every single time.

He stepped closer and brought her against him. "We'll catch separate cabs, and I'll see you at home tonight."

Over his shoulder, Lily checked a clock suspended from the ceiling. Two o'clock.

He'd taken a stream of calls while they were away. But was it too much to ask that he at least accompany her to his new house? If he'd left her belongings at her place so she could go home, sleep, then organize the things she wanted moved, she wouldn't have minded. But he'd jumped the gun and moved her into his home. And now she'd be going, alone, to a house she'd never seen.

He relaxed his grip and she stepped back to see his face. But she saw in his eyes that he'd already left. "You're running out on me." She hated the accusing note in her voice, and in that moment she hated him, for putting it there.

He blew out a breath and ran long fingers through his hair. "There's been a snag in arrangements for my father's company."

Her weariness hit her full force. In the end, it always came back to BlakeCorp. She'd lost this battle before it had even begun. A little piece of her heart died. Time to face reality. Nothing, but nothing had changed. "You don't even own BlakeCorp yet."

He shrugged, not quite meeting her eyes. "I want everything in place for when I do."

Her sorrow balled into a tight knot. His words, perfectly reasonable words, explained her situation with exceptional clarity. Theirs was a marriage on paper, one in which they would keep their emotional distance. So why should his brush-off hurt so much?

But she knew why. She'd tasted his passion again and believed it contained more than a morsel of honesty, and now she couldn't shake those memories. He'd imprinted that glorious abandon with all its endless possibilities upon her mind and soul so that it was impossible to erase.

Calling on years of practice, she swallowed and nodded. "Go."

He took his keys from a pocket and extracted a solid silver one from the chain. "Melissa should be there. I'll call her from the cab and let her know the change of plans. But just in case, here's the front door key. It's yours."

Lily took the key and turned it in her palm. It was similar to his old house key, the one she'd posted back after they'd broken up. The first time she'd realized she couldn't rely on him. Tears rose to sting the back of her nose.

Damon brushed a tender kiss across her lips. "Come on. The sooner we get going, the sooner I can get home to you."

Five minutes later, Lily sat alone in the backseat of a cab, the familiar feeling of abandonment growing stronger until it almost suffocated her.

The thing was, against her better judgment, she'd actually started to believe he could be there for her. That arranging for help—though not what she wanted or expected—was a step in the right direction.

But yet again he'd prioritized his work over her needs. Moving her into his house then letting her find it on her own showed her that, as clearly as if he'd handed her a note outlining his intentions.

She released a bitter laugh. Why should she be surprised? Based on past experience, she should have expected more of the same. For him, money came before people, even his wife and child. And *that* was why she had no future with Damon Blakely.

Six

Damon woke the next morning in his spare bedroom, curled around Lily. He smiled sleepily. What an excellent way to start the day.

He leaned in an inch, pulled her silky blond hair to the side and placed a delicate kiss to the back of her neck.

She stirred and rolled to face him, eyes opening slowly. The pleasure he saw deep in her forest-green eyes sent a bolt of satisfaction through his system…until wariness replaced her happiness.

With a primal need to banish the interloping caution, he kissed her lips, gently, teasing, the way he knew she liked. He'd rouse more pleasure in her body than she could stand…and, damn it, he'd restore that special joy to her eyes. An irresistible impulse, deep inside, demanded it.

He pulled her closer, inserting a knee between hers,

not breaking the kiss, then pulled her closer again, so his thigh pressed into the juncture of her legs.

He knew she wasn't one hundred percent happy with her decision to stay but he had more than one means of making himself indispensable. He'd give her all she could ever want with his money—materially and with staff—and all she could dream of with his body.

She was his. She and their baby.

And suddenly he knew this wasn't just about BlakeCorp anymore—not that it had ever been the whole picture.

Something more fundamental was involved, a compelling force coming from his solar plexus.

He cupped her face, channeling all his emotion into the kiss. A delicate moan of desire came from deep within her as their roles shifted and she tugged at him, reaching to his hips and finding him naked. A purr of satisfaction greeted the discovery and in return he slid her satin nightgown over her head.

He'd never get tired of feeling her skin on his. And now they were married, he never had to. For the rest of his life, he'd spend his nights making love to her and wake with her each morning. He'd drive all her doubts away.

Growling with the thrill of conquest, he rolled onto his back, taking her with him to sprawl across his ready body. Her eyes flashed with unadulterated lust and she pulled away, straightening, straddling him, raising herself into position, then lowering to bring him into heaven on earth.

His hands shot out of their own volition and gripped

her hips, planting her there, holding her firm as he bucked and buried himself as deep as possible.

Her movements slowed to a stop. She flattened her lips as that damned wariness returned, claiming her features.

She closed her eyes. "I promised myself we wouldn't do this again," she whispered.

Damon sucked in a deep breath through his teeth and held his protesting body in check while he processed her words. "We're married. It's not a sin, Lily," he rasped.

A pained expression crossed her face. "But it's not right, either."

He took a patient breath. He should have expected this reluctance. Just like on their wedding night, she clung to her doubts because theirs wasn't the traditional hearts-and-flowers courtship. But she was very wrong. They belonged together.

And now he needed a strategy before her resistance went too far. He searched her gaze, and one thing became crystal clear. She might have said she didn't want this, but she didn't want to stop any more than he did—despite her words, she hadn't moved a muscle to leave.

He reached to stroke her shoulder and along her arm. "It feels right to me, sweetheart. And maybe that's all that matters here and now." He ran his hand down her side and she shivered. "You. Me. Feeling right together."

She moved against him once and bit down on her lip. "What about afterward?"

He cupped her face. "We'll handle afterward when it happens."

He pulled her down and kissed her slowly, sensuously. "Come. Live in the moment with me." He coaxed her velvet lips, determined to make her see they belonged together.

She moaned her assent then rose up above him once more.

His hands slid up, touching her everywhere at once, lingering over her breasts and their puckered tips, moving down to slip between the place where they joined to take her higher.

She moved against him again.

"Yes," he groaned.

His eyes swept over her, silver-blond hair spilled across her shoulders, alabaster skin glowing with her desire, riding him like an erotic Lady Godiva.

How had he survived the months without her in his bed?

He gently grasped her shoulders and pulled her down, kissed her mouth hard, held her against him, as close as possible now he felt ready to explode, listened to her release echo in his ears and let it tip him over the edge, to the place where only he and Lily existed.

Boneless, he lay across his sheets with Lily's sweat-slicked body draped over him. Nirvana could hold no more pleasure than this.

Relishing the sensation, he lay still for long minutes. Then, floating down from cloud nine, his thoughts turned to the future. Their future. Their baby.

"Have you had any ideas about names for the baby?" he murmured.

A dreamy smile transformed her face as she slid to his side and stretched. She bent her elbow and propped her head in her palm. "I've got a mental list, but nothing I'm sure of. Have you given it any thought?"

A lot of thought actually, including on the drive home from work the night before. "If it's a girl, what about naming her after your gran? Pearl."

Her mouth rounded in surprise, then softened. "That's what you want? After Gran?"

He ran a finger down her cheek. "I'll be forever indebted to her—she saved the mother of my child. Expecting my own son or daughter has made me think about how she protected you."

Her eyes misted over but she smiled. "I've been thinking of that, too. And it's a gorgeous name. Pearl Blakely."

Giving thanks for this harmony, so rare between them lately, he placed a delicate kiss on her shoulder. "What about a middle name?"

Her hand fluttered to the silver heart pendant hanging from her neck. "I've been thinking Theresa would be perfect."

Damon stilled. She wanted to give his mother's name to their child? An unexpected lump formed in his throat. "I'd like that. Pearl Theresa Blakely."

Lily's hands smoothed across her naked stomach as she whispered, "What do you think, Pearl?"

Damon chuckled. "What if junior's a boy?"

Her smile grew. "I'd like Michael, for your father. I wish I'd met him."

His throat thickened again, and he cleared it before replying. "He would have loved you. Both my parents would have."

"Thank you." She swallowed then met his gaze. "I chose the first name for a boy. Do you want to choose the middle name?"

He thought for a moment. He'd considered many options last night, but only one felt right. "Andrew. Michael Blakely is from my side of the family tree, so I think Andrew from your middle name, Andrea."

Tears filled her eyes as he drew her close again. "Michael Andrew Blakely or Pearl Theresa Blakely," she said. "I like them."

He nuzzled into the curve of her neck. "And the room next door to the main bedroom—our room—would make a good nursery for Pearl or Michael. We'll be on hand during the night."

She took a moment to respond. "Pardon?"

He'd already worked out some of the details as he'd drifted off to sleep last night. It made complete sense. "I'll move the home office equipment to the room down the hall. We can knock a connecting door through—" he looked around the spare room, assessing its walls in proxy "—maybe add—"

Lily slid away and gathered the sheet around her torso. "Damon, if I've misled you, I didn't mean to. Just because we're sharing a moment here doesn't mean things have changed. Maybe I haven't made myself clear enough. Separate rooms. Separate lives." She paused with raised brows. "Pearl or Michael will have a nursery beside *my* room."

He frowned. No, she hadn't been clear at all. He'd told her on the plane he was trying to make their marriage work and she'd seemed happy. He'd thought she was giving them another chance. Granted, she'd slept in a spare room, not in his suite where all her things were, but he couldn't always follow the workings of the female mind. He'd assumed it had something to do with him not being there.

And she'd been a little reluctant making love just now, though nothing she didn't want to be talked through.

He held back a sigh and turned on a charming smile instead. He wasn't worried. He always won—sometimes the end result took a bit more work than others. But he wouldn't begrudge the effort when the windfall was as important as Lily and his child.

He took her hand and rubbed a thumb across her palm. "Lily, I meant what I said before. This feels right."

She shook her head. "There's too much at stake for me to be that simplistic. Damon, I won't compromise my baby's emotional well-being. I've told you I will not raise my child in a family where money is all-important and nothing and no one is more a priority than Daddy's work. I'll move out and raise this baby on my own before I let that happen."

His shoulders bunched and his grip tightened on her hand. "I'll make our baby a priority." He meant it down to the soles of his feet. "Securing our child's financial future is part of that. Making sure he has his grandfather's company to inherit when he's old enough *is* making our baby a priority."

He bit back the beginnings of impatience at her insistence that he wouldn't be a good father. He knew what was best for them all—being a family unit. Why was that so hard for her to see?

Lily's mouth opened and closed as if searching for words before she said, "This isn't about money. Do you know the drug addiction and suicide rates among rich kids?" She shook her head, as if world-weary. "Money doesn't buy happiness. I'm talking about love and *time* with her or him."

A memory flashed before his eyes of growing up with neither of those things, and he inwardly flinched. But he was nothing like his uncle. No question, his child's upbringing would be poles apart from his own. "I can do that, too." He leaned over and kissed the tip of her nose. "Just promise me you'll consider the nursery."

One step at a time. That's how the best deals were secured.

Lily rolled her eyes, but not before a flash of resignation surfaced. "You're not used to the word *no,* are you?"

"Actually, I am," he said with a straight face. "As a child I heard it far too many times from my aunt and uncle and I developed an allergy to it. Now I avoid it as much as possible."

The tension from thinking about his childhood eased from his shoulders before a grin tugged one corner of his mouth, softening the sentiment further. He could phrase it lightly to her but he was deadly serious. He hated being told no, and intended to hear yes from Lily's mouth sometime very soon.

She looked as if she didn't know whether to laugh or strangle him. Instead she flung back the covers and headed for the bathroom. "I have to go back to work today. We'll continue this later."

Damon laced his hands behind his head on the pillow and smiled.

A little extra work, a dose of humor, and he'd won this battle. Likewise he'd also win the war.

Lily looked around Damon's kitchen—she still couldn't call it *their* kitchen—bathed in mid-Sunday morning light…then she glanced at the ceiling.

Directly above her was the room Damon had earmarked as a nursery. She'd said she wanted the nursery beside her room, yet she'd been spending her nights in Damon's….

She shook her head and focused instead on the baking aromas that filled her senses and calmed her. Not that they'd be able to eat the entire tray of blueberry muffins, apple pie, sultana cookies, banana bread *and* fairy cakes, but she felt better having made them all. She could drop some off to Gran in the afternoon and freeze the rest.

She'd learned to cook from Gran, but had never wanted to bake this much before. Probably a nesting instinct—which made sense considering she'd repressed all other forms of that particular urge.

A nursery would have been an obvious place to channel her maternal yearnings, but she hadn't set foot in the room above the kitchen even once. It'd haunted her, though, on the fringes of her awareness where she had no control.

She glanced again at the ceiling, then felt herself turn toward the stairs, ignoring her well-developed sense of self-preservation. She climbed the stairs quickly, pausing at the top, then padded down the hall to the room next to Damon's.

They'd been home—married—for nine days and she'd immersed herself in her work at the gallery most of that time, but this weekend, her thoughts were almost exclusively on the baby and their lives together.

Slowly, almost reverently, she opened the door and slipped inside, barely daring to breathe. After that first night back in Melbourne she'd begun to temporarily share Damon's expansive room. Partly because she'd been too exhausted to move her things into the spare room, and partly because a tiny tendril of hope refused to be squashed.

Ridiculous. She *knew* they had no future—she'd made that decision already. Yet, when she was still or quiet, her heart whispered, *What if this could work? If there's a chance, isn't it worth the risk?*

She shook her head and laid her hands over her belly, feeling the comfort of the cotton and the small, hard mound beneath. Excitement for the precious child growing within her womb flared.

God, she wished it *could* work. Perhaps if she gave it a month or two, saw how it panned out…

Lily snorted a laugh. She was her mother's daughter, clutching at straws. She ran a fingertip along the windowpane and surveyed Damon's paved courtyard.

Peculiar how they'd fallen into somewhat of a routine, sharing a bed at night, acting as if theirs was a normal marriage as they left for their jobs during the day. She'd attended her checkup and been given the all clear. Melissa left dinner in the oven for them each night, even though Lily had told her she didn't need to.

Damon sometimes worked late and on weekends—

like today. So she'd eaten alone five of the eight nights, as she had when they were dating. She'd begun bringing work home for her next exhibition, on surrealists. It gave her something to do other than dwell on thoughts of this room.

The wisp of hope that her heart nurtured had inspired dreams of transforming the room into a child's wonderland, close to both mummy and daddy, and she couldn't bear to crush it completely.

She walked to the far corner, visualizing a crib draped in the finest cream lace, the place her baby would lay its head. She glanced left and imagined a chest of drawers topped with fluffy animals. If she reached out, she could almost touch them....

Downstairs, she heard a key in the lock and her heart leaped as if she were a child caught with her hand in the cookie jar. She couldn't risk encouraging Damon's confidence in his plans for the nursery, *his* plans for their future.

She slipped out of the room, securing the door behind her, then rushed down the stairs, pulse racing. As Damon's footsteps echoed across the tiled floor, she stepped into the kitchen, trying to bring her breathing back under control.

"My mouth started watering as soon as I stepped out of the car." Strong arms wrapped around her from behind and she smiled, heart still racing, as she melted back into her husband's warmth and strength. Moments like these, where she could pretend the past and future didn't exist, were glorious slivers of time where everything was perfect.

Making love in Damon's bed allowed her that same miracle, where she could block out reality and let her fragile hope take wings. Live completely in the moment.

He nuzzled the sensitive spot behind her ear and her blood heated. "I could smell your muffins from the garage, Mrs. Blakely. I swear, your baking even beats Melissa's."

Lily turned in his arms, threading her hands under his suit jacket, and kissed him. "I've just boiled the jug if you'd like a coffee and a slice of apple pie."

"I've got a better idea for my mouth." He leaned in and met her lips in a slow promise that heated her insides.

Then he pulled back, eyes roaming her face. "You're flushed. Is it from the cooking or did you rush to greet me?" His fingers brushed her cheeks. "Tell me you were upstairs starting on the nursery," he said against her lips.

Her mouth tugged to one side to disguise her grin. He just wouldn't give in. "Asking me the same question every day won't increase the chances of getting the answer you want."

He rested his forehead on hers. "It can't hurt."

His persistence gave her fledgling hope another surge of life. Maybe they could make this work….

She took a deep breath, held it, then released it in a rush. "I've decided to give us two months to see how things work out."

A grin spread across his face. He probably believed his charm had worked its magic again. Perhaps it had.

Her pragmatic side kicked herself for giving in, for being gullible enough to *believe,* but in that moment, her optimism and hope won out.

She laid her palms flat on his chest. "If, at the end of the two months, I think we have a future, then we'll discuss the nursery being beside your room. But, Damon, you need to be committed, as well."

"Sweetheart, you have no idea how committed I am to this." He captured her mouth and she lost all sense of time and place.

An eternity—or was it merely minutes?—later, he pulled back and cupped her face in his hands, his face solemn. "I'll make you happy, I swear. In fact, I want to add another vow to the ones we took in Auckland." His voice deepened. "I vow that I, Damon, will keep you, Lily, in a state of perfect happiness at every opportunity."

He kissed her lips slowly, reverentially. "I'll make *sure* this marriage works."

There was something magical in the moment, almost more meaningful than when they'd exchanged wedding vows. Almost too intense. She raised her hand to smooth the hair from his forehead. "Damon, you can't make it happen through the force of your will—"

He placed a finger over her lips. "Our wedding may have been rushed but I want this to last our lifetime. Beyond that. And I know you're not sure yet, but I'll keep working hard until you are." He kissed her top lip, then the bottom one. "I promise you."

The shrill ring of the phone on the kitchen counter snapped her back to reality. Damon reached behind him and picked up the receiver, keeping one arm firmly around her.

He answered then passed it to her, curiosity in his frown. "It's for you."

Her heart skipped a beat as she took the phone. The only person who had Damon's number was her grandmother. She'd told everyone else to reach her on her cell phone. Her stomach knotted. Even though Gran was on the road to recovery and had moved into the new house Damon had bought her with the on-site nurse, Lily couldn't help but worry.

"Hello? Gran?" Lily stepped back to lean on the counter behind her, watching Damon sample the banana bread.

"Lily Blakely?" the thin voice of an unfamiliar man asked.

One of Gran's doctors? Her lungs constricted. She clasped the phone tighter. "Yes."

"I'm Ian Crawford, one of the attorneys acting for Travis Blakely."

Relief for Gran quickly transformed into a lead weight in her stomach, one that was completely unrelated to her pregnancy. Why hadn't the attorney spoken to Damon?

"Mr. Blakely has requested that you visit him—alone, this morning—on a matter of utmost urgency." The thin voice raised a notch as if underlining his words.

Lily gripped the counter with her free hand. She hated being near Travis Blakely. He was both cruel and intimidating—an abhorrent combination. But the hairs standing up on the back of her neck whispered, as much as she might not want to, perhaps she should hear this man out. "He wants me to come alone?"

Damon's head snapped around, eyes locked on hers. He'd seen her fear. She shifted her gaze and focused on the fruit bowl on the opposite counter.

"Yes. As soon as you can get here. I can't stress the

urgency enough." The man paused then said in a rush, "Within the hour would be preferable." He disconnected with an audible click.

Lily stared ahead, unseeing, mind rushing from one implausible scenario to the next. Was this a trick? She reached past Damon to hang up the phone but he took the receiver from her, replacing it himself.

"You've gone pale." He moved closer, taking her hands and rubbing them between his own, as if trying to bring the warmth back to her cold extremities. "What did he say?" he demanded, his concern iced with anger.

She struggled to arrange her jumble of thoughts into a coherent reply. "Your uncle wants to see me this morning. Alone."

Damon's face hardened to stone. "Like hell."

Lily bit down on her lip. "His lawyer said it was urgent."

"I don't care what his lawyer says." His eyes narrowed in determination.

"It's obviously something to do with the will." Her baby's inheritance, and the lynchpin in the deal with Damon to look after Gran for the rest of her life. "He can't have anything to say to either one of us about anything else." Surely it wouldn't take long. She could face another ten minutes of that man's revolting company when the outcome meant so much to those she loved.

Damon's jaw clenched. "All the more reason why you shouldn't see him alone. I'll go instead."

A bud of resistance to Damon's high-handed manner reared its head, even as she recognized his response as concern. If their relationship had any future at all, she must keep a spine of steel and not let him dictate every choice they made. This will involved her as much as him. "What if his attorney has a question for me?"

He shrugged. "I can answer for you."

Something inside her snapped. She was tired of having decisions made for her. Her back straightened. "He asked to see me. Alone. I'm going. Alone."

Heat and approval flared in his eyes. "I was right. You'll be the perfect mother for our child. You'll be a protective momma bear." He smiled, seemingly satisfied. "We'll go together."

It was probably the biggest concession she'd wrest from him. She'd seen his determined glint before. She blew out a breath and nodded. Better she conserved her energy for facing Travis Blakely.

Lily watched Damon from the corner of her eye as he drove the distance to his childhood home. He'd been silent since he'd started the Lexus, his hands clenched tight on the steering wheel and his shoulders tense.

Finally she faced him. "You've told him about the wedding and the baby?"

Damon spared her a curt nod as he pulled off the road into Travis Blakely's large circular driveway.

She turned back and watched the mansion come into view. Stark white and two stories high, the front was the length of eight rooms, all with floor-to-ceiling windows, permanently shuttered. The only word that suited the structure was *imposing*. She supposed that was why Travis liked it.

This place would come to her baby one day. Tears stung her eyes. Although her child inheriting a home with an unhappy legacy chilled her, she knew legacies could be changed. Relief surged. Their child would never be homeless. He or she would have a rock-solid asset. This home couldn't be ripped away. Their child belonged here, and she was prepared to fight for that.

She thought of Travis and shuddered. If only it hadn't been such a soulless building.

Everything about the Blakely mansion was unbearably cold. But once Travis was gone, perhaps this house could become the loving safe haven she'd wanted for her child. Or maybe, with everything that had happened here, that was too much to ask of the bricks and mortar before her. How had Damon survived his childhood here—with Travis?

Lost in thought, she didn't notice Damon had left his seat until he opened her door. Accepting his hand, she stepped out. Even in the midst of the cocktail of fear and determination, Damon's touch still brought tingles to her fingers and simmering heat to her blood.

He gave her fingers a squeeze. "I'm right here." Despite his supportive tone, she felt the tension radiating from his body.

She smiled back and let him lead her to the front door. They were met by a short, lean man with a comb-over of long gray hairs.

"Mrs. Blakely?" His thin voice was familiar from his earlier call.

Lily nodded. Damon thrust his hand toward the man. "And Mr. Blakely."

The man sighed. "He said you'd come with her. I'm Ian Crawford. Come in."

They walked across the black marble floor through the foyer and into the vast receiving room where the party had been held less than three weeks earlier. The room, although light and airy from the two-story ceiling and masses of glass, maintained the cold, stark atmosphere of the dark foyer.

Damon's reassuring hand on her waist kept her from bolting, or losing the banana bread she'd had for breakfast. "Do you know what this is about, Crawford?"

The other man stopped and turned back. "He's ailing."

Damon's face remained impassive. "He was ailing two and a half weeks ago when I saw him."

Crawford shook his head, concern pinching his features. "He's worse. Much worse. His heart is the least of his worries now—his liver and kidneys are failing. The doctors have given him only days."

Lily's skin broke out in goose bumps. If she could ever hate a person, it'd be this old man for what he'd done to Damon. But she couldn't bear to think of anyone in pain or fear. Travis Blakely must be in both. Her newfound sympathy warred with her abhorrence for the bully, which still gripped her insides, leaving her stomach clenched and churning.

Days to live... She'd been so sure, but was this meeting truly about the will, or something less straightforward?

Crawford turned to her and shifted his weight from foot to foot. "He wanted to see you, Mrs. Blakely, most urgently." His eyes flicked to Damon, then back. "And he was insistent that it be alone."

Damon pulled her in closer. "Not going to happen."

She'd never had anyone besides Gran willing to

stand by her. Until now. The thought soothed some of her disquiet. She looked up at her husband with a softened gaze. "He's in no position to intimidate me. I'll see him alone."

Damon kept his eyes on Crawford. "No."

Crawford nervously cleared his throat. "The nurse refuses to let more than one person in his room at a time."

Damon merely grunted.

A sinking feeling enveloped her as she pictured Travis looking from her to Damon and being reluctant to talk because she'd defied him and brought his nephew. If something went awry with his will and Travis decided to leave everything to his cousin's son, Mark, what would happen to her deal with Damon to look after Gran and their baby?

She was prepared to face the devil himself if it meant protecting her child and Gran.

If Crawford were to be believed, time was running out to hear what Travis wanted to say. To ensure the will remained as it stood.

"Damon—" she swallowed, her throat suddenly too tight "—I need to see him alone."

Damon looked down at her, his ice-blue eyes calculating. "And I need to hear anything he has to say to you."

She felt the power of his demand and was acutely aware of being trapped between two powerful men. A precarious position.

But she was no longer the naive girl Damon had dated all those months ago. Coping with her relationship breakdown with Damon, and now her impending motherhood had changed her. It was up to her to ensure her family was safe. She simply had to face the lion's den.

She laid her hand over Damon's as it held her waist. "I need to do this. And Crawford said the nurse won't let us in together. I'm a grown woman, Damon. I can go alone."

A myriad of emotions crossed Damon's face before he blew out a breath and nodded once. "I'm coming with you as far as the door, though. And you'll tell me word for word what the old bastard says."

Lily smiled up at him. "I promise."

They walked the stairs behind Crawford in silence and with each step, the tension in her stomach coiled tighter. A continuous loop of questions and self-doubt ran through her mind: should they challenge the nurse to let Damon see Travis with her? How would Travis look this close to death? Was he really dying, or was it a bluff?

And always, the awareness of Damon's firm hand on her waist escorting her, his solid male warmth and strength steadying her. As much as was possible for what now felt like a trip to the gallows.

On the third step from the top she stumbled but Damon deftly caught her before she lost balance.

Outside his uncle's bedroom, Damon brushed a kiss across her forehead and released her. A muscle ticked in his jaw as he clenched and unclenched, clenched and unclenched. "Don't believe anything that tyrant says," he ground out.

Her insides went cold before she dismissed the feeling and nodded. Then she summoned all her courage, opened the door and walked through.

A grave, red-haired nurse stood beside the bed, monitoring several machines that would have looked more at home in a hospital ward. Travis lay beneath covers, looking smaller than she remembered. Lily bit down on her lip and managed to suppress a gasp. An oxygen tube ran under his nose and several other tubes came out from under the blankets. But his eyes were as sharp as ever.

She took a step closer and the nurse looked up with an unwelcoming frown. "You must be Mrs. Blakely. Are you sure your business here is a priority?"

Lily hesitated, fingers gripping the door handle behind her. "I have no idea what my business here is, or its importance. I was summoned."

The nurse passed a judgmental gaze over Lily, then across to Travis. "I think I'll stay."

The old man coughed and spluttered then, despite his obvious frailty, fixed the nurse with a commanding stare. "Go," he wheezed.

Clearly reluctant, the nurse studied Lily a moment longer before shaking her head and pointing to a button attached to the bed head. "Buzz at the first sign of a problem."

Lily nodded, still processing the scene before her, stomach in knots, as the nurse marched out the door.

"Come closer, girl," Travis rasped.

Tears of pity welled in her eyes, but she held them back, one of Gran's favorite sayings playing in her mind. *What goes around comes around.* He was a bitter old vulture who didn't deserve her sympathy. She waited for him to speak.

The wait was short.

"I have things to say…and little energy." He paused, taking several shallow breaths. "Excuse me…if I come straight…to the point."

Lily sat in the high-backed chair beside the bed in what was obviously the nurse's usual position. "Of course."

"I hear…you married him." Hate-filled eyes burned in his ashen face.

A strong urge to defend Damon from the man who'd tormented him through childhood destroyed the little sympathy she'd felt. But she folded her hands together on her lap, determined to at least hear the old man out. "I did."

"Told you why?" he wheezed.

She nodded. "He told me about the will."

He looked frustrated for a moment, as if she'd destroyed his fun in revealing that information. Then his eyes regained their sly glint.

"Know what game…he's playing?"

About to reply, she hesitated. "What do you mean?"

"I mean—" he struggled for breath "—what he's after."

"Damon wants BlakeCorp back. And I don't blame him." BlakeCorp should always have been his; of course he'd try to get it back.

"BlakeCorp…is a front—" he closed his eyes, resting them, then dragged them open again "—for his real…agenda."

The little spark of hope that had been growing during the days at Damon's house flickered, seeming more vulnerable that it'd been before.

"Your husband…wants only revenge…against me." He gasped for air, struggling as if it were a near impossible task. "Destroy me. Everything else…even you…is expendable…to his…obsession."

Her awareness shrank to just the cunning, frail man in front of her and his meaning. Expendable? To an obsession with destroying his uncle? He was only after BlakeCorp....

The thought died as she remembered a snatch of phone conversation she'd overheard when Damon had been speaking to his assistant, Macy. *"Consequences be damned. Ignore Travis's lawyers. I want that company."*

She'd thought he was talking about BlakeCorp—but, now she thought about it, why would he need to make arrangements when it would come to him via the will? The rosy picture she'd been painting of Damon began to flicker and blur.

She met Travis's reptilian eyes. "He bought one of your companies."

"Two."

She gripped the sides of her chair and brought the rosy picture back into focus. Travis was scheming again. Damon bought and sold companies every day. It could easily happen that two of them had belonged to Travis.

She would not believe the man she loved was capable of the brutality of destroying someone.

Seven

A blow of surprise slammed into her chest as she realized how her mind had phrased the thought.

She loved him.

Oh, dear God, *she loved him.*

Still gripping the sides of the chair, she dug her fingers in until the pressure turned to pain.

She'd never stopped loving Damon. And if she could love him even through this mess, she'd probably never stop.

Closing her eyes, she bit back a groan. Of course she loved him. She never would have gone along with this marriage, the lovemaking, him moving her into his house if she hadn't. She'd just been too afraid of the consequences to face the fact.

But what of *his* heart? Had all the kind words and

sweet lovemaking merely been a facade? A mask covering his true nature?

No, she *wouldn't* believe it.

Her eyes fluttered open and fixed on the ornate headboard. She wasn't naive, she knew Damon was capable of morally questionable behavior, it was why she hadn't wanted to get involved with him again. But these last few days had been *real.* He cared for her and their baby. He wasn't the monster Travis was implying.

Clenching her hands tightly on her lap, she narrowed her eyes at Travis.

"Have made…arrangements." Travis turned his head to a folder on a small table beside her.

She looked at the plain manila folder with her heart in her mouth. It would be filled with poison, no doubt about it. She didn't want to touch it, to be dragged further under the sea of chaos and confusion that already buffeted her.

Again Travis turned his head toward the folder, his pale, gnarled face burning with intent. "Important."

She hated this man, could never forgive his treatment of Damon as a child, but she'd come here to hear him out. Because he held all the cards with regard to the inheritance. She had no choice other than to do as Travis bid her.

She reached toward the folder and opened it.

Last Will and Testament of Travis Nicholas Blakely.

She bit down on her lip. Reading its contents did not mean she'd let herself be hijacked by the old man's schemes.

Travis wheezed twice, trying to speak before he gained enough control to form words. "Made changes… when knew…about baby."

Thoughts in such turmoil that her fingers felt clumsy, Lily skimmed through the first page. It was short and to the point. And then her turmoil ceased as her body went numb.

"Everything goes to me," she whispered.

Travis nodded.

She kept reading, barely believing. "You're leaving me *everything?*"

Again, Travis nodded. "For…baby. So he'll…always have…everything…he needs."

She turned the page, frowning, and slowly comprehending. He was leaving her a multimillion-dollar empire of business holdings and personal assets.

Her mind clicked into gear. *No matter what happened, her child would always be secure.* And she could look after Gran herself.

Yet, along with the relief, it felt odd to know this slip of paper afforded her the stability and financial security that had been denied her in earlier life. A heavy weight that felt as if it'd always been sitting on her shoulders fell and smashed into a thousand pieces, bringing glorious relief trickling through her veins.

But, dear God, what would Damon say?

"Money in…envelope."

Numbness beginning to lift now, Lily picked up the envelope and found a wad of cash inside.

Why had he done this? He was spiteful enough to have instigated this purely out of hatred for his nephew. And when Damon found out, he'd be outraged. She'd share everything with him, of course, but she couldn't bear to think of his reaction, or her own until her jumble of thoughts settled down into some kind of logical order.

Holding the cash in one hand and the copy of the will in the other, she looked to Travis for explanation.

"Tide…you over. Legalities…take time. Two hundred…thousand."

Lily had never held that much money in her hands. A buzz started in her ears. She had to ask. "What about Damon?"

"You don't…need him…anymore." But Travis wasn't smirking in victory, he looked strangely—earnest. "Raise baby…away. Don't let him…be…like us."

His eyes drifted closed and Lily wondered if he'd fallen asleep before he opened them again—a new, raw emotion now there. "Take…care…of…baby. Tell…him—" he broke off, eyes shining with unshed tears "—about…me."

Everything stilled—the room, her heart, even Travis—as she saw the old man show something resembling love for the first time since she'd known him. Even while a part of her wondered how this tyrant could feel this way over the seed of his despised nephew, to another part of her it made sense. Something more lay behind the man she'd thought of as rhino-tough. A small, well-hidden shred of humanity.

The door creaked open and the red-haired nurse appeared, frowning. "If he's been talking to you since I've been gone, he'll need to rest. He doesn't have much stamina."

Lily forced a smile, relieved to be set free from this room of emotional land mines, yet not wanting to leave until she had her feelings in a manageable state. Or at least till she knew *what* she felt. She put the money back in the envelope and picked up the copy of the will.

Could she accept so much money? Though, it wasn't for her—he'd done it for the baby. A baby Travis had every right to provide for. In fact, this was the same plan she'd agreed to with Damon, with one small change. Everything was in her name.

She held all the cards.

The experience was as unfamiliar as it was overwhelming. No matter what happened from here on, two things were now ensured. Her precious baby would always be safe and secure. And Gran would live out her days in as much luxury as she would accept. She could stop worrying about the future, and just live. Her face relaxed and tears stung the backs of her eyes.

This was a different financial security to being Damon's wife. Yes, that would ensure she had money, but it would have been *his* money. It could be taken again or disappear in an instant the way her father's money had repeatedly done. But this new will meant the money would be hers and the baby's, and she'd make sure that not one cent was squandered. She'd give her baby the financial stability she'd been denied.

But now Travis had done this, would Damon fight it in court?

She hesitated beside the bed, catching the old man's eye. The words *thank you* trembled on her lips but she couldn't bring herself to say them. Instinctively she knew there was more to this gift than appeared on the surface. Travis knew exactly what he'd done in raising questions in her mind, hoping to drive a wedge into her marriage.

It was time to leave, to tell Damon what had happened. Yet, she was loath to face him, his questions, the answers she needed to give and the decisions she would need to make.

And to ask the question she dreaded most of all.

Damon paced again down the corridor outside his uncle's room, his gut twisting in knots. His own childhood bedroom was at the end of the hall but he had no desire to revisit it—there were no loving memories stored there. Just the ghost of a boy huddled in the corner, crying for his parents and shaking in fear of his uncle.

Banishing the vision, he clenched his fists and turned to face the door that hid Lily. The nurse had returned a good five minutes ago. Where was Lily? What was that evil man saying to her? He'd been searching his brain to come up with probabilities, as well as contingency plans to minimize their effects. He already had his second-in-charge, Macy, on standby, ready for damage control with his business holdings.

He stared at the door, willing it to open. Lily might not realize it but that man in there was an incarnation of the devil. The man who'd taken everything from him twice. He could almost feel the ulcer form as his stomach burned.

The door creaked open and Lily slipped out, a large envelope and papers in her hand, her face as pale as fine bone china. God, what had he said to her?

Two strides and he was by her side. "Tell me what he said."

Her forest-green eyes searched his face, looking for something. "Not here," she whispered.

She was right. The old man probably had spies waiting to eavesdrop. He put a supportive arm around her and led her downstairs and out to the car. "Home?"

An emotion he couldn't identify flashed across her face but was gone within moments. "Yes."

He ushered her out and into the car, flexing his hands on the steering wheel as he drove out the driveway.

He'd fully intended waiting until they reached home before asking, but the questions gnawed at his gut. "Tell me."

She moistened her lips and took a deep breath. "He talked about our marriage. About you. He said…" She frowned and folded her arms before picking up the sentence again. "He said you didn't want just Blake-Corp. More than anything else in your life—more than me—you wanted to destroy him."

The knot of red-hot hate for his uncle exploded to life, becoming the familiar seething monster. He accelerated fast to overtake a truck. Damn that old bastard! On his deathbed and still trying to stir up trouble. Was his anger at his older brother so strong that he had to torment his nephew even with his last breath?

"Damon?" Her voice wobbled. "*Are* you obsessed with destroying him?"

"Of course I want to see him annihilated more than anything." As soon as the words were out of his mouth he desperately wanted them back, knowing she'd take them the wrong way. His gut clenched. "But there are other things I want, too," he said, backpedaling. "You, for example. Our baby."

He glanced over and saw horror in her every feature.

"Oh, come on, Lily. Don't believe the venom of a bitter old man." He reached for her hand but she drew it back, pushing herself against the door, putting as much space between them as she could.

"I didn't believe him. Not completely." Her voice wavered, then found strength—and anger. "But I do believe *you*. What I just heard you say. You mentioned wanting me as an *example*. Your wife and baby. You're too full of hatred and anger to ever see us as anything more. And I…I really thought we had a chance this time…" She trailed off, as if she couldn't bear to say any more.

He slowed for a red light, perspiration breaking out over his forehead. His chance for a future with Lily was disappearing before his eyes. No, no, this could be salvaged. "Lily, it just came out the wrong way. You know how I feel about you—about the baby."

"You know what, Damon? I *do* know how you feel about us. You desire me. You're interested in the baby, probably more than you thought you would be. But you look at us and you see one thing—access to your uncle's fortune. Everything comes back to your uncle. It's never just about us."

The traffic light changed and he accelerated, heart thumping, mind racing, trying to find a way out. The only answer he came up with was making her face reality.

He dragged in a breath. "Lily, we both went into this marriage with our eyes open. This was never a love match. You're right, I desire you. Even now when we're fighting. And you're right that I'm interested in our baby—more than that, I *want* this baby."

He ran a hand through his hair, blood pounding in

his head. He needed to get these words perfect. "You're also right that I want access to his worldly goods. Not for the money, you know that. For my father's company. It was supposed to be mine." His father had left it to his younger brother, Travis, along with all of his assets, on the understanding that he'd pass what was left, after the cost of raising his nephew, to Damon when he came of age.

But his father had been too trusting. Not a mistake Damon would make.

He swung into his garage, cut the engine and turned to her. "And if I can find other ways to hurt a man who has made it his life's ambition to humiliate me and deprive me of what's mine, then I'm not sorry about that."

She looked away from him, out the window, and spoke softly. "You don't feel anything more strongly than your hate. Our marriage—*I* can never compete. We have nothing."

Something in his chest clenched and coiled. How could she think that after everything they'd shared? He reached for her hand and interlaced their fingers. "No, Lily. We have the two of us, living as husband and wife, desiring each other, expecting our first child. That's enough for me, more than I thought I'd ever get." He laid their joined hands on her thigh, caressing the tension she was carrying in all of her body. Then she relaxed and he breathed a sigh of relief.

She turned to him, her eyes swimming with unshed tears. "Travis changed his will."

Damon felt his blood pressure skyrocket as the seething monster thrashed against his ribs, threatening to take full control, to demand answers. Yet he kept his voice evenly modulated. "Tell me."

She withdrew her hand and fidgeted with the envelope and papers in her lap. "He's leaving everything to me."

His mind sprang into action, subduing the monster, creating scenarios, calculating possibilities. He couldn't tell Lily that Travis didn't own the assets in the will to pass them on. Not even Travis or his solicitors knew. Travis's preference for secret dealings had kept him and his legal team in the dark perfectly about this bombshell.

As of this morning, Damon owned the lot. Even BlakeCorp. Everything.

He had to keep that part secret, because if Lily couldn't understand his need for retribution, she'd *never* understand this. She'd always abhorred secrets of any kind and this was the mother of them all. Perhaps if he'd told her from the start…

But now he would cover his tracks and she'd never know there had been any deception.

"He also gave me a sum of cash to tide me over until his estate is settled." She raised her chin almost imperceptibly. "I'll share everything he bequeaths me with you. In fact, I probably have to as your spouse, which is fine with me. But I'm leaving, Damon. What we had might be more than enough for you, but I can't be in a relationship with someone who's obsessed with hate and destruction."

Before he could process the words, she'd stepped out of the car and marched inside.

An hour later, Lily heard the front doorbell chime. Melissa didn't work Sundays, and she wasn't sure if

Damon had come in, so she ducked into her en suite, splashed water on her blotchy face and headed down the stairs to answer it.

Since leaving Damon in the garage, all she'd achieved was packing a couple of overnight bags. And a whole lot of crying. She'd expected him to follow her, to try and convince her to stay, and the fact he hadn't made a single move told her he was cooking up a plan to prevent her from leaving. Or he'd been called into work.

Either way, she was grateful for the time to pull herself together…to create a facade of someone who hadn't just had their world ripped out from under them.

She was in love with a man whose heart was black. He'd as much as admitted it. *And* seen nothing wrong with the admission. The devastation went bone-deep. No, deeper—she could feel the ache in every cell of her body.

Tears formed again but she blinked them back. She had no choice, she had to leave. It'd been wrong to even consider the two-month trial, she could see that now.

This was never a love match.

So clinical, so cold. He was truly his uncle's nephew. And she wouldn't subject her baby or herself to a future of such emotional desolation.

The door chimed again as she swiped her hand over her cheeks, reached for the handle and opened. On the other side stood Travis Blakely's attorney.

"Crawford." Damon's deep voice came from behind her, sending a frisson of pure want through her system. She tensed every muscle in her body to rein in the impulses the want caused. She *would not* let this man— her husband—have sway over her.

Ian Crawford, briefcase in one hand, stood uneasily, eyes on Damon but darting frequently to Lily. "I need to speak to Mrs. Blakely for a moment."

Damon's arm snaked around her waist, holding her firm. "Then you'll speak to both of us."

She recognized the gesture for what it was—an act of propriety. The burn of resentment tamped down the desire his touch had caused. But she wouldn't fight him here and now, there was no need—as soon as this meeting was over, she was out the door.

Crawford gave a resigned sigh and nodded.

Damon stood back, bringing her with him, and let Crawford pass.

Lily watched the two men with their respective missions—Crawford to pass a private message from Travis, and Damon to prevent the secrecy. She had no energy to fight anymore, and looking at the set of Damon's strong shoulders, it'd be a waste of her time trying to speak to Crawford alone. Besides, Damon knowing wouldn't affect her actions or response. She might love him, but she was beyond considering his opinion in her decisions. He'd killed that.

She focused on the visitor, wanting to be polite and offer him a drink, but instead swallowed the question, needing this over with as much haste as she could arrange.

Crawford pursed his lips, the epitome of grim determination. "I won't take much of your time. I just need to deliver my message."

Damon nodded and led them into his formal living room.

Lily, reluctantly feeling like a hostess in Damon's

home, swept a hand toward a chair for Crawford and they all sat, she and Crawford on the edges of their chairs, Damon deep in his, seemingly unperturbed by the tension the others felt.

Lily clasped the silver heart pendant at her throat and asked, "You wanted to say something, Mr. Crawford?"

His eyes flicked from her to Damon and back again. "After you left, I'm afraid Mr. Blakely's condition deteriorated alarmingly—"

Her hand flew to her mouth. "He died?"

Crawford raised a hand to stop her thought. "No, but I don't believe that time is far away." He clasped his hands together on his lap before continuing. "He's been transferred to St. Rose's. He should be there by now."

Damon leaned forward, resting forearms on his thighs. "Yet you're here instead of by your master's side."

Crawford nodded, unmoved by the gibe. "He instructed me to come and ask a favor of your wife."

A favor? She saw Damon's posture tense at the same moment the apprehension descended over her. "What does he want?" she asked through numb lips.

Crawford pulled his briefcase onto his lap, clicked the lock then withdrew a typed page. "As you may have guessed, he doesn't expect to return home from this hospitalization." He paused as if waiting for his first point to sink in. "He has left a large house full of expensive contents vacant. He would like you, Mrs. Blakely, to reside in his home, and to do so without delay."

Live in that mausoleum? The thought sent a shiver across her skin. There was not a single aspect of a home about it. Despite having known it would pass to her baby, she hadn't considered the reality of living there so soon, before she'd had a chance to make it into a place fit for her child.

Damon scoffed a laugh. "The eyesore will hardly become derelict. He has a staff."

Crawford nodded. "Employees who need direction."

Lily's mind flew to the overnight bag, packed on her bed—she'd been thinking more of her empty rental house or her grandmother's home, not an enormous building of concrete and stone.

Damon leaned farther forward, toward their guest, in an action that looked almost intimidating. "If he's worried about the security risk, why ask a pregnant woman to stay there? Why not take safety measures? Hire a security guard."

Crawford coughed. "I'm sorry, I can't answer that. I'm simply acting on instructions from my client. This was not a decision I made." He held the piece of paper out to Lily. "He asked me to type up the request in case of future legal challenges, then he signed the bottom. His nurse witnessed the signature."

Damon arched a cynical brow. "He did all this in the midst of being transferred."

Crawford nodded. "He was quite determined."

"I bet he was," Damon muttered.

Lily skimmed the page and glanced at the signatures, the germ of an idea forming. Damon hated that house. It'd be the one place he wouldn't follow her—he'd told her more than once when they'd dated that he'd see it razed to the ground before living there again.

If she moved into her empty rental, chances were

he'd move in after her. And at her gran's…well, Damon would be welcomed like a long-lost son.

But he wouldn't stay in his childhood home, he'd made that clear in the past. She swallowed. Gaining physical distance from her husband was paramount. It was her only defense against his brutal methods of charm and seduction. Especially now she'd faced the reality that she loved him.

And if this house was to become her child's inheritance, then someone had to breathe some life into it first. It needed warmth and love before it was fit for her baby.

Fate may have dealt her this hand, but she'd make the most of it.

Damon surged to his feet, fists planted on narrow hips. "Just because Travis wants Lily to live there doesn't mean she will. You can take your—"

Lily stood and moved beside him, laying a hand on his forearm. "I'll do it," she said firmly.

A muscle ticked in Damon's jaw but before he could reply, Crawford closed his briefcase, dropped a set of keys in Lily's hand and headed for the door. "My number is on that letter with the offer. Let me know if you need anything." Then he all but ran from the house.

Damon narrowed his eyes, watching the retreat. "Coward." He swung toward her and fixed her with the intensity of his unflinching gaze. "You can't live there."

Lily gathered all her courage to face the immovability of Damon once he'd decided on a path. But she had to do this, for her very sanity. She raised her chin. "I can and I will. I told you I'm leaving."

Features controlled, he grasped her fingers and

brought their joined hands to rest on the muscled wall of his chest. "Lily, he's only doing this to make sure he's driven a wedge between us. He's using you to attack me. He'd do *anything* to hurt me."

The gall of his hypocrisy astounded her for a second, before she yanked her hand free. The pain of being insignificant to the man she loved beside his obsession with destruction slammed once again into her heart. "That sounds familiar," she hissed, barely restraining her anger. "I think someone else admitted that same fault recently—willing to do anything to hurt their 'enemy.'"

"This is different." The certainty in his ice-blue eyes reinforced that he had no understanding of how damaged his dark soul was.

Her shoulders slumped as all fight left her. "It doesn't matter. I don't care why he's done it, he has. And I'm moving."

She turned to the staircase. Being this close to the man who would never truly be hers was torture, as if a thousand jagged knives pierced her very soul.

She needed to get her bags and get out of here. And haste was an absolute priority. Every extra minute in his company added another unbearable blade to the relentless attack.

Damon stepped into her path, tall, solid, inflexible. "You were looking for an excuse to leave me," he accused, eyes narrowed. "You never had any intention of giving this marriage a real go—you had one foot out the door from the beginning."

She grimaced. How could he even need to ask this? "Because the foot inside the door was dragged there, not invited in. You bribed me into the vows. Moved my furniture to your room without my consent."

He didn't get it. Just didn't get it. And her heart squeezed painfully at the knowledge that he never would.

His expression changed and for the first time since Crawford's visit, honest emotion emerged in his eyes—need. "I don't want you to go," he rasped.

Too little, too late. "We don't always get what we want, Damon. And sometimes the only answer you can have is no."

She turned and ascended the staircase, catching a flash of the vulnerability on his face as she did. But she couldn't let herself worry about him anymore. She had to prepare for the move to her new home. Alone.

Eight

After two hours of packing and driving, Lily stepped into the foyer of Travis Blakely's mansion, a cold trickle of dread running through her veins. The old man's words had repeated over and over in her mind on the drive.

"Take care of the baby. Tell him about me."

Though it might sound absurd to people who had known and despised him, Lily wondered whether Travis, in his last days, had indeed caught a glimpse of what it truly meant to be human. Whether, after leading a manipulative, selfish existence, in the end he, too, had wanted to be loved or at least remembered. The little girl in her—the one who'd yearned for her parents to notice her, to want her—understood.

His actions to Damon were unforgivable; she could

never condone or excuse the damage he'd wreaked on the vulnerable child or the man Damon had become. But Gran's mantra had always been, hate the sin, love the sinner. It was how Gran had coped with her son's treatment of his own child, Lily. Gran had made sure Lily was no longer neglected, but she'd also made peace with her son in her heart long before his death.

Lily looked from the sweeping white marble staircase to the black-tiled ballroom entranceway—each facet of the decor reflected the coldness of its owner's heart.

Perhaps loving this sinner was too much to ask. But compassion? A little compassion she could spare for a fellow human being. Or try to.

And if you allow a drop of compassion for him, her heart whispered, *shouldn't you confer the same to his nephew?*

Instinctively, her hands went to her slightly rounded belly. No. As much as she'd like to forgive and trust Damon, she simply couldn't risk it. Access visits to their child when he was on his best, charming behavior was the limit of what she could afford. Constant contact would be a danger to the emotional well-being of both her and her child. She wouldn't allow anything to blur or erase that knowledge.

A plump man with a large walrus mustache shuffled toward her, interrupting her reverie. "Oh, Mrs. Blakely, we're glad you're here."

She'd always liked the man who acted as butler and chef rolled into one. There was a small staff to help, but Thomas ran this house.

She smiled for the first time in hours—since before she'd been summoned here earlier in the day…before she'd found out about the depths of the darkness in her husband's soul.

Even as she'd left and Damon had loaded the suitcase into her car, his silence had screamed his guilt. The proud jut of his jaw had broken away her last remnant of hope.

She took the last step toward the butler as he reached her. "Thomas, you're a sight for sore eyes."

He pulled her into a bear hug, something he'd never done before.

Confused, she allowed the hug, then pulled back. "Thomas?"

Eyebrows pinched together, he shuddered out a breath and shook his head. "We've had a call from the nurse. Mr. Blakely passed away fifteen minutes ago."

Lily felt the blood drain from her face. He'd died while she was driving to his house with his last words to her replaying in her mind. The hairs on the back of her neck stood on end.

At a lock clicking behind her, she and Thomas both turned to see Damon standing framed by the opened door, at his feet the suitcase she recognized from their trip to New Zealand.

"Honey, I'm home," he said with a wry smile.

Irritation surged that he'd followed her, but she had to acknowledge that part of her had known he would. Of course he would. And that same part of her wanted to be close to him, even now. To touch his solidness and be held.

But she pushed the tumult of emotions aside because, regardless of her physical reactions and his deplorable behavior, Damon's last immediate relative, besides their unborn baby, had just died.

How would he react to the news? Probably relieved—his contempt for his uncle would barely permit more, yet she couldn't be sure. She knew only that she needed to be the person to tell him.

Lily moved to his side and sought his eyes. "Damon, your uncle passed away a little while ago."

He stiffened, eyes boring into hers, but gave no clue to which emotion the news evoked.

Thomas moved forward. "If there's anything I can do…"

Damon's eyes flicked to Thomas. "No." He shook his head, as if shaking off a passing mood. "You probably had more affection for him than anyone, Thomas, and I know that wasn't much. I'm well aware he had to pay for your loyalty."

Thomas shrugged, a confused sadness in his eyes. "He wasn't an easy man to work for, but I won't speak ill of the dead."

Damon gave a curt nod. "Tell the others that regardless of what happens with the estate, I'll make sure they're taken care of."

Lily held back a gasp. *He'd* take care of them? It was her place, surely, to take care of the house and its inhabitants? But she held back the words as they balanced on her lips. Of course Damon would think this way. And for many reasons, it wasn't the time to start arguments. She'd let it slide this once.

But just this once—she was through having her life dictated by Damon Blakely.

"Thank you." Thomas began to say more, blinked, closed his mouth then walked away.

Once they were alone, Damon thrust his hands into his pockets and looked around. "I guess this is all yours, sweetheart."

She wrapped her arms around herself in a futile attempt to ward off the ugliness of the whole situation. It seemed too cold to be calculating a dead man's assets so soon after his passing. "I'm not comfortable talking about this yet."

He let out a scornful laugh. "Come on, Lily. Don't tell me you're mourning that despot."

"No…not really. It's just…within a few hours, I've been lobbed into this house and a fortune—" *and heard the truth about the man I love and his view of me and our marriage* "—I guess I feel…actually, I don't know *how* I feel."

"Understandable. But it doesn't change the fact that you've inherited all my uncle's assets."

She looked up, searching his face for hidden meaning. "I told you I'd share it with you."

He shook his head in slow, almost methodical movements. "It's all yours. I only ever wanted BlakeCorp."

Lily felt her jaw slacken. Was he serious? "I thought you'd want it all, or at least half. Even Travis expected court battles."

"Perhaps Travis didn't know me as well as he thought he did." He raised one eyebrow and the implication hung in the air, that she'd unfairly judged him, too.

Had she? Discovering that Damon had been waging a war of destruction against his uncle without her even suspecting had shown her many things, including the more she knew about Damon, the less she knew about him.

If you allow a drop of compassion for Travis, her heart repeated, *shouldn't you confer the same to his nephew?*

Yet…Damon seemed to live for acquisitions. "Even if you hate the house, you still must have expected it'd come to you?"

He shrugged, seemingly unconcerned. "This property is small peanuts. My portfolio is worth more than ten times what Travis was at his peak. A house here or there barely registers."

She frowned and watched him walk back to his luggage, bring it in and close the door. Could it be that simple? A mere issue of sums and figures, with no consideration of Damon's driving force—ownership. Possession. Retribution.

If there was more to this laying down of his sword, he wasn't ready to share details. She could see that from the set of his shoulders. The closed angles of his face. He'd spring the surprise of his true motives on her at some stage…but this time, she'd be expecting it.

Damon was only generous when it suited his purpose. He'd taught her that well.

She wrapped a hand around her throat, knowing it was a defensive move even as she made it. "However we do it, I consider my portion belongs to our baby. And that's only if there are no challenges to the will."

He waved a hand, tossing the idea aside. "I'm the only one who'd have a claim to challenge. And I told you I won't. It's yours." He moved over to a hall table and picked up a crystal bowl in casual assessment. "Will you sell?"

"No." She swallowed convulsively. "There was some

fine print in his will that I only noticed when Crawford's letter pointed it out. I can't sell. I only inherit if I keep it so it can be passed to the baby in turn."

Replacing the bowl, he stretched his arms wide, taking in the interior of his childhood home. "So rent it out. Leave it here to rot." He lifted one shoulder then dropped it in a nonchalant gesture of disinterest. "Let the Dog Protection Society use it as kennels. But don't live in it. It's as cold as a coffin."

"I have to." Her voice wavered and she cursed it. This wasn't something she needed to be anxious about. She had a plan.

He turned back to face her, eyes trained on hers. "Why?"

She took a breath, held it, then released it slowly. "That was the rest of the fine print. I inherit only if I don't sell, and I live in it for at least twelve months."

Damon swore. "Then forfeit. Nothing is worth that."

"I wouldn't just lose the house. I'd lose everything. The money. BlakeCorp. Everything." She couldn't do it to her baby or Gran, or even Damon, despite what he'd done. They might have no future, but she wouldn't be another person to deny him his birthright. "It'd all go to your cousin, Mark."

He held her gaze, unmoving, face impassive, and a vague cloud of suspicion filtered through her mind. Why didn't he react to the possibility of losing Blake-Corp? His lack of concern didn't make sense. But before she could make any meaning of the thought, Damon closed the distance between them.

He took her hands, gripping firmly. "Travis is trying

to flex his muscle from beyond the grave." His jaw hardened. "We can't let him win."

For several seconds, she soaked up his touch, his nearness, his heat, before stepping back, out of his reach. "I have no intention of letting him win. I'm going to beat him at his own game."

His forehead wrinkled in disbelief. "By doing what he tells you?"

"No. By making this old place a home." A place of stability and security that could never be taken away. No one could gamble away her child's clothes and toys. No one would force her child to move on before she or he even made friends or settled into school. No one would ever have that power again.

She crossed her arms under her breasts, holding the thought close to her heart. "I can make it something worth inheriting." And then, despite the maneuverings of Travis, she'd have had the last say in the whole affair.

Damon regarded her with an expression bordering on pity. "This house is a lost cause." He extended a hand. "Come home with me."

Lily took a step back. She had her plan worked out. She'd be independent, a home owner. And no one, *no one,* would ever again use her as a pawn for their own ends—by buying a stake in a poker match, or marrying her to access a will—again. She squared her shoulders and met his gaze. "I'll transform it. Make it into a home. Don't worry about me, I want to be here."

He stepped closer, following her retreat, and cupped her shoulders. "I'm not leaving you and our baby alone at night waiting for thieves, or worse. By morning the world will know Travis Blakely is dead and it's no secret the contents of this place are valuable. It may have been an excuse for getting you here, but Travis was right about that. I won't leave you vulnerable."

A shudder ran down her spine at the thought of being in this cold house late at night, pregnant, alone but for staff at the other end of the building. She'd likely lie awake listening to every little bump and creak. To know Damon was down the hall…she'd be safe.

But after breaking up with him, she couldn't ask it. She licked dry lips. "The house has an elaborate security system. And three live-in staff. If it was enough to protect a sick, dying man, it'll be enough to protect me."

Damon's mouth set in a grim line. "If you're staying, then so am I." He retraced his steps to the door and picked up his luggage. "We'll take the main bedroom in the north wing."

Lily sat on the edge of the bed in the south-wing bedroom she'd moved to. She'd changed into a satin lilac nightgown and was ready to turn in, but something stopped her.

Restless, she crossed to the dresser, picked up a sheaf of papers and began to flick through the plans she'd sketched for the revamping of the mansion. She'd had the ideas and hadn't wanted to waste time, so had asked Thomas to bring her a tray instead of going down for dinner. The side benefit was avoiding another confrontation with Damon over the dinner table.

Damon. At the thought of him, her restlessness escalated and her blood heated. Thinking of the way the warmth of his hands could suffuse the fabric of her clothes to warm her right through. The seductive timbre of his voice. Memories of the hot slide of naked bodies in the dark of night.

Her core throbbed and her skin tingled with aware- ness. How would she go through her life, never lying with him again? Never rising to the heights that only he could take her?

And yet she *couldn't* give in to her body's insistent clamoring for his lovemaking. She had to keep her distance. They'd been down this path before and it led to heartbreak....

So why, she asked herself, was her hand on the doorknob?

She let out a long sigh. If she were completely honest, she had to admit something, even if only to herself. She wanted Damon with a blinding need. He was down the hall. He was her husband. And it didn't *have* to mean anything. Didn't have to mean they had a future.

The morning after they'd arrived back in Australia, married, he'd said maybe all that mattered was how right it felt when they made love, and they'd handle the aftermath when it happened.

Come. Live in the moment with me, he'd said.

Her eyes drifted closed as she contemplated sneaking into his room, climbing under the covers, perhaps finding him naked, welcoming her. The vision left her light-headed with craving.

Maybe she could live in the moment just once more....

Pulse racing, Lily opened the door and padded silently down the hall. She'd regret this tomorrow, but right now the need to touch him, to be touched, was something she could no longer deny or control.

She paused outside his door and took a long breath. How would Damon react to this late-night visit? Would he be self-satisfied that she'd come to him? Read more into it than it meant? Leaning her forehead against the door, her body yearning for him, she realized it made no difference how he reacted. She needed him.

She turned the knob quietly and edged the door open enough to slip through. Damon lay sprawled on the four-poster bed against a pile of pillows, bare chested, with a glass of red wine in one hand and the other arm up behind his head. His eyes were closed but his body was too tense for him to be asleep. A soft light spilled from a lamp, shrouding him in its golden glow and leaving most of the room in shadows.

At the sharp click as she closed the door, his eyes flashed open. His face was a picture of surprised wonderment. Within moments he'd taken in the scene, put his wine on a side table and was at her side, drawing her tightly against him. Lily trembled with want now he was holding her, now she could feel his body against hers.

"Thank God," he whispered into her hair. "I was about two seconds away from knocking on your door."

Her breath hitched at the deep rumble of his voice, but she made herself speak, to say it. "Damon, this doesn't mean—"

He leaned down, his warm breath caressing her ear as he kept her tightly enfolded against his body. "Shh."

"I just had to be in your arms again," she said, her

voice almost a sob. She reached out and twined her hands behind his neck, wanting him closer still. "In your bed."

His hands traced a path down her sides, skimming the satin nightdress, curving over her hips. "I know."

The familiar melting of her body from the inside out was as potent as it was welcome. Needing to touch him, to taste him, she pressed a kiss to his bare chest and he groaned.

"Lily, I want you so badly I can barely remember who I am."

Slowly, too slowly for her, he lowered his mouth and his lips whispered across hers. Burning for him, she raised herself onto her toes to hurry the kiss, then felt her entire body soften as he granted her request.

His lips were hungry, confident, moving over hers with such heat that she opened to him and welcomed his tongue, welcomed his teeth on her bottom lip, welcomed whatever he would do. He tasted of sweet wine and passion and she skimmed her hands over the solid muscles of his chest, up over his strong shoulders, along his back.

Just when her head began to swim, Damon pulled away, leaving them both trying to catch their breath. Their eyes met in silence, and for one moment reason broke through the fog of desire in her mind. Was this wrong? Was she making things between them more complicated? More difficult to walk away from?

Then he held out his hand and she couldn't have resisted taking it for all the world. If they had no future, then she'd give herself this gift—one night of memories to sustain her through the nights without him.

"Come with me," he said, tugging on her hand. He led her to the side of the bed, reached down for the glass of wine and lifted it to her lips. She sipped as he tilted the glass, and she felt the rich, mellow fluid slide down her throat. Then he held her gaze as he sipped from the same glass. Something about sharing the wine with him made her heart clench, as if the gesture held some deeper meaning.

He replaced the glass on the side table and smoothly lifted her nightdress over her head. The cold air nipped at her skin, contrasting with the burning heat inside her. Needing him more than air, she reached out.

"Just let me look at you for a moment," Damon rasped. He stepped away from her, his eyes feasting on her naked body the way patrons at the gallery might look at a masterpiece.

Her skin erupted in gooseflesh wherever his eyes rested, and she felt a thrill of power in her own body, felt beautiful in his eyes.

"You're the most exquisite thing I've seen in my life." Damon moved closer and she breathed him in—the woody, musky clean scent of him.

He took her left hand and guided it to the glass of wine, then he dipped her fingers into the bowl before lifting them to his mouth. Two droplets of the deep red wine dripped onto his chest before he caught her finger-tips between his lips. He circled them with his tongue, nipping gently then sucking firmly. As if a direct line connected her fingers to her core, a tug of molten heat arrowed its way through her body and she moaned.

"Damon," she breathed, her eyes drifting closed.

"Let me worship your body tonight."

Her eyes opened and she saw the promise in his eyes. "Yes. God, yes."

The droplets of wine on his chest had run a little, leaving a moist trail down his solid muscles. With barely a thought, she leaned in and ran her tongue along the path, tasting the richness of the wine, mixed with the taste of Damon's skin. Ambrosia, the food of the gods, could hold no more delight than this. All traces of the wine gone, she moved lower, tasting the skin over the ridges of his abdomen. His breath caught as she nipped, so she did it again.

His hands cupped her face and he brought her back up to meet his eyes. "Have mercy, sweetheart."

He kissed her—soft, slow and mind-blowing— bringing her closer, closer, till their bodies were pressed together. Knees like jelly, she wavered, but he held her tightly and she knew she'd never fall while he held her. How could a relationship between them be so wrong when they felt like *this* together?

With one arm supporting her, he reached across to whip the covers from the bed before lifting her and laying her across the crisp cotton sheets. Lily almost cried in bliss, knowing there was nowhere else on earth she'd rather be than in Damon's bed. Her husband's bed.

He parted her thighs and knelt between them. The vision of him leaning over her body, strong and potent, made her pulse spike. But his trousers sitting low on his hips interrupted the picture. "Have you forgotten something?" she whispered.

A corner of his sensual mouth curved. "If I take them

off, I might be tempted to take you too soon. And I want to spend much longer than that here with you."

"But I need the feel of you in my hand." She reached down to caress the hardness straining against his zipper. "Can I touch you?"

Muscles bunched across his shoulders, his chest tensed, his breathing quickened. But he rasped, "Yes."

She undid the buckle on his belt and drew it from the loops of his trousers then let it fall to the floor. A fiery need raced through her and she reached down with both hands to cup him through the fabric again, stroking. He lifted his tense body higher, up onto his toes and fists that rested either side of her shoulders.

"Lily," he groaned, then bent his head down, body still held inches above hers, and claimed her mouth.

This kiss was more greedy than the first, more demanding, more raw. He turned his head, changing the angle, and her hands slid away from his trousers, up his sides to his back, and she was helpless to do more than cling to him.

With one quick motion, without breaking the kiss, he rolled, bringing her on top of him, holding her firm against his body. The full-length contact was what she'd been craving since she'd left her bedroom, and now that she had it, a soft sigh escaped her lips. She moved, rubbing her breasts across the coarse hair of his chest, rubbing her hips against his despite the fabric in their way.

She reached for the zipper, but he caught her wrist.

"Before you slipped through my door tonight," he said, breathing hard from their kiss, "I was lying here, thinking of the things I wanted to do to you. Like this, for example." With hands gripping her sides, he lifted her torso high, arching her back, then he captured the peak of one breast in his hot mouth. He gently abraded with his teeth as he pulled with his lips, and sparks shot out from her nerve endings, flooding her body until she was limp and would have fallen but for his strong hands holding her in the air.

"Damon, I'm not sure how much longer I can stand that." She squeezed the words out as she reached to run hands through his thick dark hair.

"Then I'll stop," he said easily. Too easily. With barely time for her to catch her breath, he found the peak of her other breast and began the same sweet torture.

She bucked her hips against his, mindless, and heard his groan. He rolled them again, so she lay beneath him and he pinned her to the bed.

Looking up into his ice-blue eyes, now darker with desire, she felt her heart swell with the love for him she normally kept leashed. Tears pricked the backs of her eyes and her throat felt thick. "Damon, whatever else happens, I want you to know this is real between us. This connection we have is real and precious to me."

He kissed her tenderly. "It's precious to me, too."

He reached for the wine and, gently wrapping his arm behind her shoulders, lifted so she could sip from the glass he placed against her lips. Then, eyes locked on hers, he sipped as well. Her heart almost stopped beating with the power of the gesture; it was as if they'd toasted the importance, the honesty of their connection. He might never love her, but this was almost as good. Almost.

Damon reared back from her and allowed three, then four droplets of wine to fall into her belly button. With her skin sensitized, each droplet made her gasp.

He replaced the glass on the side table, then edged down the bed, to lick the wine from her stomach. "Making love to you has always been best when it's a little messy," he said with a lazy grin.

A delicious shiver ran down her spine as memories crowded into her mind, competing with the current sensations. "I remember the picnic at that secluded spot near the falls."

"Mango slices, dripping juice," he added as his hands trailed down along her thighs, before splaying them over her hips.

"I thought I'd pass out from the intensity that day," she whispered.

His smooth moist tongue explored farther across her slightly rounded belly, before he paused and laid a tender kiss on her abdomen. Then he moved lower still, and when his tongue plunged in the most intimate of kisses, she cried out his name.

She writhed below him, but his hands trapped her hips firmly, keeping her in place. Her muscles were melting, her bones—everything—dissolving. The only reality that remained was his mouth and its rhythmic movements. Nothing else existed. His hands slid up to her breasts to gently flick the peaks, and she truly broke free of the world, crying his name, racing higher, until she imploded and floated in a place where nothing existed beyond Damon and the way he made her body come alive.

Vaguely she felt him move to her side and pull her into an embrace that felt like home. After timeless moments she opened her eyes to find him staring at her, a puzzled line on his forehead.

She snuggled closer. "Why the frown?"

He absently stroked her side. "I'm trying to work out why every time we make love, it's better than the time before. Why I've never had enough. I always need you more."

A discussion of their marriage was the last thing she needed now. Or philosophizing on how her decision to come here tonight would impact on their future.

So instead she kept it light. "I think some things are beyond explaining." And she reached for his trousers. This time he let her unzip him and push the trousers and boxers to his ankles before he maneuvered them off to fall on the floor.

She reached to cup him again, the way she had through the fabric, but this time there was no barrier. She stroked with one hand, whisper soft, then bent to kiss the hardness.

"Lily." The word was wrenched from his throat. "You'll kill me, you know that?" He pulled her up for a quick, hard kiss, then edged off the bed to stand before her, and her heart missed a beat at the sight of his masculine beauty.

He held out his hands, but she hesitated. She'd wanted this, had come to his room in the dead of night for this, but now the culmination of her fantasy was here, she wanted to delay it. Couldn't bear it to end.

"Take my hand, sweetheart," he said softly, and smiled into her eyes.

Without another thought she reached for his out-stretched hands and he pulled her to her feet, lifting her high against him until her toes no longer touched the ground and all thoughts fled. She wrapped her legs around his waist, buried her hands in his hair.

In a haze of passion, she draped him with her body, her fingers curling and unfurling in his hair. She could feel his heart beating powerfully against her chest, his hands shifting her hips to increase the pleasure for them both.

He lowered himself to sit on the edge of the bed, the slide of skin on skin as he brought her to straddle him sending shivers up her spine. Then he lifted her again, and brought her down onto him. She felt herself expand to embrace him, rocked a little to fully appreciate the sensation.

"You said this was real and precious, Lily?" He moved in her and her breath caught. "It's more than that. It's everything."

Not wanting to confirm his meaning, she said against his mouth, "Just keep going." He shifted his hips, rocked them both higher, and she gasped.

"Lily, this is right," he said, an edge of torment in his voice. He raked his hands down her back, then wrapped them tightly around her, increasing the friction against her breasts as he moved higher in her. "We belong together."

A single tear slid down her cheek. He was right. The sensations he created in her were so beautiful, how could she have thought she could live without this? Everything else would work out. It had to.

"Yes," she whispered into his ear. "This is right."

Something like a growl rumbled in his chest and he

moved faster, higher. She reached out to brace one hand on a corner bedpost, the other hand woven in his hair, her eyes locked on Damon's.

As the power built inside her, she bit down on her lip, trying to hold on, to extend this moment of perfection as long as she could. Her grip on the post tightened, her whole body thrummed until she flew high enough to join the stars and she let go of the post and everything else, feeling Damon convulse and follow her out into the cosmos.

Nine

Lily woke in her husband's light-filled bedroom, a sleepy smile easing across her face. She stretched and reached for Damon.

The sheets were cold where his body had lain during the night. Sitting up, she looked for him, listened for sounds of the shower from the en suite, but there was nothing. A familiar ache touched her chest, but she ignored it. She'd been the one to slip into his room last night. Had gone willingly to his bed with no expectations beyond the pleasure they could bring each other. He had a right to his own movements this morning.

From the corner of her eye she saw a slip of paper on his pillow and reached for it.

"Sweetheart, I have to go into the office, but I'll be home as soon as I can. D"

Lily smiled ruefully at herself. Of course he'd gone to work. She should have predicted it.

She found her nightdress and quickly made her way down the hall to her own bedroom. During her shower, flashes of the night before filled her senses. The feel of Damon's hands on her body. The taste of his skin. The sound he made deep in his throat when he found release.

She shut off the faucet and, mind still pleasurably full of Damon, she toweled off and pulled on clothes. As she slipped on her sandals the phone rang, jolting her from the memories. She debated leaving it for Thomas, but since she was standing beside her room's extension, she picked up.

A thin, nervous voice asked, "Mrs. Blakely?"

"Good morning, Mr. Crawford."

"Oh, good. I'm glad you're home. I've discovered some rather disturbing information and wondered if I could call around to talk to you about it."

Her pulse spiked. *Disturbing information* were two words she didn't want to hear from her lawyer. "I'd rather you told me now."

"The thing is, I'm unsure of how much you already know. It's of a delicate nature."

Frowning, Lily leaned back onto the bedpost. Now the disturbing news was delicate, as well. "All I know is what you and Travis have told me."

Crawford cleared his throat. "Perhaps you should sit down."

"Please, just tell me."

He took a deep breath and hesitated before continuing. "As Travis Blakely's executor, I've been looking into his holdings before passing them on. It seems there were many things he didn't share with me or his other attorneys."

Her nails curled into her palms as she sank onto the bed. "What did you find?"

"Travis Blakely was not in possession of the assets that he willed to you."

Not in possession of the assets. The words reverberated in her head and she pressed a hand to her chest, attempting to quell her racing heart. "The house? The money?"

"He had nothing," Crawford said sympathetically, as if attempting to soften the blow. "Worse than nothing— the estate owes money in missed payments on loans."

A quick rush of panic rose to encircle her throat. "He left me a debt? I'm in debt!" Her voice sounded unnaturally high in her ears. She'd lost her independence. Her security. Her baby's security. She dropped her head into her free hand and focused on keeping her lungs breathing while all her plans dissolved into thin air.

"There's more."

Her head jerked up as adrenaline surged through her bloodstream. More? What more could there possibly be? She straightened and braced herself for worse. "Go on."

"The assets and holdings that Travis Blakely thought he owned were acquired by various companies. I've only been able to follow the complicated trail on some of them so far, and those lead back to one person. I suspect once I've traced the others back they'll end up at the same person as well."

Her heart clenched tight and she *knew.* "Damon." As

she said his name aloud, acknowledged what she knew to be true, her stomach fell away.

Crawford coughed nervously. "He really hasn't told you any of this?"

Not a word. She gripped the bedpost as her head began to spin. *Not even a hint.* She swallowed and waited until her throat relaxed enough to speak. "What do we do from here?"

"I still have quite a bit of work to do, but when I'm finished, I'll give you a full report, including the steps that need to be taken."

"Thank you, Mr. Crawford." Lily hung up with a shaky hand and closed her eyes.

He'd lied to her. He'd stood there in the foyer last night and discussed what she could do with this house, when he already owned it.

Had anything between them ever been real? The tender moments they'd shared... Him staying with her in this mansion to ensure her safety... The love they'd made last night... She gripped the silver heart on her necklace as she attempted to settle nausea that had nothing to do with her pregnancy.

And this house—the one she'd planned to make over as a permanent place of stability for her and her child— didn't belong to her. Damon had somehow acquired it.

Her legs trembled and felt weak, but she made herself stand. She had to leave. Cut ties with Damon. Now. It was unthinkable to remain here with a man who could so blatantly lie to her.

Betray her.

Burning tears filled her eyes, but she refused to acknowledge them. Instead she summoned the inner strength that had sustained her through a childhood with erratic parents.

Leaving the man who'd betrayed her as she'd never been betrayed before was the right thing to do for herself, but more important, for her baby.

She had to go.

Lily sat on a russet wingback in the mansion's formal library, feet tucked up under her, hands clenched together on her lap. On the verge of emotional exhaustion. It had been three hours since Crawford had delivered the bombshell that had shattered her heart—her life—and her bags were packed and in the car. Now she only waited for her husband to arrive.

Since Damon had rung to say he was leaving work early, she'd been on tenterhooks, alternating between sitting on this chair and restlessly toying with books on the floor-to-ceiling shelves. Her whole body was taut, like a rubber band ready to snap, but she'd forced herself to bide her time before she could confront her husband about his betrayal.

Then she must leave.

An excruciating pain stabbed her heart at the thought, but she pushed the pain aside. There would be time enough to grieve later.

The crunch of wheels over the driveway's polished gravel announced his arrival. Wanting to meet her fate head-on despite the heavy bands constricting her lungs, the pounding in her head, she rose and walked to the foyer. She listened with hyperfocus to his car door open and close. His steps on the walkway seemed to echo the thudding beat of her heart.

The door opened, then he was there, in the marble foyer with her, dominating the space. Her body was drawn by their magnetic connection even now; her heart cried out for him.

But she couldn't listen.

He walked over and dropped a kiss on her cheek. "Are you waiting to welcome me home?" he asked, a teasing note in his voice.

She swallowed, lifted her chin. "I'm waiting for you, yes."

It had started to drizzle outside—she could see the fine droplets in his dark hair and on his suit coat. Part of her wanted to shake her fingers through the waves of his hair to rid him of the raindrops, the way a wife might lovingly nurture her husband. But her love for Damon had always been her Achilles' heel.

Their marriage was irrevocably broken. He'd stood in this very foyer yesterday and lied to her about something as important as their child's home. Her hands slid to her gently rounded belly and she took a small step back.

Damon seemed to take in her mood and frowned. "What's wrong, sweetheart?"

"I know—" Her voice wobbled to a stop. She took another breath. "I know about your...scheme."

Wary now, Damon set his briefcase down, rested his hands on his hips. "My scheme?"

She gripped the silver heart on her necklace and found a strong, even voice. "I had a call from Crawford today."

He winced and muttered an oath. "What did he tell you?"

Lily felt her jaw slacken, all traces of anguish over this confrontation gone in an instant. How very Blakely of him. His first response wasn't to come clean. Wasn't to beg her forgiveness. It was a damage assessment. Her blood heated at the calculated way his heart and mind worked, even when the stakes were so high.

She looked him square in the eye. "How about we start with this house. The one *you* own."

He reached for her hand, but she took another step back, refusing to allow him that intimacy.

"Lily, I'm sorry you found out." His voice had changed, become less confident. "I never meant for you to know."

She shook her head, incredulous. "You're not sorry for lying to me? Just that you got caught? I think I need to—"

"Lily, let me explain." His eyes—his whole face— were uncertain, exposed, and that shocked her almost as much as finding out she didn't own a single thing.

She crossed her arms under her breasts, trying desperately to protect her heart from his display of vulnerability. To keep this man's sins at the forefront of her mind, how he'd callously taken every opportunity to stick the knife in his uncle's back, had disregarded her choices at every turn.

"You have ten minutes to explain how you have the deed, Damon."

She marched through the archway, then turned sharply to face him, beyond caring that he'd see her ragged breathing. "You can start now."

He sat heavily in one of the russet wingbacks, leaning over to rest his forearms on his knees. Then he looked up and captured her gaze. "I've been buying my uncle's assets since I was twenty. Travis made it ridiculously easy by taking out loans he couldn't afford and not telling his lawyers. Greed and arrogance left him drastically overextended, so I've been using dummy companies to call in the loans."

She closed her eyes briefly. Of course he had. Damon schemed and manipulated situations as second nature—why hadn't she guessed he'd already claimed back everything he thought Travis owed him? She sank into the other wingback, summoning her reserves of courage to ask for the details. "Travis knew about two companies. No one knew about the rest?"

Damon shook his head slowly, eyes not leaving hers. "I was waiting until I had everything before I told him. Everything he thought he owned—even Blake-Corp—is mine."

"Why?" Though she asked the question, she already knew the answer. She needed to hear it from him, to hear it all.

He shrugged one shoulder. "The lure of destroying him, the same way he tried to destroy me, was too strong. I've been working toward this for years, and now…" His voice trailed off.

Revenge. *It was all about revenge.*

Knowing Travis, she understood Damon's thirst for vengeance, but she could never condone it. "And now he's dead and you can't gloat." To her own ears, her voice was flat, as empty as she felt inside.

He closed his eyes, looking almost sick, or despairing. "No, that's *not* it." He swallowed hard. "I want you to keep the house."

Lily almost smiled. How noble. But she didn't need his house, or his housekeeper, or his nanny, or his millions. She never had. Another thing he'd failed to understand about her. From early in life she'd learned to make it on her own, and heaven knew she could make it on her own now. She'd look after herself, Gran and the baby.

She waved away his regret with a flick of her wrist and instead focused on the question pounding through her brain. "You didn't think, at *any* time since you proposed, to tell me about this? Even when I told you Travis had changed his will?"

His hands curled over, then he released them. "I couldn't undermine your security—I know what it means to you. You need to feel stable, and I was giving it to you."

She gasped. Was he insane? By letting her live a lie, he hadn't just undermined any sense of stability, he'd utterly destroyed it.

She set her jaw. "You underestimated me. I could have coped with losing the security—I've bounced back from worse." Her father had ripped it out from under her often enough. "But I'll *never* forgive you for betraying me with the lies all this time."

He moved smoothly over to grab one of her hands. "All of this means nothing. We're still going to have a baby, we're still going to be a family."

Lily's heart skipped a beat and she suddenly felt faint

as the reality of what he hadn't said hit home. He didn't love her. He never had or could. He still held on to too much hurt.

And even though her heart bled for his troubled soul, she wouldn't fall for his empty words. They were a pretty illusion, a means to an end.

"Don't bother, Damon. You couldn't say a single thing that would make me believe you have any feelings for me but ownership."

She was so choked up she could barely get the words out. "So the house is yours. Enjoy it." Where would she go? It didn't matter, as long as it was far from the need to control still shining from his eyes.

She took a step toward the hall entrance, but Damon moved to block her path with the solidness of his body.

"My attorney will be in touch to tell you when the baby is born and to discuss visitation rights." She stepped around him and headed for the hall, feeling as if she might be sick.

"Lily, you can't leave."

The gravel-edged rasp in his voice made her turn in time to see his face distort with grief. But she couldn't let herself believe it; she had to protect herself and her baby.

She walked straight into the hall, picked up her keys on the way and continued outside. The blood rushed past her ears so loudly she could barely hear anything else.

Damon had been right about one thing. The house was full of torment. But it wasn't in the walls. It was in the hearts and minds of the Blakely men. She would never let him have sway over her again, or warp her baby's mind into the Blakely way of life.

Ten

Damon sat in his Lexus in the art gallery car park, unfamiliar nerves squirming in his belly. Lily was just inside those doors. His wife. It had been two whole weeks since he'd seen her and, God above, he wanted her. Wanted her in his bed. Talking to him. With him during the day. Holding his hand. Everything. Just *her*. So much, he ached with it. He couldn't wait to see her hold their baby, to nurse it and bring a smile to its cherubic face.

But—he scrubbed his hands across his face—he couldn't let himself get carried away with fantasy just yet or he might lose her for good. Lose their future.

His gut clenched and swooped at the memory of her walking out the door, walking away from him. He knew now he needed to lay the blame for ruining their marriage at his own door, and it tied him in knots knowing he'd hurt her. A beautiful soul like hers was a rare treasure. Priceless.

He also knew she might never forgive him for the deception, and that was a risk he had to take. Having her pure heart in his life unquestionably made him a better man. He'd done his damn best in the past two weeks to make things up to her, and now it was time to show her the results of that work.

His pulse spiked at the thought of seeing her again. Her smile swam before his eyes, her scent surrounded him. The silken feel of her long hair made his hands twitch. He craved the feel of her skin under his fingertips, needed to have her sweet lips touch his. *Love?* Such a small and inadequate word. He was *drowning* in the depth of need and want he felt for her.

Why hadn't he realized before that he loved her? He dragged in a lungful of air and held it, trying to steady his breathing. He had no idea when he'd fallen in love with her. All he knew was he'd fallen harder than he'd thought possible.

And now it was time to show her how much.

Lily stood from her desk and stretched. Needing a break from the paperwork that had taken most of her morning, she strolled down the corridor of the gallery's office section.

As she walked, her hands moved to a familiar position—across her rounded stomach—and her thoughts drifted to her baby. And her baby's father.

Her pulse picked up at the mere thought of him,

despite all he'd done. Worse still was the ache in her heart. She missed him with every fiber of her being. Each time the baby moved she wanted to put his hand on her belly, to share it. When she had news, she wanted to call him, to hear his voice filled with warm congratulation or gentle comfort. She even missed the things he'd done for her—high-handed, yes, but done because he wanted to make her life easier....

And she missed his touch. Not just sexual, though God knew that was constant—she missed his smile, the way he'd look at her, or hold her hand.

The little things.

But she hated that weakness. She needed to settle the financial mess between them, and make arrangements for their baby's future. What was best for her unborn child had to be her *only* consideration. Divorce was definitely a priority. She couldn't possibly get over him while she was his wife.

She wandered into an exhibition on Indian Art. The space looked beautiful with the choices of artwork the curator, her friend Robyn, had made, and the swathes of fabric draped around columns. Too gorgeous to dismantle in a week. Yet it was temporary, as her whole life seemed to be. Maybe always would be. She'd really believed the house Travis had left her would be the start of a new phase of permanence. And, despite repeated evidence to the contrary, that small kernel of hope that Damon could be a part of that stable future had refused to be squashed.

Would she ever learn?

From the corner of her eye she saw a man in a crisp

tailored suit, his hair a shade darker than midnight. All the air in her lungs squeezed out as she turned to watch Damon stride toward her. His gaze intent on her, hungry and…and yes, in *pain*. His long legs strode across the room, eyes locked on hers, as if he saw nothing but her, *wanted* nothing but her.

She struggled to fill her oxygen-starved lungs.

In his hand was a single page that he fidgeted with—she'd never seen him restless before. Something must be wrong. Or perhaps he needed her signature on some business document. That must be why he'd come.

Feeling unsteady, as if she was about to fall from a cliff, she took the last steps to meet him.

It took tensing every muscle she had to stop from throwing herself into his arms—but that was ridiculous, she shouldn't feel that way. She would stay strong to her last breath. She had to.

She nodded politely. "Hello, Damon."

She saw it again…a discernible difference in his eyes—that raw emotion she thought she'd glimpsed moments ago. Pain, regret, yearning. And still he didn't speak. She clasped her perspiring hands together. Oh, God, something *was* wrong.

"What is it? What's happened?"

He shook his head sharply, as if waking from a dream. "You. You've happened."

Confused, aching to touch him, she forced herself to step back. She'd been tricked before when her body had proven itself untrustworthy. She had to think with her head and forget about her heart.

Her chin kicked up even as her knees threatened to

buckle. "You're not making any sense. What do you mean, *I've* happened?"

Expression neutral, he said, "I've come to show you something. Come with me." He extended a hand.

Yes. Even her palm burned to have the connection. Her hand began to lift before she tucked it tightly under her breasts with the other. "I'm not following you anywhere, Damon. And I'm not touching you."

He gave a wry imitation of a smile and dropped his hand. "Of course." He held out the page he carried.

She kept her arms tightly crossed. "What's that?"

He quirked an eyebrow as if he had nothing to hide, as if he was the most trustworthy man on earth. "Read it," he said, "and you'll see."

Lily bit down on her lip. She couldn't think of anything Damon could show her that would make a difference. And yet, she couldn't help but be drawn to this unusual aura he was exuding. If appearances were enough, she might almost be convinced that he'd turned over that new leaf. Where was the seductive charm, the manipulative gleam in his eye?

She held herself tighter.

It had been difficult to say no to him before. Today it was near impossible.

Curiosity piqued and, heart drawn to him, she bit her lip again and finally relented. "Okay, but I'll warn you now it won't make a difference."

He smiled, genuinely this time, and she marveled at how that expression transformed his face into something as breathtaking as a master's Grecian sculpture. "Your warning is duly noted."

She took the page and skimmed the words. It was a flyer for a new gallery; a privately owned gallery open to the public. Owned by…her grandmother!

"Would you like me to take you there?" His jaw tightened, as though readying himself to argue her refusal.

What was he up to? She raised her head to meet his ice-blue eyes. Had Damon turned to manipulating Gran?

She hardened her heart. "What have you done?"

"Something different—no games, I swear." His eyes were clear, somber. "Let me show you. Can you get the afternoon off?"

Since she'd last seen him she'd accumulated more than enough overtime to cover an afternoon. The question was whether she wanted to be pulled back into one of his schemes. But if Gran was involved, Lily had to make sure it was all aboveboard. She'd never let anyone hurt Gran.

Watching him, she felt the familiar pull of arousal and struggled against it. It had betrayed her before. He couldn't be genuine. Couldn't be.

Could he?

Hating herself for giving in, she gave a brisk nod. "I'll meet you in the car park in ten minutes."

She rushed back to her desk, shut down her computer and told her boss she'd be back in the morning. When she made it to the front door, Damon stood beside his idling dark blue Lexus.

He held the car door open for her. When he'd slid into the driver's seat and pulled out into the car park traffic, she asked, "Where is this gallery?"

"You'll see."

They traveled in silence; she could think of nothing

to say. She couldn't start the conversation about finalizing things until she'd seen what he had to show her. And there was nothing else to talk about.

Her gaze flicked to Damon and she noted the tense set of his shoulders, the way his hands gripped the wheel a little too firmly. She frowned. Why wasn't he trying to convince her to come back? Why wasn't he trying to touch her?

He pulled the car to a stop and swung into a roadside parking space in an up-market section of town, where several private galleries were located. She knew the rent was through the roof in this area. Glancing up and down the street a large, simple bronze shop front caught her eye. *Lily's Place—Opening Soon.*

Damon stepped from the car and walked around to open her door.

She swallowed, confused. "What…" But she didn't know how to finish the sentence. Too many questions to choose one to lead with.

"I'll let your grandmother explain."

Damon opened the gallery door with his key and they walked in through the secure entranceway. The airy, white room still had boxes with packing materials spread across the floor, but several sculptures in glass cases were displayed on podiums.

Drawn to them, she moved, barely aware her feet were in motion. She ran a finger along one glass case, her art-curator's eye appreciating the simple beauty of the carved marble figures.

She turned to where Damon waited, but noticed the painting on the wall beside him was a portrait of a Victorian woman, surrounded by children dressed as small adults. The one that had hung in Travis Blakely's private gallery.

"That painting is yours." She forced words through a tight throat, willing reality to return.

"It was mine. I signed it, and all the other contents of my uncle's gallery, over to your gran a few days ago. They belong here, where people can see them. Not trapped in a dark room."

Damon surveyed the painting wistfully. "Hidden," he murmured, as if to himself. "Unappreciated."

As he'd been? Confused again, her mind warning her not to believe, yet her heart aching to, she looked him over. Yes, there was something different about him. He'd given her a gift she actually wanted.

The old Damon wouldn't have even known what she wanted, nor would he have cared to find out. In his world, what he decided was best for her was always the right thing.

But now, it was as if he'd come out into the light as well, ended the years of being trapped, first by an unscrupulous uncle, and then by his own plans of revenge.

Becoming the man he would have been, had his parents lived…

A door opened from the back of the gallery and Gran shuffled in. She looked radiant—more alive than Lily had seen her in years.

"Darling," she called to Lily.

Lily rushed over and embraced her in a tight hug. "Gran, why didn't you tell me you were doing this?"

Gran looked over her shoulder at Damon. "Your

husband asked me to keep it a secret. He wanted to surprise you."

Slowly Lily turned to look at Damon, then back to Gran. Wanting, wishing—not daring to believe. "So what, exactly, has he done?"

"He set up the business side and donated his uncle's collection. He also gave us a fund for purchasing new artwork."

"A fund?" Lily's mind immediately sprang to conditions on the money Damon would have set—a lever for future manipulations. "What are the strings?"

She felt Damon move up behind her. "No strings. I sold BlakeCorp and put the money into a fund for Lily's Place. Your gran is the only signatory at the moment."

She must have heard him wrong. *He'd sold Blake-Corp?* It'd been his life's ambition. "You sold it?"

"I'd already won—taking it back from the old vulture. But it was a hollow victory." He looked into her eyes with that unashamed pain and yearning and regret, and she knew his meaning. She knew because it was the same for her. Her success at being independent was empty without sharing it with the one she loved.

Her hands fluttered up. "But selling it is so extreme…"

"I didn't want the reminder. BlakeCorp is my past. The last thing I need is a constant symbol of my mistakes. Far better it be of some use here."

Now the fervent promptings of her heart grew louder than the warnings of her mind. Could it be? Were this leopard's spots changing before her eyes?

He cleared his throat. "There's one more thing I want to show you. Come with me."

Mind in a whirl, she turned to Gran, who said, "Go on, darling. At least look at what he wants to show you."

Lily took a deep breath. In for a penny, in for a pound. She turned back to Damon and nodded.

He turned for the door and she followed, waving a quick goodbye to Gran with a promise to be back soon.

Damon tucked her into the car and pulled out onto the road. Again, they were quiet on the trip, Lily too bewildered to form coherent thoughts or questions, and Damon once more holding the wheel with white knuckles, the muscles of his neck corded.

As they turned into the street of the old Blakely mansion, she spoke tightly. "I've seen your house before, Damon."

"Bear with me a little longer." He turned into the circular drive and she noticed something odd. The front lawn was covered in new garden beds—all filled with spring blossoms. There were daffodils, roses and daisies, and one large bed in the middle was filled with lilies. Day lilies, peace lilies, climbing lilies and African lilies.

She caught her breath. From death to life… "How…how did you do this so quickly?"

"You just have to know who to ask." Still grim, he turned off the ignition and came around to her door. "Come in. Please."

She stepped out and took his hand, unrelenting surprise not allowing her to think clearly. Her gaze swept the front of the mansion, which she'd once thought so imposing. It now had a veranda added to the top story, softening the edges of its profile.

Damon led her to the door where Thomas waited, a look of relief spreading across his face. "You found her!"

Thomas reached forward and, for the second time since she'd met him, hugged her. "Welcome home, Mrs. Blakely. The place hasn't been the same since you left." He stepped back, face beaming with delight. "And now it will never be the same again!"

Lily opened her mouth to stop his train of thought from where it was going, but Damon had shrugged out of his coat, rolled up his sleeves and headed down the hall. She managed a quick wiggle of her fingers to the cheerful Thomas before they turned the corner and she lost sight of him and the door.

Damon opened the first door on the left, the formal dining room. But it wasn't formal anymore, it was full of life and informality and…love. And it looked eerily similar to the design she'd sketched for this room.

"How did you know?"

"I found your sketches after you left."

She walked in, touching the back of a wooden chair with a bright lemon cushion, running her fingers along the edge of the slab wood table. "Why?"

He gripped the back of a chair and gazed out the window for a moment before meeting her eyes. "When I found your sketches, I saw the house through your eyes. I saw its potential instead of its past. It was time for me to let go."

She thought she knew what he meant, but needed to hear it from him. "Let go?"

He walked to the window, leaning against the frame as he answered, speaking slowly. "Travis was a sadistic brute. But I've been giving him power by holding on to my anger. By transforming this house to your vision, I've reclaimed a part of myself." He pushed off the wall to stand straight and tall. "I won't let him own me."

Joy for him, for his liberty, spread from her heart to her toes and fingertips. "When? How?"

"It was you, Lily." His voice was rough, his gaze intense. "*You've* changed me."

Tears filled her eyes and she took a step toward him, but he forestalled her.

"Let's keep going."

He took her to room after room, each transformed according to her vision. She couldn't help it—the tears streamed silently down her cheeks now.

The last room was the nursery. "How did you get it done so soon?"

"I called in five teams of interior decorators. Thomas oversaw them and John oversaw the gardening team." He spread his hands. "There's still a lot more to do—the south wing hasn't been touched yet—but at least it's a home now, Lily. A home for you and the baby. You've created this."

She picked up a cuddly teddy and held it to her chest before replacing it in the crib. "No, you created it. I just had the ideas."

"Let's say *we* created it. It only needs you and our baby here. And me." Finally, at last, he touched her, his hands capturing hers, his eyes dark and pleading. "I love you, Lily. I *need* you. I've confronted the ghosts that had been haunting me, thanks to you. You gave me the template to transform myself as surely as you gave me one for the house."

She sniffed and blinked, wanting to brush the tears aside, but to do so would mean letting go of his hands, and she wasn't letting him go again. Ever. "Damon, I'm so proud of you," she whispered through a ball of aching joy in her throat.

"Wait, there's one more room I want to show you." Still grabbing tight hold of her hand, he set off for the rear of the house, almost at a run. She laughed as she rushed to keep up.

He pushed through the double doors of the mansion's private gallery, but inside it was empty.

"Everything has gone to Gran's gallery," she said.

Damon dug his hands deep into his pockets and met her gaze. "I always had an interest in art as a child. It started when this gallery was a place of refuge from my aunt and uncle. I read books about art, learned on my own."

"So that's why you knew about Monet's cathedrals."

"Yes."

"But what happened? Why didn't you follow up on your interest?"

He cleared his throat. "Travis found me here hiding one day." His hand absentmindedly ran over a scar on his left arm.

Oh, God. Her heart bled as if pierced with a dagger. She'd thought it was a *sporting* injury. She gently brushed the scar with her fingers, as if to soothe the damage. "He did that to you?"

She'd known life must have been horrible for Damon as a young boy but she'd never truly faced how grim things were until seeing and understanding the full force of this evidence now.

SAVE OVER £31 25% OFF

Sign up to get 4 stories a month for 12 months in advance and **SAVE £31.80 – that's a fantastic 25% off**
If you prefer you can sign up for 6 months in advance and **SAVE £12.72 – that's still an impressive 20% off**

FULL PRICE	PER-PAID SUBSCRIPTION PRICE	SAVINGS	MONTHS
£127.20	£95.40	25%	12
£63.60	£50.88	20%	6

- **FREE P&P** Your books will be delivered direct to your door every month for FREE

- **Plus** to say thank you, we will send you a **FREE** L'Occitane gift set worth over **£10**

  Gift set has a RRP of £10.50 and includes Verbena Shower Gel 75m and Soap 110g

What's more you will receive ALL of these additional benefits

- Be the FIRST to receive the most up-to-date titles
- FREE P&P
- Lots of free gifts and exciting special offers
- Monthly exclusive newsletter
- Special REWARDS programme
- No Obligation –
  You can cancel your subscription at any time by writing to us at Mills & Boon Book Club, PO Box 676, Richmond, TW9 1WU.

MILLS & BOON

Sign up to save online at www.millsandboon.co.uk

Damon looked at the mark, seemingly surprised at the information he'd given away. "Yes." He shrugged.

She leaned down and gently kissed his scarred forearm, then wrapped both hands around it. "I'm glad he's gone, or I'd kill him myself."

He searched her eyes, then a ghost of a smile flitted across his face. "Afterward—" his voice was hoarse as he threaded his fingers through hers "—even this room was tainted. I gave up my interest in art, but you allowed me to reclaim that, as well."

All thoughts of Travis instantly gone, joy bubbled up and overflowed. Damon may have given her gifts today, but more, he'd shown that *she'd* given *him* something priceless. No longer did she feel useless, a decoration in his life...or unloved. "Damon."

He swallowed. "You know your gran has dreams of employing you to run the gallery. Be the curator. You could select staff, take the baby to work with you. Choose your own hours. Or help her find a curator if you'd rather stay at home and be a full-time mother." He shrugged. "I could even help look after the baby. I'd like that—if you want."

The options opening before her were wonderful. Miraculous. And she melted just a little more inside at his hopes of helping with their baby. "I can't think of a single person who'd be better with our baby. But one more thing. Tell me you didn't really sell BlakeCorp. It meant more to you than anything."

He turned to her, his eyes fierce. "*You* mean more to me than anything. You and our child. I didn't want any question of that. I still have my own company and I'll still probably work long hours, but I swear to you, Lily, I'll always put you first. You'll be my number one priority…if you'll have me."

She bit her lip and took a small step closer to his heat and essence and solidity. "You truly sold Blake-Corp…for me?"

He leaned in that last inch and encircled her in his arms. "I'd do anything for you. Anything." His voice rasped with raw emotion. "Tell me I got this right, Lily. Tell me I've given you what you want most. If I didn't, just ask me for it and I'll give it to you."

"You just did. All I ever wanted was you, all of you." She hugged him tight, overcome by the emotion. "I love you, Damon. More than I thought I could bear. I've been in my own private hell loving you so much but not being able to be with you. You're all I want—you, me and our baby. Our family."

He pulled back, and his whole face broke out in the kind of smile she'd never seen from him before—just simple happiness, no shadows of the past haunting him at last. "There's nothing I want more than that, either. To live with you and our child in our home. Except…"

Her heart skipped a full beat. "Except?"

"Except maybe to live in our home with you, our baby and our next baby."

She grinned, and threw herself into his arms, holding him tight. "Oh, yes, that's a vision of the future I can support."

He lifted her chin for his kiss and she sighed, not needing a single thing more than what was in the room with her at that moment.

Epilogue

Lily finished wrapping the oil painting she'd just sold and looked up to check on Pearl. In her favorite pink "gall'ry" dress—floor length, with a full "twirling skirt"—her three-year-old daughter was dancing across the room, showing an elderly couple around Lily's Place.

A laugh of pure love escaped. She could barely believe her life, and her child's, was so perfect. Five years ago, she never would have dared to dream so big.

"She's sweet. Is she yours?" The businessman in front of the counter smiled and took the wrapped package.

"Yes, she is." Lily beamed at her customer as she returned his credit card with his receipt. "Enjoy your painting."

Maree, the full-time saleswoman, was talking to a middle-aged woman, and four other people browsed quietly through the permanent display section in the next room, so Lily sneaked over to eavesdrop on her youngest saleswoman in action.

The elderly man was looking at the landscape Pearl pointed to, and the woman leaned down to ask Pearl, "Why do you like it so much?"

Without missing a beat, her eyes wide with the importance of the conversation, Pearl replied, "It's got nice purple at a-top."

Both customers lifted their gazes to the top of the painting. The man nodded. "She's right. That pale lavender in the distance balances the painting's depth and palette perfectly."

Lily's heart swelled with pride. She supposed it was hardly surprising Pearl picked up knowledge about art after the amount of time she'd spent in the gallery since her birth, but she seemed to have an incredible affinity with colors and composition for a three-year-old.

A whoosh to her left caught Lily's attention as the front door slid open and Damon strode in, gorgeous in a charcoal business suit, pushing a baby buggy. Lily's breath caught in her throat at the sight of him and their baby. A love for her husband swelled up, so big it felt as if it overflowed her heart, spilling into the air around her.

"Daddee!" Pearl ran across the tiled floor and launched herself at Damon, who caught her in an effortless move and swung her into the air.

Lily's face broke into a smile. She loved her work in

the gallery two afternoons a week, but her favorite time of the day was when Damon dropped in with baby Michael to pick them up, and she had her husband and two beautiful children in one place. Damon had been so supportive—delegating work and taking one afternoon off to allow Lily this time in the gallery. The other afternoon, today, Gran had Michael, and Damon collected him on the way home.

Damon sidestepped the buggy, still with Pearl in one arm, and reached for Lily. "Sweetheart," he murmured before kissing her lips slowly and tenderly.

Lily melted as the familiar rush of desire almost made her knees buckle. His effect on her had only deepened over the years—she could still barely stand to see him and not touch him, even if just holding his hand. She wound an arm around his neck and held him closer.

"I missed you," he said against her lips.

"And me?" Pearl chirped. "Did you miss me?"

Damon's smile for their daughter made Lily's heart sing. "And you, munchkin. So much that Michael and I had to come and get you."

"Yay!" Pearl hugged her dad tighter as Damon released Lily to push the buggy through the gallery and into the staff area out the back.

He checked on Michael, who was sleeping soundly, then deposited Pearl back on the ground. "And to give you some news."

Lily glanced at her darling eight-month-old, her fingers twitching to pick him up, but hating to disturb his sleep.

"News?" Pearl asked, voice excited.

Damon nodded. "Gran is coming over to spend the night with you and Michael."

Lily smiled and her skin tingled with anticipation. Another of Damon's impromptu nights out. She could never guess when the next one was coming or where they'd be.

"In fact, Gran is at our house now." He turned from Pearl to Lily, and dropped his voice. "So we just need to change and then we're going out."

Gran's health had improved so much, probably from a lack of stress as much as anything. But still, it was re-assuring to know that Thomas and Melissa—who now worked together in running the household—would be around to do any work, leaving Gran to have fun with Pearl and Michael.

"So what should I wear? Where are we going?"

He grinned, used to her fishing for their destination. "Dress up…but make sure it comes off easily." His gaze turned to smoldering as he raked it up and down her body.

Lily glanced over at Pearl, who was busy packing up her lunchbox and toys. Then she took a step forward and ran a finger down her husband's chest, pleased by his sharp intake of breath at her provocative move.

She blinked innocently. "There's nothing I can do to convince you to give me a hint?"

He captured her finger and pulled it up to his mouth, biting gently on the tip, and she felt the touch down to her core. "Choose shoes you can wear in the helicopter," he rasped. "And, sweetheart, be prepared to follow through on that promise in your eyes."

She laughed, low and husky. "I love being married to you, my husband."

His eyes suddenly became serious, filled with love and certainty. "And I love being married to you, my wife."

* * * * *

Seducing Samantha was definitely a perk he hadn't expected, but one he would thoroughly enjoy.

She wouldn't deny him. He'd seen the look of desire and passion in her eyes, felt it in her kiss. She was a woman, and women had needs just like men. He intended to meet her needs until he got what he wanted.

His list of wants was simple: Samantha in his bed, his resort back and Stanley Donovan's empire obliterated.

SEDUCING THE ENEMY'S DAUGHTER

BY
JULES BENNETT

Published in Great Britain 2011
Harlequin Mills & Boon Limited,
Eton House, 18-24 Paradise Road, Richmond, Surrey TW9 1SR

© Jules Bennett 2010

ISBN: 978 0 263 88090 8

51-0111

Harlequin Mills & Boon policy is to use papers that are natural, renewable and recyclable products and made from wood grown in sustainable forests. The logging and manufacturing processes conform to the legal environmental regulations of the country of origin.

Printed and bound in Spain
by Litografia Rosés S.A., Barcelona

To Grace and Madelyn.
I followed my dream to lay the path
for you to follow yours.

Jules Bennett's love of storytelling started when she would get in trouble as a child and tell her parents her imaginary friend "Mimi" did it. Since then her vivid imagination has taken her down a path she's only dreamed of.

When Jules isn't spending time with her wonderful, supportive husband and two daughters, you will find her reading her favorite authors, though she calls that time "research." She loves to hear from readers! Contact her at julesbennett@falcon1.net, visit her website at www.julesbennett.com or send her a letter at PO Box 396, Minford, OH 45653, USA.

Dear Reader,

What better setting for vengeful seduction than an exotic island? As an author I love forcing the ugliness from people's lives by dropping my characters and their problems smack into the middle of beauty, leaving them no choice but to embrace it.

Brady is a man who will let nothing stand in his way of gaining back his family's resort…especially not Sam Donovan. His vindictive plans take a slight twist when Sam turns out to be sexy, business-savvy Samantha. And Sam is too busy earning her place in her father's empire to give in to Brady's charm.

I hope you enjoy this exotic romance between two strong-willed business moguls who teach each other to step out of the stuffy boardroom and onto the sandy beaches to enjoy the simple things in life like a swaying palm tree or ocean breezes.

Happy reading!

Jules

One

"I'm sorry, sir, but the Tropical Suite isn't available until tomorrow."

"That's unfortunate, since I'm here now."

Samantha Donovan took a deep, calming breath, approached the registration desk and pasted on the umpteenth smile of the day. Running a high-class resort was certainly straining on her jaw muscles.

"Is there a problem?" she asked.

The tall, impossibly good-looking stranger turned his darkened gaze to her. "My room is unavailable."

Because she'd been in toe-pinching Jimmy Choo shoes all blasted day, Sam leaned an arm on the marble counter and directed her attention to the young employee at the computer on the other side of the registration desk. "Mikala, what is the problem with the Tropical Suite?"

The young Hawaiian girl punched in several keys; her hands shook as they hovered over the keyboard. "It seems Mr. Stone's reservation was entered into the computer for his check-in as tomorrow."

"But as you can see, I'm here today."

Sam didn't blame the man for having a bit of irritation to his voice; she was a bit irritated herself and had been since her father came up with this preposterous plan to make her gain his respect and a place in his company by getting their family's newly acquired Kauai resort up and running smoothly.

"Mr. Stone," Sam said with a soft yet professional tone. "I cannot apologize enough for this misunderstanding. We could upgrade your room and offer the Honeymoon Hideaway at no additional charge. I know that suite is available, because I just saw the couple off to the airport personally."

Another part of the job her father hadn't warned

her about. Not only had the resort been operating at a loss, they'd had to lay off workers. Now, as manager, Sam found herself playing taxi driver, maid, occasionally a waitress in one of the three restaurants and yesterday she'd had to unclog a commode in the Sands Suite.

Not the luxurious position her father had made this job out to be. But she would persevere, no matter what daunting tasks she had to take on.

This once five-star resort was the newest piece of property owned by her father and brother. Details weren't given, but Samantha knew the takeover hadn't been pretty or easy, so she needed to use all her energy and then some to make sure the guests were happy, the staff was well paid and the grounds were kept immaculate.

No problem.

"Is the room clean?"

The guest's question snapped her out of her self-induced pity party. "Yes, sir. Mikala, please make the necessary changes in the computer and I'll show Mr. Stone to the suite myself."

The man had a garment bag over one broad shoulder, so Sam reached for the extended handle of the single piece of black luggage.

Now she could add bellboy—or bell girl—to the growing list, providing Sam a diverse and impressive résumé, if her father chose to boot her from the company for good.

"Ma'am." The gentleman's voice drifted over her left shoulder. "I can take my own bag."

Not slowing her pace one bit, Sam replied, "Guests don't carry their own luggage."

She hit the button for the elevator, glanced up to see what floor the car was on and tried her damnedest to ignore the sultry, woodsy scent of this handsome guest.

"What kind of gentleman would I be if I let you carry my bag?"

Glancing to the side, Sam couldn't help but notice how well his shoulders filled his navy business suit or how nice his golden, tanned skin looked against the dark material.

Why was this man alone? She couldn't believe a man who dripped with charm and sex appeal didn't have a busty, leggy blonde draped over his arm. Granted she'd been here only six short months, but she hadn't seen too many singles.

"What kind of hotel would I be running if I had guests take their own bags to their rooms?"

Just as the elevator dinged, he lifted a dark brow. "I'm not going to win this fight, am I?"

She merely smiled over her shoulder as she stepped on to the empty elevator. Once upon a time the two lobby elevators had probably been full of laughing families and honeymooners, but not anymore. Sam wasn't sure what happened, all she knew was that her father had handed her this new resort and she was going to make it the best in Kauai, the world for that matter, or she would drop over dead in her Jimmy Choos trying.

The next time she contacted her father—he never contacted her—she'd bring up the fact, yet again, that in Kauai traditional resorts were going by the wayside and those with luxurious day spas or upscale Bed and Breakfasts were the only way to go. Of course, coming from her, she doubted he'd believe the new concept. Perhaps that's why the hotel had been in financial trouble before. Poor communication and/or lack of interest to upgrade in an attempt to compete with the other tourist hot spots.

If her father didn't listen, and soon, she feared they'd be caught in the same dilemma as the previous owners.

Since his wife's death, Stanley Donovan cared for nothing but himself. Samantha had been pushed to the back of his mind. Well, she was still his daughter whether he wanted to put forth the relationship effort or not.

Sam rested the bag's handle against her hip and

hit the button for the penthouse floor. "Did you have a nice flight?"

"As a matter of fact, I did, considering I have my own jet." A smile spread across his lips as he glanced down to his suitcase. "If you're the manager, why are you playing bellhop?"

"Mr. Stone—"

His dark gaze darted back up. "Brady."

"Brady," she said, instantly liking the strong, confident name, not to mention the way his coal-like eyes raked over her. "Because I'm the manager, I have to fill in when and where someone is needed. By the time I would've found someone to take your luggage, I could've done the job myself. Besides, even though there was an error in your reservation, I want you to be confident that we will do everything to make your stay pleasant."

The elevator came to a halt, the doors slid open. She motioned for him to exit first.

"That's quite a speech," he told her as she stepped beside him. "You even have a pleasant, professional voice. It sounds as if you've used those same words once or twice before."

Sam swallowed the lump in her throat, inserting the key card into the slot of the only door on the floor. "Mr. Stone—"

His hand slid over hers, sending shivers all

through her overworked, underappreciated body. "Brady, please."

Because she couldn't deny the low, seductive tone of his voice, Sam lifted her gaze only to find his eyes held more of a punch than his sultry voice and warm, strong hand.

Dark, rich brown eyes shielded by half-lowered lids roamed over her face, pausing at the lip she chewed on.

"Brady," she replied, cursing herself for allowing, even for a moment, emotions she didn't have time for to creep up. "I assure you, there are no problems with Lani Kaimana. We're happy to have you and I guarantee you'll have a pleasant and relaxing stay."

His bedroom eyes traveled back up her face, a corner of his full lips tipped into a smirk, but his hand remained enclosed around hers. "I'm sure it will be pleasant, but I don't know about relaxing. I'm here to work."

Sam forced herself to remember her task. She slid her hand from beneath his and jerked on the cool metal door handle. As much as she'd like to chat with Mr. Charming, she had a resort to save from despair.

"What exactly does Lani Kaimana translate to?" he asked.

"Royal Diamond." She swung the door in to reveal the spacious dark green and bright white suite. "I'm sure you'll be happier in this suite. Even though it's the honeymoon suite, it's the only one on this floor, so you shouldn't be disturbed. There's a king-size bed, a Jacuzzi, wet bar and Internet access."

Stepping across the threshold, Brady studied his surroundings, while Sam continued to study him. She'd seen plenty of men in business suits before, but as her eyes continued to roam over Brady's broad back, she couldn't recall seeing a single man who filled out a tailor-made jacket so well.

"This is amazing. The view through those balcony doors is absolutely breathtaking." Brady turned to face her. "I can't believe this room isn't booked year-round."

Sam took a step into the romantic suite, her eyes betraying her by drifting up to the king-size canopy draped with white sheers in the far corner perched on a stage just for the bed. An image flashed through her mind of this sexy, too-good-to-be-true handsome man stretched out beneath the crisp white sheets—wearing nothing but the sheet.

She looked back to Brady; a smile danced in his eyes as if he knew where her thoughts had wandered. "Yes, well, that's what we're working on," she said.

"How about if you discuss your plan of action with me over dinner?"

Stunned, yet flattered, Sam shook her head. "Brady, I appreciate the offer, but I cannot have dinner with you."

"Because you don't date guests?"

"No, because I'm too busy." Though now she would have to make a vow not to date guests. The topic had never come up before.

He cocked his head to the side. "Too busy to eat? How about if I come to your office?"

Obviously this man didn't take kindly to rejection. And Sam was pretty positive he hadn't heard a negative word from a woman in his lifetime.

"Thank you again, but I can't." Sam moved toward the door in an attempt to get away from his sexy scent and those piercing eyes before she gave in to temptation. She couldn't help but wonder just how many women fell into those bedroom eyes. "If you need anything, please just ask."

"Actually, there is one thing."

She peered over her shoulder. "Yes?"

"You know my name, but I don't know yours."

"Samantha Donovan, but everyone calls me Sam." She grinned. "I own the resort."

Samantha Donovan?

All this time he'd expected *Sam* to be a man. How could he not have known his worst enemy had a daughter? And a stunning one at that.

Brady slipped his smart phone from his jacket pocket and punched in the number to his brother, Cade. Not having all the facts on a resort he intended to take over was unacceptable. How the hell had this vital piece of information not been caught before?

"Hello."

"Cade, why the hell didn't I know Sam Donovan was a woman?" Silence filled the other end. "I assume you didn't know, either?" Brady asked.

"I had no idea. Are you in Kauai?"

"Yes." Still astounded, Brady stood in the same spot he'd been in five minutes ago when *Samantha* had walked out the door after dropping the bombshell. "Not only that, but I was escorted to my suite by the Donovan heir herself. I thought old man Donovan had two sons, not a son and a daughter. I can't believe this."

"Why did she escort you to your room? Didn't they have a bellboy?"

"I thought that odd myself. I guess they are still not back up and running like Stanley thought they'd be." Knowing his worst enemy was faltering pleased Brady. "Sam came up with some excuse as to why she was pulling double-duty."

"Sam?" His brother chuckled. "You're already using a nickname? Sounds like you're better off than running into her uptight, arrogant brother, Miles."

The epiphany hit him hard. "Cade, you're a genius. I'll call you later."

Brady disconnected the call, more pleased now than he had been only moments ago. If he hadn't been blindsided, he would've come up with this plan before calling Cade.

Seducing this woman may prove to be a bit of a challenge, but challenges were something Brady lived for. He wouldn't be in the position he was today without taking on numerous risks.

Besides, he hadn't been lying when he'd told Sam he was here to work. She didn't need to know his agenda was to gain information from the resort's employees and figure a way to overtake this property from Stanley Donovan in one swift, surprising move.

Just as the old man had done.

Stanley Donovan had wanted Lani Kaimana for

years, but waited until Brady's father had fallen ill with terminal lung cancer. Brady still couldn't believe his father was gone, but he had to push forward. His father wouldn't have wanted him to dwell on the loss but move on to gain back what had been taken.

Even though he'd had time to grieve, Brady still felt guilty about concentrating solely on business. The way he worked himself made him appear, to outsiders, as coldhearted. But he knew, deep in his heart, his father would've wanted him to do anything to gain back Lani Kaimana.

Brady had no intention of letting this beautiful piece of property remain in the hands of such a ruthless business tycoon for one second longer than necessary. He'd come here with the sole purpose of gaining information to use against the Donovan empire and he had no intention of leaving without it.

But now his agenda had changed, and he intended to work strictly on Samantha for the information.

This plan was getting better and better by the minute. Just the thought of entertaining such a sexy competitor had his heart accelerating.

He hadn't known what to expect once he arrived in Kauai. Actually, he'd planned on spying on Sam, assuming the Donovan son was running the place, but now that he knew Sam was actually Samantha, he'd have to pull out all the stops. Dinners, romantic strolls along the beach, some "accidental" one-on-one time. Oh, and of course, flowers. Didn't every romance begin with something as innocent as fresh-cut blossoms?

Seducing Sam would be a pleasure—his and hers. He wasn't vain enough to deny the fact he could indeed keep Sam pleasured. Now all he had to do was find a way, a reason, to remain close to her. He had to gain information to take over this resort. Period.

Two

Brady examined his "honeymoon suite" closer now that he was alone. The bed was definitely the centerpiece of the room even though it was up on a platform in the corner. The white, sheer fabric draped over the four-poster demanded attention. He had no problem imagining Sam in that bed with him, and from the look he'd seen on her face, she'd been imagining the same thing. Yes, seducing her would be no problem and an added bonus.

Hopefully she'd be so consumed with her newly inherited duties, she wouldn't notice him prying into her personal and professional business.

Setting his seductive thoughts aside for the moment, Brady walked around the room. The open floor plan of the suite no doubt would have the intimacy level soaring. The Jacuzzi tub was in the opposite corner of the bed, just outside the bathroom. The tub, more than big enough for two, gleamed sparkling white with towels folded like swans around the edge of the porcelain.

A pale yellow sofa, mahogany desk and a small dinette table were all on the other end of the spacious room. The wall directly across from the entryway held an impressive set of French doors, which overlooked the vibrant blue ocean with white-capped waves.

Brady made his way over, shifted the filmy, white curtains aside and stepped onto a wide balcony overlooking the water. A soft, gentle breeze glided through the air, the scent of salt water wafted up from below and the crashing of the waves made him feel at home. Even though the decor had changed a bit throughout the hotel since he'd been here last, the romantic ambiance remained.

He'd grown up on a beach and had never gotten the love of the water out of his system. Adding to that, he'd always envisioned taking over this Kauai property.

The whole island had always been peaceful, a section of the world away from all the hustle of his daily life in San Francisco. He wished he could take some time to himself to enjoy the white sand, refreshing breeze and cooling water.

Perhaps one day he could talk Sam into relaxing on the beach with him. Of course, that would take a great deal of persuasion on his part, but he was a patient man. And if he could get her into a bikini, well, that would be worth the wait. Picturing her in nothing but strings and triangle-shaped material had him eager to put his game plan into motion.

Leaving the beauty of the land behind him, Brady stepped back into his room. He pulled his smart phone from his pocket and checked his e-mail. Nothing too pressing.

He punched in the number to his office, hoping to catch his assistant before she left for the day.

"Stone and Stone."

"Abby, I was hoping to catch you."

"I was finishing up for the day and Cade just went home. What can I do for you, Brady?"

He pulled out the small desk chair and took a seat. "I just wanted to let you know I may be in Kauai a bit longer than expected. I'd like you to forward any calls I may receive regarding Stanley or Miles Donovan."

Abby paused, he assumed to jot down his request. "Is there anything else?"

"Not at the moment. If you need anything you can either call me or let Cade know," he said.

"We'll be just fine."

Brady laughed. "I doubt the two of you could go very long without me to be your go-between."

"I'll have you know we haven't had one argument since you left," she assured him.

"Just make sure you keep your claws in until I return."

Abby laughed. "Will do. Have a nice trip."

Brady disconnected the call, confident his business was in capable hands between Abby and his younger brother and business partner. Even though the two were always bickering like siblings, Abby was the best assistant they'd ever had.

Brady figured the two of them would finally call a truce and just get together, but so far, no. All the sexual tension in the office was really starting to get to him.

Before Brady had left, Cade had asked if he could come instead. But Brady was more than ready to get this vengeance started and knew Cade would be too soft or emotional when it came to the dealings of their late father.

And now that he'd seen Sam, well, he didn't want Cade anywhere near this siren.

Which reminded him, he needed to get the ball rolling with the seduction of Sam. God, he'd named the mission—Seduction of Sam. Oh, well, every war had a name. Right?

He picked up the hotel phone on the desk and dialed the concierge.

"Good afternoon, Mr. Stone. What can I do for you today?"

"I'd like to have some flowers delivered."

"Not a problem. Do you have a price range or a specific style in mind?"

Brady thought for a moment. Sam needed something to make her smile, to make her stop and think of only him. "I'd like a large arrangement of exotic flowers. The price doesn't matter. I want the most extravagant, colorful arrangement this lady has ever seen."

The young male on the other end chuckled. "Yes, sir. Do you have an address and name of the recipient?"

"I want the arrangement delivered to Samantha Donovan in her office here."

"Oh, well." The man stumbled over his words. "We'll get right on that, Mr. Stone. What would you like the card to say?"

Brady relayed the message he wanted, had the charge billed to his room and thanked the helpful employee.

Now all he had to do was wait.

In the short time he'd talked with Sam, he already knew she was too nice not to thank him personally. Hopefully she would come up to his room and do it face-to-face. That would gain him some of the alone time he needed.

With the first step of his plan already in play, Brady pulled his laptop from his suitcase and decided to get some work done.

After all, destroying every last Donovan was going to take some time. He almost hated that someone as angelic-looking as Sam had to get mixed up in this. After all, she may be a total innocent, but she was a Donovan.

And the Donovan's were responsible for the downfall of his father's empire.

Don't forget to take time for yourself.

Sam read the card once, twice. Okay, at least three times before she smiled and realized who'd sent the most obscene amount of flowers she'd ever seen.

She'd come back to her office after taking care of a minor kitchen-staff argument to check her messages. But her desk had been hidden beneath a tall crystal vase with striking flowers in various vibrant shades.

Sam hated the fact she immediately smelled each and every bud. She'd never received flowers before and this was a heck of a way to start her collection.

On a sigh, Sam knew she needed to take a moment and thank the man behind the impressive, not to mention expensive, bouquet. Could something this large and exquisite be called a bouquet?

Even though her Jimmy Choos were still biting into her little toes, she forced the pain aside and made her way to the top floor. She really didn't have the time in her hectic schedule to talk with Brady Stone, not that she minded thanking him, but she knew their next conversation wouldn't be a simple thank-you.

He'd try to get her to dinner again. And, once again, she'd turn him down. No matter how she desired to give in, she would not allow her mind to be muddled with a smooth talker. She'd learned her lesson long ago where smooth, charming men were concerned.

Once in front of the honeymoon suite, Sam smoothed a hand down her pale pink designer suit and tapped on the door. When the door swung open, Sam had to focus on breathing.

Brady had taken off his jacket, rolled up his sleeves to expose tanned, muscular forearms, unbuttoned three—she counted them—buttons of his shirt and stood holding on to the edge of the door with a wide, knowing smile on his face.

"Samantha. Please come in."

Because she knew it was rude to refuse, she stepped inside. The man had been in this overly spacious room for only a few hours and already his masculine scent enveloped her. He'd made the room his own by setting his laptop up on the desk, a pair of Italian leather shoes sat near the foot of the bed and his clothing hung in the open closet area.

Without any effort on his part, he'd already made a lasting impression. She had no doubt he left a lingering impact on all the ladies he encountered.

"I want to thank you for the flowers." Lacing her fingers together, she turned to face him as he closed the door. "I have to say I've never seen quite an arrangement."

With his hands in his pockets, he offered her a wry grin. "How did you know I sent them?"

Sam rolled her eyes. "Well, let's see. You're

the only man in the past six months to ask me out. Other than my father, my brother and the employees here, I don't even talk with men, so I did the whole process of elimination thing." Feeling a bit flirty, she added, "Plus, I'm just smart."

Brady's soft, soothing chuckle settled in the crackling air between them. "I like a woman who has brains behind all her beauty. However, I can't believe I'm the only man to ask you out in the past six months."

Oh, he was good.

"Believe it. I've been too busy working to socialize."

He took a step closer, then another. He came so close, in fact, Sam had to lift her gaze to hold his. Brady was taller than she'd first realized. At five foot six, Sam hadn't had to tip her head for too many men, especially when she wore her heels.

"All the more reason for you to have dinner with me and take an hour to yourself." He brushed a strand of hair from her shoulder. "It's the least you could do after I sent you flowers."

Sam smiled. "Are you trying to guilt me into having dinner with you?"

"Only if it's working," he said, stroking a finger down her cheek.

She eased out of his reach. "You like to touch, don't you?"

His hand lingered in the space between them. "Problem?"

"I—I'm just not used to it, that's all."

Again, Brady grinned, reaching for her face. "I bet you aren't used to stuttering around a man, either, but you're doing a nice job of it."

She swatted his hand. "I most certainly am not."

Heat rose to her cheeks. Sam knew she needed to get out of this room before she made a complete fool of herself.

"Don't get your back all up," he said, dropping his hand. "You actually gave my self-esteem a boost."

Sam laughed. "I'm sure you really needed the extra confidence."

His grin widened and she found herself mesmerized by his perfect white teeth.

"A man always needs confidence. Especially when getting turned down by a beautiful woman."

Yup, he was smooth. More than likely he'd had his fair share of experience wooing women. And she seriously doubted he'd been turned down by too many, if any.

"I'm sure you'll find plenty of ladies at the resort or on the island to keep you occupied." She cocked her head to the side. "I thought you were here to work?"

He shrugged. "That doesn't mean I can't enjoy the company of a beautiful, sexy woman."

His compliment swept through her like a cool, gentle breeze, leaving goose bumps all over. She didn't want to be charmed by him—or anyone for that matter—but she found herself melting with each word he spoke.

What happened to not getting sucked in by smooth-talking men?

She cleared her throat. "Well, I'm sure with your confident attitude, you'll find someone to occupy your free time."

Brady threw his head back and laughed. The rich, robust sound vibrated through the air, through her, reaching each and every nerve she had, making them tingle.

"I think you just called me arrogant."

Heat rose to her cheeks once more. She'd definitely overstayed her allotted time. "I most certainly did not. Now, if you'll excuse me, I need to return to work. Thank you for the flowers."

He closed the gap between them, coming to stand inches from her. "I apologize if my words upset you." He reached up, stroked her jawline with the pad of his thumb. "I can't help but think you're too busy taking care of this resort and not yourself."

Sam stepped back, unable to think when such a potent man was touching her. She swallowed the lump in her throat. "I'm taking care of myself just fine. Thank you for your concern."

Just as she turned to go, he spoke. "If you change your mind about dinner, let me know."

Throwing a grin over her shoulder, she nodded. "Thanks again, but no. Have a nice evening, Mr. Stone."

Three

She'd purposely used the more formal name to prove to him, and to herself, she was indeed a professional. Making time for anything other than business was simply inconceivable.

As she stepped from his suite into the elevator, she knew she would have to watch herself for the duration of his stay. A man like Brady Stone could be easily led on and Sam wasn't about to be the one to stroke his ego. Nor was she about to stroke anything else of his.

She hadn't lied when she'd said she was too busy to have dinner. Just as the elevator dinged on the bottom floor, her stomach growled, betraying her former decision. She'd grab a pack of crackers from her emergency stash in her desk drawer and get back to work. She'd already used up enough of her time chatting with Mr. Desirable Businessman.

No way would she allow this charming, ever-so-sexy man to sway her judgment toward men—correction, toward powerful, cocky men.

After years of being under her father's controlling thumb and always trying to compete with her brother, Samantha had had enough of being overpowered. She didn't want or need a man. Being alone served her purpose in life just fine. Besides, being a career businesswoman didn't leave much time for a love life. She was still young. If she chose to have a love life, she could. But right now, she didn't even have time to think about companionship, much less jump into a relationship.

So why did her face still tingle where he'd briefly touched her, caressed her? Allowing a strange man, who just happened to be passing through her resort, affect her in such a way was just absurd and something she didn't have the time for.

Yes, he was sexy. Yes, he was smooth. And, all right, yes, she was attracted. But that was it.

Nothing could come between her and her goal to please her father.

Chin high, shoulders back, Sam breezed through the lobby, pleased to see people checking in at the registration desk. If her father would only let her take the reins, she had no doubt the resort would be booked year-round. Unfortunately, she was still under his thumb.

Why couldn't her father see her for the savvy woman she'd become? Sam hated the strain they'd always had on their relationship.

Each time she spoke to him, she hated the urge she had to call him sir. Nothing was casual and Sam always felt their conversations were solely about business. What few conversations they had. Every time she tried to talk to her father, he came up with some excuse as to why he didn't have time. There was always a meeting, always a client or always an employee in his office.

In short, there was always something or someone that came ahead of Sam. She should be used to it, but in fact, she wasn't. She didn't want to get used to the idea her own father put everything ahead of her.

Feeling the start of a headache, Sam made her way through the lobby, down the wide, marble-lined hallway and into her cozy office. She'd purposely chosen an office at the end of the hall so she could concentrate on work and not be disturbed unless absolutely necessary.

Though since coming here six months ago she hadn't spent too much time inside these four walls. The majority of her time had consisted of catering to guests and making sure all her employees were happy. That is, the employees they had left.

Just before her father purchased the resort, the previous owner had had so much financial trouble they'd had to lay off fifty workers. Not only did the layoff put a strain on the employees who were still here, but the ones that were let go were hardworking and desperately needed.

Sam had each of their names and contact information. And just as soon as this resort was out of the red, she intended to bring them all back… if they hadn't gone elsewhere.

Sam's eyes focused in on the vase of vibrant flowers that still adorned her desk, reminding her of the man she was trying her hardest to block out. She moved the arrangement to the small mahogany table in the corner.

Taking a seat at her desk, she opened the top drawer and pulled out a bottle of aspirin. After taking three, she slid out of her shoes and wiggled her toes until she felt each one crack. She actually thought she heard them sigh with relief.

She tugged open her bottom drawer to reveal her junk stash and grabbed a pack of peanut butter and cheese crackers. She knew she'd have orange crumbs all over her suit, but she just loved these little things.

After popping one into her mouth, she got to work checking this week's numbers and comparing them to last week. Unfortunately, the hunger headache had yet to ease up. She really shouldn't go so long without eating.

There was just so much to be done, but she had to concentrate on one task at a time or she'd become overwhelmed and never accomplish a thing.

Closing her eyes, she leaned her head back against her leather chair and polished off the rest of her snack. With her career teetering on a fine line as far as her father was concerned, she didn't have time to take breaks—regardless of hunger or headaches.

She tried to concentrate on her breathing, on the plush carpet beneath her bare feet, on the sweet fragrance wafting from the flowers. On anything other than the fact her head felt like a volcano ready to erupt.

Moments—perhaps several—passed when a

knock sounded on her door. On a groan, Sam lifted her eyelids, blinking against the harsh light.

"Come in."

Her door opened, but instead of seeing a person, she saw a stainless-steel serving cart slide through the opening. Sam jerked upright in her seat.

"What's all this?" she asked as the head chef of their high-class restaurant stepped through the door behind the cart.

"Dinner." The middle-aged man smiled, lifting the silver lid to reveal one of her favorite dishes. "The special of the day, Ms. Donovan. Seared, toasted-macadamia-nut mahi with citrus aka-miso sauce."

Sam's mouth watered at the sight of the crusted filets. "But I didn't order anything."

"No, but Mr. Stone did. Should I just leave this cart here or would you rather have it over there?"

Still speechless, Sam pushed back from her desk and stood, brushing off the inevitable orange crumbs. "Thank you, Akela, I can take it."

"Enjoy your evening, Ms. Donovan." He smiled and closed the door behind him.

The strong, mouthwatering scent drew Sam to the serving cart. She pulled off another silver lid and sucked in a breath when she saw her favorite dessert, lemon cake.

Her eyes darted to the oversize arrangement in the corner, then back to the tempting dinner. She couldn't stop the smile from spreading across her lips, just as she couldn't stop herself from going back to her desk to call Brady and thank him once again for his kindness.

Just as she reached for the phone, it rang. Thinking the caller on the other end was Brady making sure his surprise arrived, she lifted the receiver, ready to offer her gratitude for the meal, but reiterate the fact she was too busy to socialize.

"Sam Donovan," she answered, still smiling.

"Samantha."

Her father's commanding voice, calling her by her full name, wiped the smile off her face just as sure as if he'd slapped her. It sounded nothing like the smooth way Brady had said her name earlier.

Her spine stiffened, her sweaty palm gripped the phone. A business chat with her father was not what she needed right now.

Too bad her pain medication hadn't taken effect yet.

"Dad, what can I do for you?"

"I haven't heard from you in a week. What is the status of my resort?"

She hated how his voice always sounded so

demanding, so cold. But even more, she hated how he referred to Lani Kaimana as "his resort." Weren't they a family? Sam knew if Miles were here in her place, their father would be a bit more considerate.

Sam walked around the edge of her desk and sank into her chair. The stiff leather groaned, mimicking her reaction to this unexpected phone call.

"I was just getting ready to cross-reference the numbers from last quarter and forward them to you. If you'll give me an hour, you'll have them."

An impatient sigh filtered through the phone. "Samantha, the day is nearly over. I expected the report this morning."

"I've been busy today and I just now got a chance to sit in my office and pull up the spreadsheets."

Her father's sigh filtered through the phone. "I'm not interested in your excuses. Is there anything else I should be aware of?"

Her gaze focused first on the flowers, then the dinner. She refused to admit her mind and her time had been spent on a handsome businessman passing through. That would definitely not sit well with the business tycoon on the other end of the line.

"No, there is nothing else you should be informed of."

A knock on her door jarred her from her thoughts.

"I'll be waiting on that report, Samantha."

Listening to her father's edgy tone, she watched as Brady poked his head in. She motioned for him to hold on.

"I'll get it right to you," she assured her father. "If there's nothing else, I have someone in my office waiting to talk to me."

"I'll check back later in the week."

As usual, he hung up without a goodbye. Sam knew he didn't even treat his business rivals this rudely, so why did he act so cold toward his own daughter? Why did Miles deserve all the praise, all the love? And why did she always let her father's hurtful tone and words get to her?

She should be used to this. After all, she'd been treated like the black sheep for more than twenty years now.

Was it her fault her mother died? Was it her fault she looked exactly like Bev Donovan? According to her father, yes.

"Bad time?" Brady asked from the door.

Sam shook her head and smiled. "Perfect timing,

actually. I was just getting ready to call you and thank you for the dinner."

He stepped into her office. "May I close the door?"

"Sure." Sam came to her feet, clasped her hands in front of her and hoped she came across as professional and that professional side hoped he wouldn't pursue a date. The woman in her hoped he did. "Looks like you're getting dinner with me after all."

"No, this is just for you." He motioned to the cart. "I do want to take you out, but I know you're busy. At least this way you may be forced to eat."

How could a woman's heart not melt at that? The man was not pushing his way to get what he wanted, he was genuinely concerned for her welfare.

Sam took in Brady's casual appearance from his khaki pants to his mint-green polo shirt. She'd thought the suit was impressive, but the way his cotton shirt stretched across his shoulders and chest made her rethink her original thoughts. What would he look like without a shirt?

"Are you okay?" he asked, bending down to look her in the eye. "You're looking a bit pale. Do you have a migraine?"

"Yes, but I'm fine."

Brady moved around the side of her desk, studying her face. "Why don't you sit down and I'll bring the food to you?"

Before she could protest, his firm hands settled on her shoulders, easing her back into her seat.

"Brady, I appreciate everything you've done, but I have to get a report to my father and I'm sure you have better things to do."

He made his way across her office and wheeled the cart closer to her desk. "Your father won't care if you eat, and I have nowhere else I'd rather be."

Sam wiggled her mouse to wake up her computer. "I need to get this report cross-referenced and sent to him within the hour. After I'm done, then I'll eat."

Brady frowned. "Anything I can do to help?"

Sam tilted her head. "I can handle it on my own."

"Is that your polite way of asking me to leave?"

Coming to her feet, she smiled. "I don't mean to be rude, but I am rather busy."

He spread his hands wide and shrugged. "Since I arranged this nice meal, it's my duty to make sure you eat it. I'll just have a seat over here and wait for you to finish."

She didn't have time to question his actions. If

he wanted to keep her company, that was fine with her, so long as he didn't interfere with her work. Besides, she kind of liked the idea of someone worrying about her. When was the last time that had happened?

Before her mother died. Before her world changed. Before she was forced to grow up before she was ready.

Having Brady's attentiveness somehow made her spirits lift. The allure of having a perfectly handsome stranger take notice may be cliché, but it was also downright thrilling. Perhaps she should take the time to enjoy Brady while he was here if only she could add extra hours in the day.

While Sam worked, Brady sat across from her desk with his long legs extended, ankles crossed. He'd tipped his head back and laced his fingers over his flat abdomen. Even though he wasn't exactly looking at her, his presence was overpowering. His masculine scent combined with the dinner he'd ordered made her fingers fly across the keyboard. She wanted to take just ten minutes to herself and enjoy the dinner. And the man, if she so chose.

She checked and double-checked the numbers before sending them on to her father. Finally, she pushed back from her keyboard, tilting her head from side to side to work out the kinks.

"All done."

Brady's gaze came back to hers as he straightened in his seat. "Now will you eat?"

"Yes."

He quirked a dark brow. "Promise?"

Sam cleared a space on her desk, while Brady gathered dinner. He placed the main dish in the middle of her desk and grabbed the bottles of water from the cart. But instead of taking a seat, he went to the arrangement in the corner, plucked out an exotic purple flower and handed it to her.

"I would put the vase in the middle for a little romance, but I wouldn't be able to see you."

Sam took the flower he'd extended to her. "I didn't know a dinner for one could be romantic."

With his charming, killer smile, Brady took a seat across from her. "You're not alone yet. Don't ruin my romantic gesture."

His matter-of-fact tone sent shivers through her. "You're so determined to spend time with me when I've made it clear I'm too busy to socialize. Don't get me wrong, I'm flattered, but I feel like you're wasting your time. I'm not even sure I could spare two minutes."

Brady shrugged. "It's my time to waste. But I see this as time well spent. When I see something

I like, I go after it. You strike me as a woman who does the same."

She eyed him over the food. "You're right. I do."

And she wanted Lani Kaimana to be the best tourist attraction on the island of Kauai. If only she could get her father to see things her way and listen to her ideas. Or just listen to her, period.

Too bad Brady Stone had entered her life at this particular point in time. She'd love to throw caution to the wind and see where this harmless flirtation led. Perhaps, once her life settled—please, God, let that be soon—she could afford to indulge in some Brady time.

True, she never wanted a serious relationship again, but she had a feeling Brady wasn't a long-term kind of guy. A man with so much sex appeal more than likely stuck to one-nighters.

What would it be like to be held by those strong arms? What would it be like to ignore what was right and proper? Would she be able to let her stiff, boring lifestyle go and see where her desires led?

Like everything else in her life, she could only fantasize. Until she claimed her rightful place in her father's company, she couldn't indulge in any desires. No matter how her body ached.

Four

Brady couldn't believe his luck. Well, luck only played a small part. He had to give proper credit to his charm and Sam's moment of weakness. He loved when a last-minute plan came together.

Still smiling, Brady stepped into his suite, pulled his phone from his pants pocket and dialed his brother.

Cade answered on the first ring. "Hello."

"You have no idea how close I just came to uncovering all the ammunition we need." Strutting over to the French doors, Brady took pleasure in watching the waves crash against the sand. Much like Mr. Donovan's business would come crashing to an abrupt halt in the very near future.

"What happened?" Cade asked.

"I had a very nice dinner sent to Ms. Donovan's office. When I stopped by to make sure she'd received it, she was getting ready to send the report." Brady breathed in the fresh, floral scent of the island. "I hung around by using the excuse that I wanted to make sure she ate. She never second-guessed me. I'd say I'll have that information we need within a week."

Cade let out a low whistle. "That is some fast work, brother. And you claim I work fast with the ladies."

Brady's eyes darted to the four-poster bed in the corner; yet another image of Sam sprawled out between the silky sheets stirred his emotions. "Nothing went on between me and Sam, I just happened to be in the right place at the right time. Unfortunately, I wasn't able to get close enough without arousing suspicion."

"You've been there two days," Cade said. "I'll say you're making remarkable progress. Do you really think you can get those numbers within a week?"

Making his gaze focus back on the dark, mostly deserted beach, Brady thought of the petite blonde down in her office. He wouldn't let his hormones hinder his business dealings.

"Yes."

"Fantastic. May I ask how you were so close to the report?"

"I was in Sam's office and she had a migraine."

Brady ignored the lump in his throat as a twinge of guilt flashed through him at taking advantage of her in a moment of weakness. But then hadn't her father taken advantage of his during a moment of weakness? Turnabout was fair play…and all that.

"She needed to get her report to Stanley and I offered to help."

Cade chuckled. "Man. Too bad she didn't let you send it."

"When it comes to her business, she wants total control." Something he had to admire. "She's a Donovan, after all. Even though I've only seen her sweet, angelic demeanor, she may very well be like her old man beneath the surface. And I'm just attracted enough not to want to see the ruthless side of her."

"I have a feeling when she finds out who you are and why you're giving her so much attention, you'll be seeing more than ruthlessness." His brother laughed. "Call me if you uncover anything else. And I don't mean Ms. Donovan herself."

Brady disconnected the call, cutting off his brother's continuous chuckle.

Brady wanted nothing more than to retrieve those numbers and get them back to Cade, but seducing Sam would take time and patience. Two things he didn't possess.

The Donovans had only been in control for six months. Six months ago when Brady's father had been battling lung cancer and struggling to keep his cooperation from going under, Stanley Donovan had swooped down like the vulture he was and took Lani Kaimana.

Stanley had always been known as a callous businessman. And from the conversation he'd overheard between Sam and her father, Brady figured Stanley had no problem being a menace to his own daughter.

Brady had seen the look of defeat when she'd hung up the phone, giving him the feeling that old man Donovan was not only a shark with competitors, but also a class A jerk with his family.

But none of those facts or images negated that Brady and his brother had a job to do and until

Lani Kaimana was back in the Stone family, Brady wouldn't back down from seducing Samantha.

Soft white sand slid between his bare toes as Brady strolled along the pristine beach between Lani Kaimana and the Pacific Ocean.

In a way, Brady couldn't fault Stanley Donovan for taking this bit of property. Who wouldn't want to own a piece of paradise and make money from it in the process? But what he did fault Stanley for was taking advantage of a sick, dying man, stealing a resort from his floundering company and aiding in the possible demise of an empire.

Hands fisted at his sides, Brady crushed the sand beneath his feet with each step.

With Brady's father gone, Stanley's reign over the Stones would end. Brady and Cade were young strong men who wouldn't be run over by a shark like Sam's father.

A gentle breeze floated along the water, sending whitecaps ruffling to the shoreline. This was the perfect weather for a romantic walk on the beach. Lately when he thought of romance, his mind immediately drifted to Sam. Of her sweet, innocent smile. Her sassy yet flirty mouth. The way her curvy, petite body looked in her clean-cut suits.

She was a woman meant for romance, for long

walks along beaches just like this, for evenings spent in five-star restaurants. Not for running herself ragged to appease an ass of a father.

No romance, he told himself. The breathtaking ambiance of the evening had muddled his mind. His reason for being here was pure business. Nothing more.

Then as if his fantasy and dreams came to life, Samantha Donovan was standing just ahead of him. She still had on her perfectly pressed suit, but she held her shoes by the strap, dangling from a finger at her side.

Her long golden hair floated and danced around her shoulders as she stared out onto the horizon. As Brady approached—thanking God for this stroke of luck—he wondered what thoughts were running through her head.

Did she have worries, doubts? Was she taking a break from her hectic position?

"Beautiful, isn't it?" he asked as he came to her side. When she turned to look at him, she jerked back as if she realized he wasn't talking about the orange-and-pink sunset.

She quickly masked her surprise by turning back to the water. "I don't get out here often enough."

"You really should. The fresh scent and evening

breeze will ease your mind and make you forget all your troubles."

She cast him a sideways glance. "I doubt that."

With a deep sigh, Sam turned in the opposite direction and began walking. Brady didn't wait for an invitation, he simply fell into step beside her.

When she glanced over, he smiled. "It seems a waste to walk on this beautiful beach alone, especially with a sunset as breathtaking as that one."

"Do your smooth moves normally get you the ladies?"

His grin widened at her bluntness. "Always."

The soft laughter he'd come to expect from her floated along the breeze and warmed a spot deep within. Brady didn't want to be warmed by her, he wanted information he could use to crush her family…even if that meant her. He couldn't help who got caught in the crossfire.

"So what are you doing out here?" he asked. "I didn't take you for the type to take breaks."

"I started feeling claustrophobic in my office and needed to do some thinking. I'm still working," she assured him as she tapped the side of her head. "I'm just doing it in here."

The water lapped up around their bare feet,

splashing up onto her shapely calves and wetting the folded edges of his khaki pants.

To onlookers, they probably looked like a couple out for a romantic stroll. And hopefully that's how Sam would see his presence, but in reality, he was laying the groundwork for destruction.

"You know the old saying about all work and no play?" he kidded.

She stopped, turned to him. "Why do I have the feeling you get plenty of play in?"

A strand of her fair hair came around and clung to her pink, glossy lips—her kissable lips. With the tip of his finger, he swept the hair aside.

"Maybe because I do." He watched her pale blue eyes widen with acknowledgment. "Maybe if you added a little more playtime into your life, you wouldn't be so stressed."

Her defiant chin tilted. "I happen to love what I do and if I wanted to play, I would. I can take an hour to enjoy life."

"Fine, then. When you want to forgo some work and see what else life offers, come find me." He turned, but glanced over his shoulder. "Oh, Samantha, playtime with me takes more than an hour."

He strolled off, literally into the sunset, and let her chew on that tantalizing thought.

* * *

Sam strode through the open lobby, inhaling the refreshing salt water of the early morning. If only her life were as sunny and bright as the sunshine beaming in through the doors and windows.

After a meeting with the disgruntled grounds crew, Sam had finally appeased them by explaining that a new budget was being looked over with all employees of Lani Kaimana in mind.

She did not, however, mention the fact that the new budget she was looking over wouldn't allow for too many raises until she could see how well the resort operated since switching ownership.

Unless her father listened to her, there would be no turning this resort around. He'd purchased the piece of property when it was operating at a loss, something they couldn't fix overnight.

She knew her father trusted her or she'd never be here to begin with. So why couldn't he also entertain her ideas?

Just as she turned toward her office, she saw Brady. She hadn't had much time to think of him this morning, but she'd spent plenty of time last night tossing and turning between her lonely sheets.

She took a moment to appreciate such a fine specimen of man. And, considering he wasn't looking her way, she allowed herself the satisfaction of raking her gaze over his broad, muscular body.

His crisp white polo shirt did amazing things to his golden, sun-kissed biceps. And the way his faded denim covered his long legs as he ate up the ground made her wonder why she'd never noticed a man this way before.

Allowing her eyes to linger longer than necessary only made her heart beat faster.

Was this just a case of good old-fashioned lust? Did she just find Brady Stone appealing because he was a stranger passing through? Because he'd given her flowers, a nice meal and was there to comfort her when she'd not felt well?

Oh, and the walk on the beach. Planned or not, that had been the most romantic moment of her life. And that proved how pathetic a life she'd been living.

So, why now? Why *this* man?

Before she could answer her own questions, Brady turned his head. His eyes locked with hers and a knowing grin spread across his face.

Damn. She'd been caught staring.

Oh, well, she couldn't undo the damage now. With her shoulders back, chin up, Sam made her way toward him.

"Good morning," she greeted with a smile.

Brady nodded, offering a warm smile of his own. "Morning."

"I forgot to thank you again for the flowers, dinner. When I ran into you last night, my mind was elsewhere." She kept her smile going, not a hardship when looking at such a magnificent man. "Are you still enjoying your stay?"

"So far."

Another happy guest. "If there's anything I can do to make your visit more pleasant, don't hesitate to ask."

His grin kicked up a notch; a naughty gleam twinkled in his chocolate eyes. "I bet I can come up with something. Is that an open-ended invitation?"

She'd walked right into that one.

The way he looked at her—as if he knew where her thoughts had traveled since meeting him— made her palms dampen. Add mind reading to his impressive personal résumé.

After their few short conversations, she should've known where his mind, and other body parts, would go with her innocent comment. He was a guy, after all.

"I do have a tight schedule," she told him, hoping she sounded professional and not like a nervous schoolgirl. God, couldn't she make up her mind? "I'd be willing to accommodate your needs. I mean—"

He leaned into her ear. "I know what you mean, Sam." Easing back, he smiled. "When can I expect you to...accommodate me?"

Sam glanced around the nearly empty lobby. "Umm..."

Brady eased back and chuckled. "How about we start with a dinner *not* in your office?"

She so wanted to say yes. Did she dare take some time for herself? "I don't know, Brady."

"We already shared a romantic walk in the sunset," he reminded her. "Dinner isn't nearly as romantic as that."

He had her there. Besides, the man was just passing through on business. What could one meal hurt? She wasn't going to start a time-consuming relationship with him.

"Are you free tonight?"

"Absolutely. I'll take care of all the arrangements." He reached out, easing a strand of hair from her shoulders. "Meet me in my suite at six."

Before she could tell him she couldn't possibly meet him that early, he'd walked away. And Sam recalled the rule she'd recently made about dating guests. Oh, well, she'd never been a rule breaker, so doing it once wouldn't hurt.

She watched him cross through the lobby and exit into the breezy summer day. Dear Lord, the man looked just as good going as he did coming.

Sam forced herself to concentrate on the rest of her hectic workday, but her mind betrayed her. Instead of figuring out how to bring more tourists to her father's newly acquired resort, all she could think of was how long she'd gone without sex.

And why was she even thinking about sex? It wasn't as if she were going to be intimate with Brady tonight or anything. She didn't even know him. But he was clearly interested in her and that had her thinking of the two of them tangled between sheets.

Sex. Even the word hadn't been on her mind since trying to gain her father's respect and a place in his company. She'd put all her personal desires aside in order to concentrate on her career.

Her whole life, Sam had wanted to be important to her father. Her mother had passed away years ago, leaving shattered, five-year-old Sam and eight-year-old Miles behind to be raised by a business mogul who knew nothing about raising little girls. Good news for Miles.

She'd gotten through her life just fine on her

own and she liked to believe that's what made her strong. Sam knew she didn't need anyone to lean on, especially not a man. Actually, she was a bit thankful her father had made her stand on her own two feet. She shuddered at the thought of being one of those clingy women.

But a little flirtation—and maybe more— with Brady Stone seemed to be rejuvenating her depressed state. Seeing him just a few stolen moments here and there helped her hectic days pass with much more pleasure.

When her eyes started to burn from glaring at a computer screen for too long, Sam glanced to the corner of the monitor.

Oh, God. It was 5:59.

She quickly saved the proposal she'd been working on and turned her computer off. She took a swig from the tepid bottle of water on her desk and turned off her lights.

After racing down the hall to the elevator and getting on, she sagged in relief against the cool metal.

But then stiffened as she caught her reflection in the steel doors.

Oh, this was not good. How could she continue her flirtatious, so-far-harmless fling with Brady if she looked like she'd pressed her suit with a crimping iron?

Strands of hair tangled around her shoulders. Her makeup had worn off, her concealer giving way to her dark circles. She not only looked rumpled, she had the appearance of a haggard raccoon.

Oh, yeah, she was looking good.

The elevator dinged on the top floor. Sam took a deep, calming breath and stepped out, fully intent on backing out of the dinner date.

She knocked on his suite door and waited. But when the door flew open with a smiling Brady standing on the other side, her recently rehearsed speech fled her mind.

Five

"I thought you'd gotten a better offer," he said as he motioned her in.

"Not a better offer, but I do have to cancel." She remained in the hallway, trying not to look beyond the alluring man to the candlelit dinner by the French doors. "I ran later with work than I intended and I'm a mess. Perhaps we can do this another time? Say when I have time to freshen up?"

He reached for her hand, pulled her inside. "Nonsense, you're here now and you look beautiful as always."

Sam allowed herself to be drawn into the lion's den.

Why did she feel like prey for this overpowering man? And why did she let him persuade her decisions?

Because she liked being needed, even if only for a while. And because she was a woman. A woman who found herself a little too attracted to a total stranger. So what if her appearance wasn't perfect? Obviously, he didn't care, which just proved yet another point—Brady Stone obviously wanted to be near her for no other reason than because he enjoyed being with her as she did him.

A mixture of enticing aromas filled her senses. Between the scrumptious-smelling dinner and Brady's fresh, masculine scent, her reasons for leaving fled her mind.

Sam's gaze traveled across the suite, through the patio doors where the sun still remained high in the sky. A small, intimate glass table with one tapered candle and two plates covered with silver domes beckoned her closer.

"Looks like you've thought of everything." She crossed the plush beige carpeting. Being alone with Brady in such a personal atmosphere made her nerves jitter with excitement, her heart pound with anticipation. "I hope you didn't go to any trouble."

"None at all," he assured in that rich, deep tone that gave her chills.

A delicate pink rose lay beside one of the table settings. Twice in just over twenty-four hours this amazing man had brightened her dull days with a touch of beauty.

"This looks lovely," she told him, turning around.

He smiled, taking one long stride after another until he came within a foot of her. "It goes with the company."

Why did such come-on lines work so well when they came from his mouth? No grown woman with any sense would fall for this smooth-talking charmer. Obviously, where this man was concerned all her judgment flew out the window. And for some unknown reason, she didn't care.

"I don't know how good my company will be." She looked up into his dark eyes, breathed in his hypnotizing scent and trudged on with her plan to get out of his presence. "I haven't stopped since this morning and I'm afraid if I sit, I may fall asleep in my plate. So, you see, not good company."

His eyes darted to her lips. "Then I'll have to do something to keep you awake."

Before she could even take a breath, he stepped closer, his mouth claimed hers.

The shock only lasted a moment before pure pleasure took control. Brady's arms wrapped around her waist, pulling her taut against his hard, lean body.

She had no choice but to answer his demand with one all her own. She didn't want to take the time to consider how much time had passed since she'd been held this way, kissed this way. Nor did she want to acknowledge the fact she needed the intimacy more than her next breath. And she certainly didn't want to think about how fast Brady was moving. So what if she'd only known him two days?

His tongue parted her lips. She let him in.

She slid her arms around his neck, threading her fingers through his thick, wavy hair. No way would she let him ease back, not now that she'd tasted him.

Brady's hands splayed across her back, his fingertips dug into her suit jacket, creating an arousing friction from the warmth of his hand and the satin material on her bare skin.

A moan escaped. Hers, his? She didn't know. Did it matter since their mouths were fused as one?

He nipped at her bottom lip. "I've been dying to do that for two days."

Breathless, Sam opened her eyes. "I'm glad you didn't wait any longer."

"I don't normally attack women, but I can't control myself around you."

"Attack? If only I'd get attacked like that more often, maybe I wouldn't be so caught up in work."

His soft chuckle vibrated through his chest and against hers. "Are you awake now?"

"Huh?"

"You said you were tired."

Disappointment flooded through her. She unlaced her hands, releasing her hold on him and stepped back. "Oh, um, yes."

"Now, don't get your back all up again."

"I don't know what you're talking about," she said, even though she'd knowingly tilted her chin and straightened her shoulders.

He closed the short gap she'd created. "I was just using your tiredness as my excuse."

Sam placed a hand on his chest before he could lean down again. "You don't strike me as the kind of man who needs an excuse to kiss a woman. Especially if you always kiss with such... passion."

Brady's enticing smile widened. "Passion? Does that mean you'll stay awake and keep me company?"

His scorching stare roamed over her face, doing nothing to squelch the desire that had erupted inside her.

Perhaps dinner was a mistake. How could she concentrate on anything else other than the desire to get completely naked with this man she'd known for only forty-eight hours?

His heart beat in a calm, easy manner beneath her palm. Obviously he wasn't as worked up as she.

Did she affect him in any way whatsoever? Was his attention toward her typical as with any other woman? There wasn't a shred of doubt in her mind that Brady had more experience in the sexual department than she.

"Look," she said, removing her hand from his chest, distancing herself from temptation. "I'm running a resort, so my time is pretty limited. I don't even know if I have time for a fling."

Brady's intense stare lasted only a second before he erupted into laughter. "Do you always speak what's on your mind?"

"There's no misconception that way."

"I'm not into flings, either." His eyes darted

back down to her lips. "I want to spend time with you while I'm here. Tonight we'll have dinner. No pressure."

Before she could answer, her cell vibrated in her pocket. "I have to take this," she said, pulling out her phone.

"Take your time. I'll pour us some wine."

He moved away, giving her the privacy she needed. Without bothering to glance at the caller ID, she flipped up her phone. "Hello."

"These numbers are unacceptable, Samantha."

Glasses clinked over her shoulder, but the noise did nothing to drown out her father's anger. "What do you mean?"

"The number of guests is down ten percent this quarter. I trusted you to bring the numbers up."

Sam stepped farther away from Brady. "I'm doing what I can. If we could sit and talk about my ideas—"

"Not this again." Stanley grunted. "I just want you to do what I sent you to do. Don't second-guess me and don't forget who's in charge."

Sam jerked as if he'd slapped her. Thankfully, the love seat was nearby. She sank onto the cushions. "As if I could."

"Are you in your office?" he asked.

Sam's gaze darted to Brady. "I had to step out for a moment."

Stanley let out a sigh. "Perhaps you should concentrate on your work instead of socializing, Samantha. My resort won't run itself."

Sam ended the call, suddenly not in the mood for dinner—or Brady. Her father always managed to toss cold water on anything good in her life. She found it sad the man did nothing but stew about business and finances.

No wonder her mother had been unhappy.

Brady's grip on the wine bottle tightened. He had a feeling his plans for the night had just evaporated. And for the first time in his life, business wasn't in the forefront of his mind.

The hurt and the confusion in Sam's eyes had him placing the bottle on the table and crossing to her.

She glanced up when he brushed a strand of hair off her shoulder. "Are you okay?" he asked.

Pushing to her feet, she stood, her body brushing his. "Just business." She pasted on a fake smile. "But I'm afraid I won't be very good company tonight. Could we do this another time?"

Because he knew she didn't want to appear

weak, especially in front of a virtual stranger, he nodded. "Absolutely."

She hadn't said who was on the other end of the call, but Brady knew. Speaking with Stanley Donovan was obviously upsetting to everyone.

He escorted Samantha to the door, all the while cursing her father. Besides the fact Brady needed to get information from Sam, he'd planned on doing a little seducing, as well.

But more than that, he hated the fact the old man could wipe the light right out of Sam's eyes in a matter of moments.

He couldn't afford to let her innocence and vulnerability get to him. Business was business. He had to keep telling himself that or he'd be pulled under by Samantha's sweet way.

She turned to him once they reached the door. "Thanks for going to all the trouble."

Without another word, she opened the door and left.

Brady turned only to have the cozy table by the patio doors mock him. This was not how he'd planned the evening. Granted he'd planned a little seduction and a little deceiving, but he certainly hadn't wanted Sam to leave hurt and confused.

With a tightening in his chest, Brady moved to the desk, picked up his phone and dialed Cade.

"Hello."

"We have a problem."

"What's wrong?"

Brady walked back to the sitting area, taking the warm seat Sam had just vacated. "Stanley just called Sam and, from the one-sided conversation I overheard, he's mad about the report she sent."

Cade muttered a curse. "Did she say anything about the call?"

"She's too discreet to discuss business with me." Brady rested his elbows on his knees and rubbed his forehead. "My concern now is Stanley finding out about my stay here. I need to step up my game plan."

"Sounds to me like he's just as much of a jerk to his own daughter as he is to everyone else."

Brady had gotten that impression, as well. How could a father be so harsh to his own child? How could *any* man treat Sam with such disrespect?

God, he was no better than her father. Disrespect? Brady had disrespected Sam from the moment she'd walked up to the registration desk to assist him. Backing down now, though, was not an option he would even entertain. Sam would get caught in the crossfire, but there wasn't a thing he could do about it. Business always came first. Period.

Besides, he owed this mission to his father. This

property had been purchased and the first shovel of dirt dug by his dad when Brady had been only ten years old. The name Lani Kaimana was chosen by his mother. She'd always wanted to live in Kauai and his father had made sure she always had a place to come to. Lani Kaimana had been his family's first resort, and Brady needed to bring ownership back to its rightful place. So Sam's feelings, and his for that matter, could not interfere with his conquest.

"What do you want me to do?" Cade asked.

"Nothing. I just wanted to give you heads-up in case Donovan decides to make a move on another property."

"Keep me posted."

"Same here," Brady said. "Talk to you later."

As he disconnected the call, Brady knew he should find Sam and make sure she was truly okay. But first, he'd let her have some privacy.

He hated that he had to use her feelings to his advantage, but he had no choice—not if he wanted to ruin Stanley Donovan. Brady had never let his hormones control a business transaction and he didn't intend to start now.

Brady pocketed his key card and left his suite. He had no clue what room Sam occupied here, or even if she stayed on the grounds. All he knew was he needed to find her.

He'd start with her office and go from there. Once he made sure she was okay, he could return to his original agenda.

Six

Two days. Two whole days had passed since he'd seen Sam—not for lack of trying to find her. Obviously she was busy and didn't want to be found, but Brady wasn't giving up. He had to get Sam, get closer to her.

He made his way down the wide marble hall for the umpteenth time in the past forty-eight hours.

She had to return to her office sometime. Clearly she was a hard worker and not someone to sit behind her desk all day and delegate orders.

Surprisingly, her office door was ajar. He peeked his head inside, expecting to find Sam at her desk nursing another migraine. But her office was empty.

Being a man to take advantage of every opportunity, he stepped inside the spacious room and took a seat at her desk. He hadn't planned on glancing at the paperwork lying on top of the desk calendar, but, well, it was there and he couldn't resist.

His eyes roamed over the budget proposal, his mind agreeing with each number he saw. Not only that, Brady found himself intrigued by the renovation ideas she'd listed at the bottom. This woman had smart business sense—unlike her father. Perhaps business was her forte after all. His respect for her kicked up a notch.

With ideas like the ones listed on the paper, Lani Kaimana could be the most prestigious resort in the world. The ideas had to be Sam's. Stanley couldn't come up with something this good, this fresh and new.

If old man Donovan listened to Sam, this resort would be absolutely packed. Brady only wished he had someone as talented and passionate about her work in his corner.

A brilliant idea popped into his head and he nearly jumped out of his seat with excitement.

He needed to get Samantha Donovan on his team.

But first, he had to gain back the resort.

God, if all his plans fell into place—and in the order he intended—not only would he have his property back, he'd have Samantha as a major asset to his company.

"Looking for something?"

Brady jerked, his gaze locking with Sam's. The muscle in her jaw clenched as she stood leaning against her doorway, arms crossed over her chest. He'd been so absorbed in her proposal, he hadn't heard her come in.

Brady cleared his throat. "You."

She made her way toward her desk, coming to stand beside him. "If you're done snooping through my business, I have work to do."

In no hurry to leave, Brady leaned back in the creaky, leather chair. "I won't use much of your time. First of all I wanted to make sure you were all right. I was worried the other night."

"I'm fine. Thank you."

"Good. Second—" he pointed to her paperwork "—that's some pretty impressive stuff. Are you planning on a major overhaul of this resort?"

Sam let out a short, clipped laugh. "If I had my say."

He came to his feet, ready to lay his own proposal on the line. "So, those plans aren't set into motion?"

"I wish."

"What I saw impressed me," he told her, trying to smooth out his path.

He couldn't have her doubting his trust and presence now. He'd come too far and had too much to lose.

"Really?" Her tone softened as she leaned a hip against the desk. "Why is that?"

"I own a real estate company with my brother and we specialize in renovating resorts and businesses. You really know what you're talking about here."

Her eyes darted to the open file. "Thank you."

"I'm serious," he reiterated. "You've got good business sense."

"I appreciate that, even though you were snooping."

She placed a hand on the desk and leaned her body onto it, drawing his attention to her simple, white button-up shirt as it drew across her breasts. Her attention, however, was on the file.

He redirected his attention. "Your figures are impressive."

Sam's mouth quirked up as her eyes darted to

his. "I know what you think of my figure. Now, I have to get back to work if you're done chatting about useless ideas."

Brady resisted the urge to kiss her again. "First of all, I meant the figures here." He pointed down to the file he'd been caught reading. "Second, these are hardly useless."

"My father disagrees."

Brady placed his hands on her shoulders. "Then we'll make him understand."

Samantha's brows drew together. "I barely know you. Why would you offer such a thing?"

"Listen to me before you make up your mind." His heart beat so fast he feared she'd hear the thumping. "This resort has more potential, and from the look of your proposal, you know it, too. I have properties I'm acquiring that I could use input on from someone with such verve for renovating."

Her eyes roamed over his face. "I appreciate your enthusiasm in my work, but I still don't understand why you'd want to do this. Aren't you here to work yourself?"

Her unsureness didn't faze him. He had an agenda and he would see it through.

"I overheard your conversation with your father," Brady told her. "I know he doesn't appreciate you or your ideas. I see what you have to offer and it shouldn't be wasted."

She shook her head and glanced away. "This isn't a good idea. Now, if you'll excuse me, I have to get back to work."

Brady nodded and exited her office. He'd let her chew on the suggestion he'd planted in her head and see how she felt once she calmed down.

And once he let Cade in on his plan, there would be no way Sam could refuse the two Stone boys.

Sam studied her proposal, warmed at the thought someone took her seriously. But she wasn't giving up on her father. If she gave up on her dream for this resort, she'd regret it.

Just like she regretted ever talking to Brady Stone. He'd planted an idea in her head and she wished she could erase the tempting thought from her memory.

Could she trust a virtual stranger to help her rejuvenate this resort? Heaven knows he'd done wonders in reviving her once-buried sexual urges.

But this was business, and she had to keep her personal emotions locked away.

Running this resort was her one—and probably only—chance to prove herself to her father. If, and that was a big *if,* she let Brady in and confided in him, what would stop him from using her weakness to open a greater resort right next door? Kauai was a growing island and the last thing she needed was another competitor.

Sam laughed. Obviously her father's cynicism had rubbed off on her. Her gut told her to trust Brady. Besides, at this point, she needed someone in her corner.

Sam took a seat at her desk, picked up her phone and dialed her brother's office line. His secretary put the call through immediately.

"Sam." Miles's low, silky voice came through the phone. "What's up?"

"Has Dad talked to you about the resort?" she asked.

"I know he's upset."

Miles paused, just enough to arouse Sam's curiosity. "About?"

"Ask Dad."

Sam eased back in her seat, tucking the phone between her shoulder and her ear. "I'm asking *you.*"

He sighed. "It's not my place to say."

Frustration flooded through her. "The more you and Dad keep me out of the loop, the more damage you're doing to the company. Communication is the key to running a good business."

Miles laughed. "Sounds like you need to take your argument to the top, little sister."

"I'm an equal here," she told him. "I need to know what's going on that you're not telling me."

"All right. Dad is concerned that if the numbers don't go up he'll have to bring someone else in as manager or, as a last resort, he'll have to sell. He's giving you six more months."

Shock and disbelief settled into her chest. "What?"

"Now you see why Dad was so insistent on you turning the place around," Miles explained.

"How could the two of you keep something this vital from me?" she demanded, gripping the phone.

"It wasn't my idea."

Without saying goodbye, Sam hung up on her brother, more upset now than she'd been before.

With her blood pressure rising, she punched in the number to her father's office. He answered on the second ring.

"Samantha, I'm very busy. Can this wait?"

Obviously he'd looked at his caller ID, so why did he even answer?

"No, it can't." For once he would listen to

her, and she would come before his precious company.

"Make it fast."

Sam crossed her legs, rocked back in her leather chair. "Why the hell wasn't I informed that I've been working on a probationary period?"

"I didn't feel it necessary to inform you."

Sam gripped her padded armrest. "Miles knows."

Her father sighed. "Sam, let it drop. You just take care of my resort."

Blood pulsed through her head. Her teeth clenched.

"Fine," she told him. "I'll take care of everything on my end."

Once she'd hung up the phone, Sam forced herself to breathe in slowly and exhale the same way. She needed to calm down and think before making any rash decisions.

She'd tried. Nearly all her life she'd tried to gain her father's respect. As an adult she'd practically begged him to earn a place in his company. Now she saw what he was really doing. As if she were a child, he seemed to just pat her on the head and humor her, giving her small jobs to keep her out of his hair—and even that was temporary.

Well, no more. She was more than ready to be

appreciated, more than ready to be taken seriously as a businesswoman.

She wasn't sure what step to take next, but she knew one thing, she was done being pushed around by her father and her brother. Controlling men were officially a thing of her past. From here on out if they didn't see her for the talented career woman she'd become, she would do what she wanted, what was best for her. Risky decisions may come back to haunt her, but she had to do something drastic—or at least consider her options.

And if her father and Miles didn't appreciate her, she knew of someone who would make them.

Seven

Brady had just folded his last pair of khakis and placed them in his suitcase when someone knocked on his suite door.

Who could that be? He hadn't called down for the bellboy yet.

He opened his door and smiled at Sam.

She clasped her hands together. "I'd like to talk, if you have a minute."

He motioned her in. "Please."

She stepped in, bringing her soft, jasmine scent with her. Brady inhaled one good, deep breath.

Enough to fill his lungs with the sweet aroma of Sam and just enough to entice him even more.

He closed the door and turned. "Is something wrong?"

"Depends."

Sam's gaze darted about, her teeth worried her bottom lip. She was nervous about something, and he should be glad. But instead he was concerned.

He gestured toward the sofa. "Have a seat."

Sam glanced across the room toward the bed, noticing the almost-packed suitcase. "Are you leaving?"

"I need to get back to the office for a meeting with my attorney. I was hoping to see you before I left."

She took a seat on the couch and crossed her elegant, bare legs, allowing her pale blue skirt to inch up just that much more on her tan thigh. Brady swallowed hard and resisted the urge to adjust in his seat.

"Well, then, I'm glad I caught you before you left." She rested her elbow on the arm of the sofa, clasped her hands together and tilted her chin. "I've been thinking about your proposition."

Did he dare hope she'd reconsidered?

"But first I want to know if you were serious when you said you saw more potential with this resort, because this place means everything to me."

He knew the feeling. Lani Kaimana *was* his family. It was the backbone of his father's legacy and the foundation they'd used to build upon. The Stone's literally *made* this place, and he would not see his bitter enemy destroy it over bad business decisions.

From this angle of attack, using Sam and her ideas, he could not only have the resort updated, but he'd be doing it all at the cost of Stanley Donovan.

Priceless. Absolutely priceless.

Her questioning eyes held his gaze, so he answered honestly. "Absolutely. I never lie about business."

She cleared her throat. "In that case, I'd like to discuss working with you on some plans. That is, if you'd planned on coming back."

Brady couldn't stop his mouth from dropping open. He'd never guessed she'd actually come to him. Oh, sure, he'd hoped, but what made her change her mind in such a short amount of time?

"May I ask why the sudden change?" Now he did shift closer to the edge of his seat—every fiber of his being was aroused. "Last we talked you weren't even considering the notion."

"Let's just say I had a rude awakening. I'm not committing to anything, but I'd like to discuss how you intend to help me."

Oh, he intended to help her. He had to stay in control of this situation and use it to the advantage of his company.

The thrill of being one step closer to destroying the Donovans rushed through him.

He reached out, brushed her hair from her shoulder. "Perhaps when I get back we can have dinner and discuss my plans."

"A business date?" she asked.

"We'll start there."

With a laugh, she came to her feet. "I don't think that's a good idea. Perhaps my coming here was a mistake."

Brady stood, as well, and, just as Sam turned, grabbed her arm. He couldn't let her leave, not when he was so close to getting what he wanted— and he wanted her. In his business. In his bed.

Her eyes met his, and he couldn't ignore the spark of desire. It practically radiated from her baby blues, from the heat in her body beneath his touch. This woman wasn't getting away so easily.

"Nothing about you being here with me is a mistake," he whispered. "Nothing."

Common sense went straight to hell as he

lowered his mouth to hers, all the while keeping his gaze locked. He waited for a sign, something to make him stop. But when she parted her lips and fluttered her lids, he knew he'd received a sign… just not the one he'd expected.

His lips touched hers and a flood of emotions took over. Desire, passion, want. Need.

The sweetness she offered with only her mouth made his knees weak.

He'd never gotten weak knees over a woman before.

Opening her lips, she welcomed him in. His tongue swept through and, other than his hand on her upper arm, they remained apart.

But, God, he wanted to grab her and drag her down to the sofa. How easy this would be to have her clothes off and satisfied.

He knew she wanted this as much as he did, so why wasn't he taking what he'd wanted since he met her?

Because a woman like Samantha should be handled with care. Obviously something she wasn't used to. He intended to show her a different side of himself—one she wouldn't expect. One that would be impossible to dismiss.

Seduction was key in reaching his goal. He could tell Sam was the type who pretended not to need anyone, but deep down, she wanted the affection, the love.

Brady kissed the corners of her mouth and eased back.

"That's why we would have a hard time working together on this," she murmured, lifting her lids.

Her swollen mouth only looked more inviting, especially now that he'd tasted her again. "Because we can't contain our attraction?"

She nodded, her eyes darting back to his lips.

He stroked his thumb along her arm. "I don't see why we can't keep business separate from pleasure."

"What happens when we decide we've had enough of each other?" she asked. "Does your offer to help cease?"

Enough of each other? Since he hadn't had her yet, he couldn't imagine getting enough of the lovely Sam Donovan.

"You make it sound as if we're already sleeping together."

She shrugged. "Are you saying we wouldn't if we continued to see each other on any level?"

Brady swallowed the lump in his throat. "You do really speak your mind, don't you?"

"Are we or aren't we sexually attracted to each other?"

"We are."

Her heavy-lidded eyes roamed over his face. "I assumed sex is what you wanted from me."

Why did that sentence sound so, so...dirty? Even though he did want to sleep with her, why did he feel like he was cheating her, and himself, of something more?

"I won't lie. The thought of you naked in my bed is more than appealing."

She smiled. "This is all moving a bit fast for me. I mean, I didn't even know you a few days ago and now you want me to trust you with my business and my body. I keep asking myself what you'll get out of all this."

Brady wasn't surprised at her hesitation. This was a woman who would make a man beg and not even realize he's doing it. Damn if he didn't wish they'd met under different circumstances.

He couldn't very well tell her what he'd get out of this appealing offer.

"What I'll get is the satisfaction of helping a woman I've come to admire gain her equal footing in her father's company." He stroked her shoulders. "I know how hard this industry is. Besides, I'll get a side benefit of seeing you, touching you."

She shivered beneath his touch and Brady refused to let the guilt creep up. He reassured her with a soft kiss to her lips before drawing away. He had to maintain some distance every now and then to keep his own emotions from getting boggled up in this mess.

"I do have to get back to my office," he told her. "I'll be returning to the island in a week or so. I plan on purchasing a vacation home in the area and I want to keep my eye on it."

Samantha nodded. "I can't wait to get started on the resort proposal."

"And my personal proposal?"

She lifted one perfectly arched brow. "I'll let you know."

Flying several thousand feet above the Pacific Ocean in his private jet, Brady turned off his cell. He didn't feel like chatting with Cade anymore about Lani Kaimana or Sam—*especially* Sam.

Brady had called Cade when he'd first boarded his jet and explained the progress he'd made, but his brother zeroed in on Sam, claiming Brady was getting in too deep with her.

Cade didn't understand. Hell, Brady didn't understand himself what was going on with his emotions. But he did know he had to keep trudging on with this plan.

Sam would get hurt, that was a fact. But would

he? Doubtful. If he had the resort back how could he be remorseful?

Perhaps Sam had gotten under his skin, but so what? Obviously, from the way she'd kissed him last night, he'd gotten under hers, as well. He just had to stay there.

Their sexual chemistry would just make his plan flow that much smoother. He intended to not only get Samantha Donovan in his bed, but gain back his lost property. There was no reason in the world he couldn't have both.

As far as he was concerned, she didn't need to find out who he was, and thankfully most of the staff had been replaced since his father's ownership, so he wasn't recognized.

Brady watched the pillowy white clouds pass beneath him as he settled deeper into his leather sofa. Samantha was definitely a perk he hadn't expected, but one he would thoroughly enjoy.

She wouldn't deny him. He'd seen the look of desire and passion in her eyes, felt it in her kiss. She was a woman and women had needs just like men. He intended to meet her needs until he got what he wanted.

His list of wants was simple: Samantha in his

bed, his resort back and Stanley Donovan's empire obliterated.

When he returned to Kauai, he wouldn't leave again without each item on the list checked off.

Eight

"The old conference room needs to be cleared out." Sam nestled the phone between her ear and shoulder as she typed up her budget plan for the new day care center. "I want that whole area emptied because we're turning it into a day care for parents who want some alone time."

"Are you sure, Ms. Donovan?" the head maintenance man asked. "This is the first I've heard about this."

Sam resisted the urge to sigh as she went on. "I'm sure, Phillip. The conference room hasn't been used for as long as I've been here and nothing is scheduled. We still have the ballroom for receptions, so if need be, we can hold meetings in there. Now, please, clear out the room and let me know when the job is done so I can get a construction crew in there to build some dividers."

"You're the boss."

Yeah, she was. If only her father would see that.

Samantha reviewed her notes and saved the file. No, the day care hadn't been approved by her father, but if she wanted to get ahead in his company, and gain his approval, she had to take initiative. Now parents could take at least a few hours to themselves, maybe have a nice lunch or a romantic walk on the beach.

Romantic walk. On. The. Beach.

No matter what she did, her thoughts always drifted back to Brady Stone and his ridiculously affecting charm. She'd never been one to fall for smooth talkers before.

Physically, Brady had left, but the potent man still lingered in her mind, in her office where he'd had dinner for her and along the beach every time she glanced out the window.

Damn. She wished she had more willpower where he was concerned, but she was a woman and he was an extremely sexy man who, for some insane reason, found her attractive and actually wanted to help her. How could she even try to resist?

Samantha shook her head, hoping to clear all the Brady thoughts from her mind, and came to her feet. She needed to get out of her office and make sure all was running smoothly in her—*her*—hotel. After all, this resort was her baby, and she intended to spoil it.

Even though she and Brady were going to work on this together, she planned on getting a jump start before he returned. Hopefully her days would go by more quickly and she could fill the void he'd left.

"Abby, hold my calls, I need to talk to Brady."

Brady led the way up to his second-floor office.

"What's up?" Cade asked, closing the office door behind him.

Brady took a seat behind his desk and rested his elbows on the glossy mahogany top. "I'm going back to the resort in a few days."

Cade nodded, resting his hands on the back of the leather wingback chair opposite the desk. "Has she given you any ammo we can use against her old man?"

"None, yet. But I have a feeling with a few more one-on-one occasions, it's just a matter of time before I can really pump her for information."

"Just be careful," Cade warned. "She'll discover who you are eventually."

He hoped like hell she didn't. "I'll have the information we need to destroy the Donovans beforehand. Trust me," Brady said. "I'll get what we need. I just want you to be aware that I may be on the island for a while. I don't intend to come back until the job is done."

Cade shook his head with a laugh. "An exotic island, a beautiful woman—albeit the enemy—and a plan of seduction. Man, you get all the cushy, rewarding jobs."

Brady grinned, resting back in his seat. "Just part of being the oldest."

"Just make sure you get this done right. We don't want to let Dad down."

Brady held his brother's stare. No, they wouldn't let their father down. And that was all the reason Brady needed not to fall under Sam's spell.

"What the hell is this I hear about a day care?"

Samantha held the phone away from her ear

as her father's booming voice punctured her eardrum.

She should've known she'd be ratted on. Was she in a corporation or junior high?

"Who told you?"

"It doesn't matter," he scolded. "Maybe you forgot our numerous conversations where I not only didn't authorize this preposterous plan, I flat-out denied your request."

"Yes, I remember," she agreed like going against the great Stanley Donovan was no big deal. "But I am the manager and I see what's going on here and what the patrons want. Many couples would like some private time to enjoy the tranquility of the island without kids running around and screaming at them. Surely that's something you could relate to."

That last sentence slipped out of her mouth before she could think, but once the words were out, she didn't regret them. Stanley Donovan had never been a hands-on father. Quite the opposite. Before the death of Sam's mother, Bev Donovan had done it all. After her death, well, Stanley paid nannies and eventually shipped his daughter off to boarding school in Switzerland.

"As of this moment, you will be checking in

with me at the beginning and end of each business day."

Sam slammed her fist into her desk. "What? You can't be serious."

"I'm dead serious. If you can't follow my directions, you will have to report every day and let me know what your plans are. I want to know everything from the number of guests to the number of rolls of toilet paper in the storage room."

Rage filled her. "This is not how you treat Miles."

"Miles doesn't go behind my back."

Samantha gripped the phone. "Fine. You'll get your daily report, but don't blame me when your resort fails because you were too bullheaded to see some changes need to be made."

"Your attitude needs some major adjusting, little girl, or you'll find yourself out of a job."

"I bust my butt around here and have never been given any praise, much less a thank-you. You have no idea what I do."

"Things that I don't agree with," he inter-jected.

"I won't let this resort go belly-up. You seem to not care about it, but I do."

Slamming the phone down, Samantha gained a

slight bit of satisfaction in the fact that her father was still talking. She'd really just about had it. She'd never been treated like a problem employee and she'd certainly never hung up on her boss, but she'd never worked for her father before.

Her hands shook from all the anger pumping through her. She counted to five, then ten, and even when she got to twenty, she was still enraged.

How dare he speak to her as if she were a child? He didn't take the time to discipline her when she'd been young, why would he start now?

Sam shoved back from her desk and stood. She needed to take a walk, cool off and then resume her duties that would continue to go unappreciated.

She flung open her door and slammed directly into a wall of solid muscle and sexy man.

"Whoa." Brady grabbed hold of her arms. "What's the hurry?"

She stared up at him. "What are you doing back?"

His soft chuckle penetrated the wall of anger she'd erected. "I told you I'd be back."

"But you only left three days ago. You said a week."

He shrugged. "I got done earlier than expected. Besides, I missed you."

Those three simple words melted her, made her knees weaken.

How could he have known just what she needed and how on earth did he know she was having a really, really bad day? For anyone else, she would've made an excuse to be alone but with Brady, well, she wanted his company.

She reached up, wrapped her fingers around his wrists. "Can we talk?"

"Of course."

With his hold still on her arms, he backed her into her office, shut the door with his foot and captured her mouth.

On a sigh, she molded into him. Like a starving woman, she took everything he offered as she slid her hands up his arms and curled her fingers around his strong, muscular shoulders. His wide hands slid around her waist and drew her closer... as if she'd go anywhere now. She tasted his need, his desire and she was almost certain he could taste hers, as well.

Heat pooled between her legs, her nipples pressed achingly against her silky bra. The need for this man gave her no choice but to respond to his arousing kiss.

If this man could make her damp with just a kiss, what would he do to her in bed?

Nine

Brady didn't relinquish his hold as he eased his mouth from hers. "I've been thinking about that for days. I knew you'd be worth the wait."

Confused, stunned and incredibly turned on, Sam opened her eyes and peered up at him. "I don't think we should be doing this."

"Why not?" His brows drew together.

Good question. She had to push aside her desire and longing to recall the excuse she'd rehearsed in her head.

"Because I don't move this fast," she said through her thick voice. "Not that I'm not incredibly attracted to you, but getting a quickie in my office isn't my idea of romantic or professional."

He studied her face, his thumbs still caressing her neck. "I appreciate your honesty, so I'll be truthful, as well. I want to lay you down on that desk and make you scream. Romantic or not, that's my fantasy."

Her nipples tightened at the erotic image. "Brady." She placed her hands on his hard chest, his pecs fitting perfectly in her palms. "Think about this. If we have sex—"

"*When* we have sex…"

Rolling her eyes, she laughed. "Let's just enjoy each other while you're here on business. If we get to know each other, and things progress at a natural, slower pace, that's fine. No expectations. Okay?"

His chocolate eyes turned serious. "Fair enough. But I should warn you, I won't stop trying to fulfill my fantasy."

God, when he spoke in that low, seductive tone she wanted to take him up on the desk offer. But she couldn't—not yet. Her career had to come first no matter how much she wanted Brady.

But just once in her life she wished she'd be a bad girl and put her personal needs first. Why did every fiber of her being have to be so damn good all the time?

* * *

After an hour of concentrating on breathing, Sam was able to get back to work. She honestly didn't know how much more willpower she had left. She liked to think she had quite a lot, but she feared if Brady kissed her again, she wouldn't even be able to define the word *willpower*.

Brady told her he'd be busy with conference calls the rest of the afternoon, but he'd like to see her tonight if she had the time.

On one hand she appreciated the space he offered, but on the other, she wished he'd tell her he couldn't wait another minute to strip her down and get to know every inch of her body and to hell with business.

If he told her he couldn't wait to be with her, that he wanted to spend the night, she'd cave with no regrets.

But he'd been a gentleman and told her he respected her decision. How could she be so tough with her willpower when he had her defensive walls crumbling?

Her cell rang just as she was about to pull up the upcoming-guest list for the following week.

She slipped the cell from her Prada jacket pocket. "Hello."

"Sam, are you busy?" Miles asked.

"No. Are you calling to scold me, as well?"

Samantha settled back in her seat. Getting a call from Miles was better than her father, but not much.

"Dad doesn't know I'm calling," he explained.

"Aren't you afraid you'll get grounded?" she joked.

"Will you be serious for a minute?"

She sighed. "Fine. What is so urgent that you had to go behind father's back and call the enemy?"

"You're not the enemy, Sam."

"Whatever." She waved a hand through the air. "The reason for this call is…"

"Dad is making some major changes and your little stunt didn't help. Things are getting chaotic around here, so if you could lay low and just do what you're told, that would really help."

Samantha snorted. "You're kidding, right? I'm doing double the work of anybody else in his company and receiving little to no recognition and you want me to lay low?"

"I take it you don't know about the changes?"

Sitting up in her seat, Sam feared she wouldn't like what she was about to hear. "Do you really think he'd tell me anything? Besides, he was too busy berating me."

Miles paused a little too long for her liking.

"We've hired a new V.P. He will be taking my place and I will be taking Dad's place. Father plans on retiring soon."

Her heart sank. Obviously she hadn't been considered for this promotion. She was a Donovan, but not enough of one to be part of the family's major decision makers in the corporation.

"Did he even consider me for a higher position?" She almost hated to ask.

"No."

"This is unacceptable," Sam all but shouted. She didn't know if she wanted to punch something or cry.

After all she'd done for that company, how could they do this? Did they not have a caring bone in their bodies? She knew the answer, she just didn't want to face reality.

As usual, the Donovan empire reigned above all else. Even her feelings.

Obviously her father and Miles had had someone in mind for a while or the hiring process would've taken longer.

"Sam?"

"I've got to go."

She disconnected the call, and for the second time that day she needed some fresh air. Unfortunately, this time when she opened her door,

Brady wasn't there to greet her with open arms and a mind-numbing, toe-curling kiss.

Samantha made her way through the lobby and onto the beach. She slid off her Gucci sandals and hooked the straps around her fingers.

Now that she'd had time to absorb Miles's bombshell, she realized she was beyond pissed, beyond hurt.

Samantha knew she wouldn't get any more work done today, so she decided to do what she always did when she was upset and wanted to take out frustrations on something. She went back to her room at the resort and cleaned.

Oh, there were plenty of maids, but Samantha would rather have them cleaning up after an actual guest than herself. Besides, she didn't dirty too much considering most of her time was spent in her office or milling about the hotel making sure everyone was happy.

Sam threw on her sloppy clothes. She had no intention of going anywhere for a while.

With tattered exercise shorts and a white tank, she grabbed her bucket of cleaning supplies.

She scoured her bathtub until it was sparkling white. She searched for dust bunnies to attack and found only one. She reorganized her clothes in her closet and still, still wasn't satisfied with her self-cleansing.

She had, however, worked up a nice sweat. Just as she was about to make use of her freshly cleaned tub, someone pounded on her suite door.

Sam glanced down at herself and hoped it wasn't an employee needing to talk. She was not exactly in boss mode.

She glanced through the peephole and groaned. Be careful what you wish for.

With no other option than to be seen at her worst, Sam opened the door.

Brady's eyes raked over her. "Cleaning day?" he asked with a smile.

"Yeah. What are you doing here?"

He shrugged and stepped in. "I was hoping you'd take me up on the dinner I offered earlier."

He turned to face her, looking so GQ in his white T-shirt, dark jeans and black belt and sandals.

God, she had to look like a madwoman in his eyes. The hair she'd yanked into a ponytail had halfway fallen and her makeup surely had worn off by now.

"I wish you would've rang my room first," she told him.

"Had I called, you would've found some excuse not to see me."

Maybe. "I'm such a mess, Brady. I've scrubbed my tub and reorganized my closet. I'm really not at my best."

"You look cute to me." He kissed her forehead and strode into her small yet cozy living area as if they'd not just met a little over a week ago. "Go ahead and finish. I'll just watch some TV until you're done cleaning."

Defeated and a little pleased that she hadn't scared him away by her appearance, Sam followed him. "I'll be right back."

He picked up the remote, clicked on the flat-screen television. "I'll be waiting."

Sam rushed into her bathroom and ran a tubful of scalding-hot water to relax her tight muscles. She made sure to shave and wash with her jasmine-scented body wash.

It may have been a quickie bath, but when a man like Brady showed up at your front door, you had to at least try to look feminine. Freshly shaven legs and some scented lotion would go a long way.

As she towel dried she wondered why her heart beat like a sixteen-year-old's. This was a man she'd shared multiple kisses with. A man she was starting to care about and she believed cared for her, too.

A man who'd made his intentions clear. He wanted her. Bad.

* * *

Brady wasn't known for his patience, but for Sam he would make an exception. No, for the fact he was going to take the resort out from under her, he'd make the exception.

He wanted information and he wanted it yesterday.

But most of all, after that passionate kiss in her office, he wanted his hands on her again. He needed to feel her against him, needed to hear her soft groans.

Unable to concentrate on any program, Brady turned off the TV and settled back onto the plush, floral sofa. Behind him Sam's soft footsteps padded from her bedroom, and he smiled. Already her jasmine scent filled the room, making him all the more eager to touch her.

"Nothing on TV?" she asked as she took a seat beside him.

"Nothing important."

She'd left her hair damp, making the golden blond seem more dark honey. Her face was pink and she'd thrown on a pair of white cotton shorts and a black tank. And he was pretty sure there was no bra considering her nipples were pressing against the cotton.

"I've had a really bad day, so if you want to dine with me, can we just do room service?"

"Room service is fine."

Actually, spending an intimate evening in her suite, on her playing field, was perfect. Being in her own atmosphere would make her more relaxed, more open to share. He hoped.

Because he couldn't go another moment without touching her, he placed a hand on her bare thigh. "What do you want?"

She swallowed, her gaze darted down to his lips. "Anything. I'm starving."

That made two of them.

"I didn't realize how much I missed seeing you until I was gone," he told her. And much to his surprise, he wasn't lying.

Her hands came up to frame his face, and he was completely lost. Her soft touch aroused him, her trust humbled him, and Brady knew—just knew—he was going to hell for sure.

Ten

Before he could say another word, she pulled him in, capturing his mouth.

Dear Lord, this woman knew what she wanted. Talk about a complete turn-on.

Her lips prodded his until he opened, allowing her tongue access. She tasted minty and cool as if she'd just brushed her teeth.

He ran his hands up her dainty, bare arms, easing down the straps of her tank. With just the tips of his fingers, he glided over the smooth slopes of her breasts, pleased when she arched into him.

Dipping his hands inside the shirt, he grabbed

her bare breasts. Sliding his thumbs over her nipples proved to be satisfying for both of them, as they let out dueling groans.

Her hands slid down to his shoulders where she held on tight. Brady wanted more. He left her mouth to trail open-mouth kisses down her neck, across her collarbone.

Sam let out a moan when he moved his mouth lower.

He plucked a nipple into his mouth. Just as Sam let out another groan, the suite phone rang, the piercing sound cutting through the heavy breathing.

"I have a machine," she panted.

After the third ring, the machine picked up and Sam's soothing voice filtered through the air, asking the caller to leave a message.

"Samantha—" Her father's voice boomed through the room, and she all but froze in his arms. "Call me immediately. I'd better hear from you within the hour."

Rage filled him, but he suppressed the urge to curse. Did the old man have to ruin *everything?*

Sam pulled back, adjusted her tank and glanced up at him. "I'm sorry. That's my father."

Brady had to smile, he couldn't let her know he

already knew the voice of the devil. "Go call him. It sounds urgent."

"Everything's urgent with him, except what's important."

She went into her room, closed the door and left Brady wondering what she meant. Stanley was definitely a bastard, but to his own daughter? He'd suspected so before, but he'd heard the gruffness, the irritation in the old man's voice.

A part of Brady felt sorry for Sam, but the other part of him knew he couldn't get emotionally involved. He had to gain back this resort for his own father's sake.

Lani Kaimana held a special place in his heart and he wouldn't let it go, no matter what blue-eyed beauty crossed his path.

But the way she'd melted into his touch had him wondering what if. If they'd met in San Francisco at his office, would they have become lovers on their own without his driving force pulling them together?

Yeah. No way would he have let Samantha go without trying—at the very least—to date her.

But right now he had access to all the ammunition he needed to destroy Stanley Donovan. While "helping" Sam, he would have her permission to look into files no enemy should see.

After several minutes of waiting, Brady picked up the phone in the living room and ordered room service. Some strawberries, finger sandwiches, wine. He didn't want anything major and he wanted things he could feed to Sam.

He needed to get back to the seduction he had going before Sam's father interrupted their evening.

But when Sam exited her bedroom with her cell in hand and a look of defeat on her face, he knew his plans for the evening may have just headed south.

"Everything okay?" he asked, coming to his feet and guiding her to the sofa.

"Just personal business."

"Want to talk about it?"

She nestled her head in the crook of his arm. "My father just made some decisions that I'd hoped he'd reconsider. Obviously he doesn't care about others' feelings."

"I don't know what's going on, but if you want to talk…"

She smiled up at him. "Thanks. I'd rather not."

Of course not. That would've been too easy.

"How about a movie?" he suggested. "I ordered room service, and it should be here any minute."

"Bless you."

While they waited on room service, they agreed on an action flick and, much to Brady's surprise, she'd not only seen the movie but loved it.

Great, now they had something in common other than Lani Kaimana and sexual attraction. As if he needed yet another reason to have his defenses soften toward this woman.

When the food arrived, Brady took care of tipping the waiter and moved the silver cart beside the couch.

"Do you have a blanket?" he asked.

Her brows drew together. "Are you suggesting a carpet picnic?"

"Do you mind?"

A beaming smile spread across her face. "I'll be right back."

They spread the thick, cream-colored comforter from her bed in front of the couch and took a seat with their food, wine and glasses.

While the movie rolled in the background, Brady hand-fed Sam strawberries and nearly groaned when her tongue darted out to lick the juice running down his hand.

"This was the best idea," she said.

"You're the one who wanted to stay in," he reminded her.

"True, but you ordered the food."

He grinned. "Maybe we're just a good team."

Once all the food was gone, the wine empty, Brady settled with his back against the couch. Sam came to rest between his legs, her back against his chest. He wrapped his arms around her and, more than his next breath, he wanted to rip off that thin tank so he could feel her skin on his.

But he had to take this at her pace. The pace that was damn near killing him.

By the end of the movie, Sam was asleep.

Sam awoke in her bed, in the dark. With Brady at her side. Alarmed, she sat up.

"What?" Brady jerked. "Are you okay?"

Her eyes focused in the dark as she glanced back to him. "Um…how did we get here?"

"You fell asleep," he told her in a husky, sleep-filled voice. "I carried you in here."

Sam glanced back to her nightstand and groaned. "It's nearly 3:00 a.m. I'm so sorry, Brady."

"Sorry for what?"

When she turned her head, their lips nearly connected. "For falling asleep on you."

His gaze dropped to her mouth. "Do I look upset?"

She licked her lips. "You look turned on."

"I am."

"Are you going to make love to me?"

"Yes."

She moved a hand up his T-shirt, over his shoulder and threaded her fingers through his hair. "Good."

He reached out, circling her wrist with his strong hand as his mouth came crashing down on hers. Both eager, frantic, they came to their knees with their mouths still fused.

Hands were everywhere, tugging at shirts, pulling on waistbands. Sam didn't recall wanting a man with everything in her. Nor did she recall loving how a man kissed so much. And Brady Stone could make her forget the world existed with just one hot, steamy kiss.

When he eased back to remove her shirt completely, his eyes widened. "You have no clue how long I've wanted you."

"I have a good idea."

In no time at all their clothes were strewn about and they moved down on the bed together as one. Bare skin to bare skin. Lips to lips. Chest to chest.

The feel of his solid erection against her heated skin only made her hunger for more.

Instead of coming together, Brady rained kisses

over her face, her shoulders, her chest and on down her abdomen. Instinctively, her legs parted as he settled between them.

He rested his hands on her inner thighs, spreading her before he tasted her. Sam arched off the bed, grabbed hold of his hands with her own and groaned. His cool mouth made quite the contrast to her heated center.

With slow—agonizingly slow—kisses he continued to devour her as she writhed against him.

Just when she thought she couldn't take the assault anymore without screaming, he eased back up her body. "You taste so sweet, Sam."

"Take me," she pleaded. "Don't make me wait."

She reached into her nightstand drawer and pulled out a condom. Brady took the foil wrapper and in no time had himself sheathed.

He moved over her, spreading her legs wide with his hard thighs.

She eased her knees up, allowing him total access. Sam held on to his taut shoulders as he entered her in one swift move. The burning quickly gave way to pleasure.

Brady stilled, then as if a dam had broken free, he started moving his hips. His head dipped down to take a nipple. The soft, moist suction of his mouth combined with the hard, frantic pace of his hips nearly drove Sam insane.

She couldn't keep her eyes open another minute. Her fingers tightened over his muscled skin as he pulled out and thrust back in. Over and over again.

Sam cried out. She saw the bursts of light behind her lids. Warmth spread through her as she wrapped her legs around his waist, tilting her own hips to feel more.

"Yes, yes."

Brady captured her cries with his mouth. His tongue mimicking their lovemaking.

Her inner muscles clenched, and Sam let out one long moan.

Tingling sensations sped throughout her body as the climax rolled through her. And just when she thought she couldn't take any more, Brady pumped in and out in fast, frantic motions. Finally, his body shuddered, his hands gripped her thighs. Sam held on as his body tightened with his release.

When the tremors ceased, he rubbed his palms over her belly, her breasts. "Are you okay?"

"Ask me again when I can catch my breath."

Brady chuckled as he eased off the bed. In the distance she heard him running water in the bathroom.

Her body was beyond tired, beyond satisfied. The man knew just where and how to touch a woman. He wasn't a selfish lover; if anything he cared more about her needs than his own. Why had she put him off for so long?

He didn't hesitate to climb between the rumpled sheets with her once again. Wrapping his arm around her waist.

She rolled over, pressed her backside into his front and relished the fact that she was in Brady Stone's arms. They'd made love and she couldn't be more pleased with her life right now.

Except for the fact her brother and father were still trying to control her, Sam was doing well. And even though they'd all but cast her aside, she knew in the long run, she'd be better off if she got out of the company for good.

She didn't want to be involved with anybody who thought they knew what was best for her. She wanted to be on equal terms with the men in her life. So far, Brady had proven he thought her his equal. Perhaps she should reconsider his business proposal. But right now, business was the last thing she wanted to think about.

She couldn't berate herself for allowing her lack of self-control to interfere with business. So far, every time Sam had needed someone, Brady had been there. And now that she'd shared her body, she knew trusting him with the business of revamping the resort was the right decision.

If the man was half as thorough with business as he was in bed, Sam was quite certain that she'd made the right choice in going against her father's wishes and partnering up with Brady.

In the end, her father may just thank her.

With Brady's soft, warm breath on her neck, Sam drifted off to sleep, thankful she'd finally given in to her desires.

Eleven

"Sometimes I wonder what would've happened if my mother had lived."

Sam's soft voice drifted through the darkened room. Her back nestled into Brady's chest and he knew this intimate moment was about to get even more so. His heart was softening toward her even though he'd tried to steel himself.

Even so, he still had an agenda. Sam couldn't, wouldn't, get in the way of his takeover plan. He knew, though, he wouldn't be able to keep his feelings for Sam out of this mess. He'd tried.

Dammit, he'd tried, but Sam was a stronger force than he could handle.

He couldn't think about that now. Right now, he had to ignore the jab of guilt and keep trudging along with his plan of demise for the Donovans.

Moonlight flooded her spacious bedroom. All was quiet. No cell phones, no e-mails, no meetings. Right now, nothing existed but Sam.

"I often wonder the same thing about my mother," he confessed. He'd never, ever discussed his family with a woman. Especially in bed.

"It's hard growing up without them, isn't it?" she asked.

He swallowed the lump in his throat. "Yeah."

"I like to think she'd be proud of me."

Brady smiled in the darkness. "I didn't know your mother, but I'm sure she would've been."

"How do you know?"

He ran a finger down her side, dipping in at her waist and back out at her hip. "Because I know the woman you've become and I have to believe all the good in you stems from her. I have no doubt your mother is looking down on you with a smile on her face."

Sam turned in his arms. "I hope so. I only had her for a short time, but I miss her every day."

Because she was opening up, Brady kept the

focus on her instead of talking about his own loss, reliving the nightmare. "Can you tell me about her?"

"She was beautiful." Sam's eyes misted, though a faint smile adorned her lips. "I remember her long blond hair. I loved brushing it and wishing my hair would be like that someday. She had a rich smile that would light up any room. And she cared. She truly cared about people and tried to put others' needs ahead of her own."

Brady tucked a stray tendril behind her ear. "Sounds like someone else I know."

Bright blue eyes came up. "I've been told we look exactly alike. My father used to tell me how beautiful she was."

He didn't want her happy memories destroyed by thoughts of her father. "Go on about your mother."

"She stayed at home to care for me and Miles while my father worked." She laughed. "My father was always at work. The only time I saw him was when we'd have parties for his colleagues or around the holidays. Mom always made sure we never wanted for anything, and we didn't. At least, I didn't. Since Miles is older than me, Dad would take him to the office sometimes, but I stayed home with Mom. Occasionally, she'd go into the office and help him with some paperwork, but for the most part, she stayed home.

"We'd make cookies or watch a movie. Sometimes she'd take me shopping. When I showed interest in dancing, she signed me up for dance classes."

Silence filled the room. Brady didn't coax her. He knew discussing this was hard for her. After all, he'd lost his mother when he was eleven and his own father only six months ago.

"One day we were running late for my class, and she was speeding," Sam said softly. "The weather was beautiful. The sun was shining and I was so happy because we were going to go get a puppy after my class. I was going to name him Baxter. But we never made it."

Brady continued his journey over her silky skin, hoping to relax her. "You don't have to tell me."

A tear escaped, sliding down to her hairline. "A car pulled out in front of us," she continued on as if she hadn't heard him. "I just remember my mother screaming then the sound of metal against metal. I was in the back, but I can still see the look in my mother's eyes in the rearview mirror just before we hit the other car."

Brady's heart ached for Sam. As she struggled to form words, he stroked her bare shoulder.

"She didn't die until we reached the hospital. There was internal bleeding," Sam explained with a sniff. "I only had a few minor injuries. Cuts, bruises, a broken collarbone from where I jerked against the seat belt. I overheard the doctors say I was lucky to be in the backseat."

"But you didn't feel lucky." It wasn't a question. Brady knew both the little girl and the woman sitting beside him had survivor's guilt.

"No," she whispered. "Why did she have to leave me? I needed her. I need her now."

Just as he pulled her into his embrace, she broke. Sam buried her head in his chest as sobs tore through her.

He knew, without a doubt, that no one had held her and let her cry this out. Nobody had been there for this little girl when she'd needed someone the most. Certainly not Stanley Donovan.

Years of emotions poured from her. The helpless feeling that swept through Brady only made him angrier with Sam's father and brother. And angry with himself. He didn't want Sam to hurt anymore, but he knew she would once all was said and done. So what right did he have to offer consolation now?

Had anyone been there for Sam when she'd needed them? Had Stanley grieved alone at the loss of his wife? Had he ever bothered to talk to Sam about the woman they both lost?

Brady wasn't sure what he would've done if he hadn't had Cade to lean on. And vice versa.

Minutes, maybe hours passed before Sam lifted her head. "I'm sorry for that."

Brady stroked her damp hair away from her face. "Crying? If you ask me, you're long overdue for an emotional meltdown."

"Did you have an emotional meltdown when your father passed?"

Images of throwing his glass of bourbon against his bedroom wall and cursing everything and everyone around him filled his mind. "I did. People deal with death differently, though. But I had Cade and he had me."

She settled her cheek against his chest and wrapped her arm around his waist. "I guess I just needed to talk about her. You'd think I'd be used to life without her."

"She was your mother. I don't suspect you'll ever get used to being without her. I never have."

"The older I get, the harder it is to cope. I want to make the right choices in life, but I don't have anybody to give me advice or listen when I need to talk."

Brady kissed the top of her head. "You have me, Sam."

"For how long?"

He didn't bother answering.

How could he when he was unsure himself? What started out as a vendetta was slowly turning into something less sinister…at least where Samantha was concerned.

He gathered her close and prayed he would make the right decision for Sam. It was becoming more and more clear that Sam was going to get caught in the middle of this ugly war. It was only a matter of time before she became a casualty.

Brady ran a hand down his face and glanced back to the computer screen where he'd pulled up the San Francisco newspaper. The headline was still at the top of the page. Easing back in his leather chair, he dialed his brother's office line.

The second his brother picked up, Brady said, "News sure got to the paper fast."

Cade sighed. "I can't believe they're already making the announcement."

The headline of the paper continued to stare back at him: Donovan Heir Takes Control.

The caption was complete with a picture of Miles with a smug grin.

Of course, this piece of news wasn't so new to Brady or Cade. They knew of the change in positions and the fact that Sam's father was retiring, thanks to the ever so clever snooping of their assistant, Abby.

It didn't matter who sat at the helm of the Donovan empire, Brady intended to crush them.

"This does take the Kauai property into a different direction," Cade said.

"Not necessarily," Brady countered. "We knew this announcement was coming. Actually, Sam may need me now more than ever."

"Had she mentioned this to you before?"

Brady shook his head. "No. Honestly, I doubt she knew until the last minute."

"So, she's nothing like the Donovan men?"

"They're polar opposites."

Cade let out a low whistle. "She's got you, doesn't she?"

"No." Brady shut down his laptop and came to his feet. "I think I'll make a call to the new CEO and offer my congratulations."

Cade laughed. "Let me know how it goes."

Brady disconnected the call and dialed the Donovan offices, which happened to be close to his own San Francisco office. As he waited for the receptionist to put his call through, he gripped the receiver so tight he heard a slight crack.

"Miles Donovan."

Brady walked to the open patio doors and leaned against the door. He took great pleasure in being at the resort when his enemy on the other line had no clue.

"Miles. Brady Stone. I hear congratulations are in order."

"What do you want?"

"Just to say I hope you run the company better than your father did, for your sake."

"Is that a threat?" Miles demanded.

"Not at all." Brady breathed in the fresh salt water. "But just because you're in charge now doesn't mean you're going to be able to keep Lani Kaimana."

"Oh, I'll keep it, Stone. I'm not surprised you're trying to get that back after your father's death, but don't waste your time. I'm in charge now and I intend to keep everything that's mine."

Brady rubbed his smooth chin. "Well, good luck. You may be in charge, but I have an ace in the hole."

There was a slight pause on the other end and Brady wondered if Miles had heard him. He waited another few seconds.

"What's the matter, Miles? Worried?"

"You don't have squat. You're just running off at the mouth."

Brady shrugged, knowing the gesture would come across in his tone. "Don't say I didn't warn you."

He hung up feeling better about the business, but sick to his stomach that he'd inadvertently used Sam.

Granted, from the beginning he'd always planned to use her as a conductor, but now that he'd done so, there was a sudden ache in his chest.

Brady turned away from the beauty of the white sand and frothy waves. He couldn't admit, even to himself, that the night with Sam had been too intense, too close to his heart. She'd somehow managed to chisel her way around the steel wall he'd erected around his emotions.

But what could be done now? He didn't intend to back down and the damage was already done.

There was nothing to do but stay on target.

Twelve

Sam knew her father blamed her for the death of Beverly Donovan. If only he knew the impact his harsh words over the years had had on her.

She'd overheard him one night talking on the phone, to who she didn't know. He'd said if Bev hadn't been in such a hurry to get Sam to her dance class, she wouldn't have died.

Little did her father know, her mother had been miserable for the past couple years of their marriage. Sam had discovered a journal her mother had kept. Within the thin pages, Bev had remarked time and again how she wished her husband would be as loving as he used to be, not work as much and pay more attention to Sam.

Sam had never picked up on the tension, if there was any, between her parents. Perhaps her mother would've left her father, perhaps not. Beverly Donovan was a strong, incredible woman and Sam wanted nothing more than to be just like her.

She already had the looks part down pat. But Sam wanted her mother's love of life; she wanted that vibrancy people saw when her mother would enter a room.

The chirping of her cell phone jarred her from her thoughts.

She didn't want to talk on the phone. She wanted to go see Brady. After two weeks of not being with him, she wanted to scream.

He'd told her Cade had to be out of the office for a few days, so Brady needed to return to San Francisco. Business was most definitely his life. Sam just hoped she was part of it, too.

Fastening her last gold hoop in her ear, Sam grabbed the phone from her nightstand and answered. "Hello."

"Sam."

Her excitement dropped. "Miles."

"Have you had any guests within the last week

or so question you or the staff on the status of the resort?"

She rested a hand on her hip. "I haven't and the staff hasn't said anything. Why?"

"I'm almost certain that our main competitor is going to be making an appearance in an attempt to gain information to take the resort from us."

Horror filled Sam. "I won't let that happen."

"You may not be able to stop it. If something doesn't seem right, call me or Dad."

"Yeah, right. I can handle this, Miles. I will call you if I discover someone is pumping the staff for information, but I'd rather walk over hot coals than call Dad and explain I need his help."

"Samantha, be reasonable."

She sighed, not wanting to hear any more. "I have dinner plans. I have to go."

She hung up, pleased that Miles thought enough about her to include her in the business, but horrified at the thought of the beautiful place being taken from her. She'd come to think of this as her home, her life.

The knock on her door brought her back to the fact Brady was here. She was more than eager to see him again, make love to him again.

With one last glance in the mirror, Sam gave

a nod of approval at her strapless white dress and gold T-strap sandals.

By the time she opened the door, she was as giddy as a schoolgirl.

"Hi," she greeted him.

His eyes raked over her, thrilling her and making her want to forget the restaurant entirely.

"You look amazing," he whispered as he stepped over the threshold.

She'd barely gotten the door closed behind him before he spun her around and crushed his mouth to hers, wrapped her in his inviting embrace and made her knees turn to rubber.

She couldn't deny the fact he could make her forget her own name with just the touch of his lips.

But before she could even wrap her arms around his neck, he'd released her mouth, but not her body.

Dazed, Sam fluttered her lids and focused on him. "What was that for? To prove we're still combustible?"

Moist lips tilted up into a smile. "That was because you looked like you could use something to take your mind off whatever put that sad look in your eye."

Sam ran her hands over his crisp navy blue

dress shirt, settling on his hard pecs. "Your tactics worked. But let's not discuss my personal issues. You're here now and I'm dying to get you naked again."

He kissed her once more. "You have the best ideas."

Needing to feel more of him, Sam moved her hands around to his back, lifted the hem of his shirt and slid her fingers along smooth, taut skin over well-toned muscle. A low moan escaped him, vibrating through his chest.

With a smile on her face, she glanced up. Brady's eyes were closed. Sam placed small, short kisses on his neck, his chin, his jawline.

Suddenly, as if he couldn't take another second, Brady shoved her back against the door and lifted her dress. "You're a little minx," he growled.

With her body burning with need, she unbuttoned his shirt, slid it off his shoulders and made quick work on his belt, button and zipper.

Then, in one swift move Brady yanked her bikini panties. The tear pierced the air a split second before his hands found her most intimate spot. Spreading her legs wide, she granted him the access they both desperately needed.

He slid his finger over her center, penetrated

her, and she cried out. Bucking her hips, she held on to his bare shoulders.

"More. I need more."

Brady removed his hand, gripped her waist and lifted her so her body wedged between the door and his chest. "Wrap your legs around me."

The second her ankles locked behind his back, he drove into her. The fullness of him had her tilting her hips once again, eager to take all he could give.

Brady caged her body, leaving her no room to move. He was in complete control and she loved it. For once in her life, she liked being controlled by a man.

Hips pumping, warm breath ragged in her ear, Sam couldn't get enough of this potent man. He consumed her every fiber.

All too soon, she felt herself rise. She tried to increase the pace, wanting to get to her release, but Brady remained in charge.

"You're ready, aren't you?" he purred in her ear.

She couldn't piece together a response, instead she bit her lip and whimpered. Just then Brady moved in such a fast, frantic pace, Sam knew he must be close to his own release.

She turned her head, capturing his lips with

her own. Tongues mimicked bodies as they rose together and held on for the climax.

They shuddered together, lips still fused as one. Nothing ever felt so intense, so perfect. Once the tremors ceased, Brady kissed her softly and eased back until her feet were once again on the carpet.

When he slid his hands up under her dress and removed the flimsy garment, Sam didn't protest. She didn't have the energy to. She'd never been taken in such an urgent way before, as if he couldn't live another minute without touching her.

The idea of being desired so much had her body humming for more all over again. What had she done to deserve this attention, this affection from such a remarkable man?

"We need to freshen up again," he murmured against her ear.

"But we have reservations."

He nipped at her chin. "I'll change them."

"I'm too tired," she protested as he scooped her up and headed toward the bathroom.

"Then I'll just have to do all the washing."

They dined in a romantic corner booth complete with candlelight. Brady, though, was having a hard time concentrating on anything other than the way Sam's bare shoulders looked in her strapless white dress. She'd pulled her hair up, leaving some tendrils down to dance around her tan shoulders.

She looked like a woman who had been thoroughly loved.

He'd seen the looks men had passed her way when they'd entered the restaurant. Jealousy didn't take over, though. No, Brady was glad they were looking. She was his, and he was proud of her.

Since when did he think of Samantha as his? If he didn't put a stop to these emotions he would fall for her.

"I've been thinking about going ahead with the spa," Sam said, drawing him back to the conversation.

"What?"

"I think we need to go ahead with the plans for the day spa." She rested her slender arms on the table. "I've already been in contact with a contractor. Would you mind looking over the plans he sent?"

"Not at all."

"Are you okay?" she asked.

Was he?

He faked a smile and nodded. "Fine. Just thinking about work. My brother is holding down the office until I return."

"You're lucky to have him."

Brady couldn't deny that. "We'll look over those plans after dinner. Moving ahead with this major renovation will put more of a rift between you and your father."

Sam's eyes misted. "Since he's not in charge anymore, I don't think he has room to criticize. Besides, my brother doesn't need to know every decision I make."

He reached up, covered her hand with his. "Your father hurt you with this new change in positions."

"I should've known I would never be considered for anything more than a hotel manager."

The way she put herself down and expected to be overlooked was heart-wrenching. How could he make things better for her and still gain control over the resort?

He couldn't. Which meant he had to choose.

Thirteen

Samantha held the stick, stared at the two pink lines and didn't know if she wanted to throw up or jump up and down. But it had only been two weeks since they'd slept together. And they hadn't used a condom. The realization hit her hard.

A baby.

Brady's baby.

She sat on the edge of her bathtub and took deep, calming breaths. Okay, the breaths were deep, but not calming.

Other than being one day late for her period, which was always regular, she had no symptoms.

She placed a shaky hand on her still-flat abdomen. More signs would come soon enough.

What would Brady think? They hadn't even spoken the three most important words that should be spoken *before* making a baby.

Even though she did love him. She wouldn't be this deep into a relationship if she didn't. She wouldn't have opened up about her mother, her worries as a businesswoman, if she hadn't fallen for him.

When the burning of fresh tears threatened, Sam came to her feet, placed the stick on the edge of the counter and went to dress for work.

She'd had to go to the pharmacy early this morning for the test and pray that no one recognized her. That's all she needed was for news to travel back to her father, her brother or worse, Brady, before she could tell him.

How would she break this life-altering news?

She hoped Brady was happy, but she understood if he didn't want a family. He was, after all, a businessman with a chaotic schedule. How would a wife and baby fit into the mix?

And who's to say he would even want to marry her, she thought as she grabbed her Kate Spade handbag. Honestly, she didn't want Brady to marry her because he felt obligated to. Marriages that started out of obligation usually ended in disaster.

They were still getting to know each other. Actually, they hadn't even spoken about how far this relationship had progressed.

Did Brady even consider them a couple? Was he just with her while he stayed on the island for business?

She stepped onto the elevator, and because the doors shut leaving her all alone, she placed a hand on her flat tummy and grinned.

"I love you already," she whispered.

If Brady took the news well and was excited, Samantha would have to make more life-altering decisions.

Working under Miles would probably not be good in the long run.

And even though she hated to give up Lani Kaimana, she knew making a life with her baby and Brady would be better in the long run.

After all, how could she work fourteen-hour days and take care of a little one?

God, all the what-ifs swirled around in her head as she passed through the lobby.

Employees nodded and smiled, and Samantha wondered if they knew. Could they tell she was going to be a mother? Could they see it in the silly smile she knew she wore on her face?

She needed to speak to Brady as soon as possible. She couldn't wait to tell someone the news. But this was also the one time in her life she'd dreaded. How would she cope with a child without her own mother? Who would give her motherly advice?

A lump formed in Sam's throat at the thought of going through this without her best friend.

God, what an emotional wreck she was. This pregnancy thing really did take a toll on emotions. Hadn't she just been smiling five seconds ago?

She headed down the hallway to check on the progress of the spa. The contractor had started on the renovations last week and Sam was already hearing the buzz about guests who were eager to return.

"There you are."

Sam turned to the male voice and was shocked to see her brother.

"Miles," she greeted as she gripped her purse tighter. "What are you doing here?"

"I came to check things out," Miles said.

Sam clasped her hands together instead of balling them into a fist like she wanted to do. "You mean to check up on me."

"I'm looking out for my property, Samantha."

She quirked a brow at him. "I certainly hope you don't consider this your property. If I recall, I'm the one that has been here busting my butt since we acquired it and you just slid into dad's seat."

"Let's not get petty," Miles suggested. "Could we talk in your office?"

Sam hesitated a split second before she stalked off, leading the way. The sooner she found out what he wanted and got him out of here, the sooner she could track down Brady and see what their future held.

Because she wanted to keep the upper hand for as long as she could, Sam stepped behind her neatly organized desk and sat her bag at her feet, but did not take a seat until her door was firmly closed and Miles was seated across from her.

"Now," she said getting comfortable in her leather chair. "What is this impromptu visit about?"

Miles eased forward in his chair. "As I told you on the phone, I have reason to believe one of our main competitors is here or will be on his way."

"Yes," Sam agreed, trying to keep the irritation out of her tone. "And, as I told you, I can handle it and I would call you if I thought something was up."

"I'm also taking this opportunity to check out

the whole resort," Miles went on as if she hadn't spoken. "I was shocked when I heard you were going ahead with some rather expensive plans. We really don't have spa money in our budget."

Deep breaths, she told herself, deep breaths. In, out. "We will have a nice return on our investment. Trust me. And if there was a problem that I couldn't handle, such as a competitor coming in, I would've called you."

Miles stared at her for what seemed like eternity before nodding. "Let me see what's going on with the spa area."

"Fine." She came to her feet. "But we have to hurry. I have a busy schedule."

She opened her door with a jerk, the not-so-subtle way of letting her brother know she was not happy. After she gestured for him to go ahead, she closed and locked her door behind her.

A bit of her tension eased as they entered the open lobby and Brady stepped off the elevator looking extremely sexy in khaki shorts and a green polo.

She turned to her brother. "Excuse me just one minute."

With a smile and a quick stride, Sam made her way across the marble floor. "Hey, are you going out?"

Brady closed the gap between them. "I was going for a walk on the beach. Care to join me?"

"You don't know how much I'd love to, but I have something I have to take care of first." She stood on her toes and kissed him on the cheek. "I'll come find you later."

"What the hell is going on?"

Samantha jumped around at the booming sound of Miles's voice. "Excuse me?"

"Miles," Brady said.

Sam threw a look over her shoulder. "You know my brother?"

"Oh, he knows me all right," Miles confirmed. "He probably knew you, too, before he ever stepped foot here."

Samantha's heartbeat kicked up. From the tension surrounding her, the tone in the two male voices and the look of murder in both their eyes, she had a feeling this scene was about to get really ugly.

"Let's all go back to my office," she said quietly.

"I'd like to talk to you alone," Brady said.

Miles laughed. "I'm sure you would, Stone. Let me guess, you've been working my sister in the romance department trying to get in on some company secrets?"

Her once-beating heart dropped. "What?"

Brady took her arm and turned her around. "Sam, please, let me talk to you alone."

The pleading look in his eyes made her want to go with him, to hear what exactly was going on. But the logical side of her knew whatever he had to say could possibly destroy them.

Oh, God. The baby.

No, she could not get upset. She had to remain calm. There was someone depending on her now.

"Don't listen to him," Miles said. "He's a liar."

Sam turned back around. "You have no right to talk to me about liars. You and Father kept secrets from me from day one on this job and if I want to talk to Brady, I will."

"Do you know who he really is?" Miles asked.

"His father used to own this resort." Miles paused when the elevator dinged and a couple stepped off. "Let's step over here out of earshot of our guests."

Shaky legs carried Sam around the corner with the men. They stood in an empty hallway that led to the conference room she'd wanted transformed into a day care. But suddenly, nothing mattered but the truth.

"Has Brady told you he intends to steal this property back from us?" Miles continued.

"I'm not stealing anything," Brady said in a cold, flat tone. "I'm simply taking back what my father used as the foundation of his enterprise and your father stole at a moment of weakness."

Sam's head was spinning. She held up her hands. "Wait. Brady's family owned this before we bought it?"

"Stole it," Brady corrected.

"How could we steal it?" she questioned.

Brady rested his hands on his hips. "Ask your father and brother."

A wave of dizziness swept over her. Sam settled her back against the wall and prayed she wouldn't pass out.

"Just tell me one thing," she said. "Did you know who I was before you came here?"

"You're his ace in the hole. Right, Brady?" Miles asked. "I assume when you called me the other day you were referring to my sister."

God, this wasn't happening. This was just another cruel trick fate was playing on her. How could she have been so blindsided, so in need of affection that she'd completely let all common sense dissipate?

Samantha wanted out of this mess. She wanted

to go back to this morning to when she'd first discovered she and Brady may have a solid future together. She wanted this nightmare to be just that…a nightmare. But she knew she wouldn't be waking up anytime soon. This was reality and now she had to deal with it.

"You called my brother?"

Before or after we made love, she wanted to add. Made love. No, that's not what they'd done at all. Suddenly everything she thought they'd shared was tainted by lies.

"You had this planned from the beginning, didn't you?" she whispered because tears clogged her throat.

Brady's eyes held hers. "I came here to confront a Sam Donovan, who I thought was a man, so yes, in a sense."

"Convenient I turned out to be a woman." Sam's stomach turned, bile rose in her throat. "So you decided to use me."

Brady didn't bother to answer seeing as how she'd made an accusation, not asked a question.

"Can we talk?" Brady whispered, his coallike eyes searching her face.

"I think I've heard enough." Samantha pushed off the wall and willed the nausea to cease. "I'm going to my room. I want both of you out of my hotel by the end of the day. Miles, I'll speak with you later regarding my status with the company."

"What does that mean?" he asked.

"It means I'm not sure I can continue to work for you."

She walked slowly away from the men. How could she continue to work for Miles when she was having the enemy's baby? Miles—and her father—wouldn't understand.

The excitement she'd felt earlier had vanished, but the one thing that remained was the fact a piece of her was still in love with Brady. Well, the Brady she thought she knew.

How could such a loving man be so conniving, so vindictive?

Samantha barely made it back to her suite and into the bathroom before she fell to her knees and threw up.

Fourteen

By the time Monday rolled around, Brady was more than ready to battle with Miles over Lani Kaimana. He was just glad Cade was going to the meeting with the attorneys he'd had scheduled over another property. No way could he have gone and tried to discuss business today.

Brady's temper had still not settled back down from the hurt he'd seen in Sam's eyes caused by Miles's ill-timed interference. Not that there would've been a good time, he thought.

And how could he place the blame solely on Miles? Wasn't Brady the one who'd set out to seduce Sam? To gain her trust and access all the company's dirty laundry to use against them?

But, dammit, he hadn't known he'd come to actually care for her.

Now the need to take away everything that mattered to Stanley and Miles was stronger than ever. Everything they cared about would become his.

After all, they'd taken away a portion of his father's legacy and Samantha.

Would Sam see his way of thinking? She, more than anyone else, knew the kind of men her father and brother were. She also knew the kind of pain that came along with losing a parent and how you just wanted to lay blame with someone.

Hadn't she blamed herself for the death of her mother? Surely she would see Brady's side of things once she cooled off and could think rationally.

God, was he practicing his speech to her or trying to convince himself?

Sitting in his San Francisco office, Brady tried to catch up on his work, but the thought of Cade with the attorneys right now only made him anxious to move forward with building back their father's company.

He glanced at the digital clock on the lower right-hand corner of his computer screen. The meeting had only been going on ten minutes, and that was if they got started on time.

Hell, who was he kidding? He couldn't even concentrate on the new property they were obtaining. All he kept thinking of was Sam's tearful recollection of her childhood and the fact she wanted Lani Kaimana just as bad as he and his brother did, but for totally different reasons.

He thought of the way she'd made love with him, pouring all her emotions into their intimacy. The way she'd opened up about her feelings growing up and losing her mother.

But most of all, he couldn't stop thinking about the hurtful look in her eyes when she'd found out the truth.

He would find a way to make this right, to make sure she got everything she ever wanted. No matter what he had to barter or pay, he'd make sure Samantha stayed on at the resort. He no longer wanted it for himself.

And that thought made Brady freeze.

That statement confirmed his love. He'd only recently discovered the emotion, but wasn't sure how real it was. Now he knew. How could he have not seen the whole picture until now?

True, he'd started this vendetta out of revenge and he still wanted to make the Donovans pay, but somewhere along the way, obtaining the property turned into making Sam happy. Truly happy for once in her life.

Brady knew what he was about to do was perhaps the dumbest business move he'd ever made. Hell, forget *business* move, this was the dumbest move—period.

He was tired of sitting around moping, tired of being alone and worrying about her. So he got into his Navigator and decided to do something.

Twenty minutes later, he pulled up in front of the Donovans' office building and killed the engine. If Sam knew what he was about to do, she'd probably be more furious—if that was even possible. But Sam didn't know, and as far as he was concerned, she didn't need to know.

More than ready to confront any and/or all of the Donovans, Brady stepped out into the sultry summer heat and made his way into the cool, air-conditioned building. Stepping into the lion's den didn't sit well with him, but at this point he'd go head-to-head with the devil himself if he could prevent any more pain from slipping into Sam's life.

"Can I help you?" The petite, elderly receptionist greeted him with a smile. Obviously she didn't know who he was.

Brady returned her smile and stepped forward. "I'd like to see Miles Donovan, please. I'm afraid I don't have an appointment, but this is a pressing matter."

The woman shuffled around the papers on her desk and looked over what Brady assumed to be Miles's schedule. "He's free for the next twenty minutes. Let me make sure he's up for a visitor. May I tell him your name?"

"Brady Stone."

He had to give this lady credit, her smile barely faltered before she picked up her phone and dialed the extension.

Brady glanced around the cold black-and-chrome office. There was nothing warm and inviting about the waiting area, nothing that greeted the clients other than the receptionist.

Black leather chairs, chrome-and-glass tables with a few *GQ* magazines, no plants, no pictures on the white walls, not even an area rug over the dark hardwood floors.

"He'll see you now, Mr. Stone."

Turning his attention back to the woman, Brady smiled. "Thank you."

"His office is the last door on the right," she said, motioning down the long, narrow hall.

Even though the door was closed, Brady didn't

bother knocking. Rude, yes, but considering the man on the other side of the door, Brady didn't care.

"Hell must have frozen over for you to darken my office." Miles came to his feet, motioning for Brady to have a seat across from the large oak desk. "Either that, or you're here on my sister's behalf."

Brady didn't take the chair that was offered. He'd rather stand. Getting comfortable in this office wasn't likely.

"I want to call a truce," he said. "Samantha doesn't need to be caught in the middle of this feud."

Miles shoved his jacket back from his waist and rested his hands on his hips. "You have a lot of nerve, Stone. You tried to seduce my sister, when she had no idea who you were, in order to gain information about this company and now you're worried about her welfare?"

Brady swallowed, ignoring the guilt that crept up. "I'm here to make sure she doesn't get hurt any more."

"I don't intend to hurt her. And I suggest you move on. The resort and my sister will no longer be your concern."

"On the contrary," Brady said. "Sam and Lani Kaimana are very much my concern."

Miles chuckled. "You can't be serious about pursuing Sam. You used her as leverage to get back Lani Kaimana."

Anger bubbled inside Brady, but he pushed it down for Sam's sake. "Well, now I'm not using her for anything. You may find this hard to believe, but I care for her."

The muscle in Miles's jaw clenched. "Care? I doubt you care for her. Although I'm sure you care about everything we own, so maybe you'll continue to charm her. You may even resort to begging in order to get her to come back. Whatever it takes in the name of business. Right, Stone?"

How on earth could Miles think so little of his sister? Had their father been so cruel to Sam that Miles could just toss her aside?

Brady clenched his fists at his side. "I don't care what you think. I'm only concerned with Sam."

Without another word, he exited from the office. Maybe the meeting hadn't gone so well, but what had he expected? The Donovan men weren't known for their ability to get along with others. Perhaps that's why they were failing so miserably at their business dealings as of late.

But he would put forth an effort only for Sam.

Brady called Abby and informed her that he'd be spending the rest of the day out of the office. He also left a voice mail for Cade to call after he'd finished with the attorney.

He needed to clear his head. No way could he work with all the anger and rage that flooded through him. Added to that, he had to go back to Kauai, force Sam to hear his side and plead for forgiveness. She may never, ever forgive him, but he had to make sure she understood his actions.

Brady's head fell back against the seat. He couldn't pinpoint the exact time he fell in love with Sam. And he *was* in love with her. There wasn't a doubt in his mind. He'd never felt this way about another woman. Never wanted to be their protector, their provider, their lifetime partner.

Lifetime. His heartbeat quickened, from excitement and eagerness—and a slice of fear.

How could he go on if she chose to never forgive him? He could never love anyone as much as he loved Samantha.

He'd never backed down from a fight and he didn't intend to start now. Not when it truly mattered.

Brady exited his Lincoln and headed up the narrow steps to his suburban home. He wanted a chance at a relationship. He wanted to start off strong and grow from there. He wanted to give her the life she'd never had, a life she deserved, full of love and happiness.

With plans already forming in his head, Brady unlocked his front door and prepared the speech in his head.

Fifteen

Dread, sadness and loneliness enveloped Sam each time she stepped into her childhood home. How had she managed not to go insane all the years she'd lived here?

The marble floors gleamed, the chandeliers sparkled, sending a vast array of shapes and colors down and, as usual, not a thing was out of place. No shoes by the front door, no keys lying haphazardly on the secretary inside the foyer. No sign of life.

The house was just as it had been after her mother's passing.

Sam rubbed her arms against the chilly aura and

ventured on. She should've called ahead, but she didn't want any more harsh words than necessary with her father.

Stanley Donovan was in the first place Sam looked...the same room he'd lived in all her life. His office.

She stood in the doorway, staring across the room to the man who was her father, but had always seemed more of a stranger than anything.

He still used the same old oak desk. His floor-to-ceiling bookcases provided the backdrop, stretching the length of the wall.

He was no doubt in his element.

But instead of the robust, domineering man she'd recalled, Stanley looked old. His hair had gone from silver to mostly white and had started retreating from his forehead. His hands, which held on to a file probably containing his latest stock report, were wrinkled.

He rubbed his head with a weathered hand and Sam couldn't help but feel pity for him. All his life he'd concentrated on making money, working the next deal, but he'd missed everything that mattered. His family.

Samantha settled her hand on her stomach and entered the room.

"Dad."

Stanley jerked his head, dropping the file onto the neatly organized desk. "Samantha. What brings you here?"

She stepped farther into the den. "We need to talk. Actually, I need to talk and I need you to listen."

"Sounds important." He crossed his hands over his small, round belly and leaned back in his chair. "Does this have to do with business?"

She laughed, taking a seat across from him. "Everything always comes back to business with you, doesn't it? I guess in a way, what I have to say does center around business."

"Miles told me you turned in your resignation."

"Yes, but that's not what I want to discuss." Sam willed her cowardly nerves away and focused on the mission she came for. "I want to know why you always treated Miles different from me."

"I don't know what you're talking about," he said. "And I can't believe you'd even ask such a childish question."

"Childish? You know good and well you treat the two of us differently. You always have. Since Mom's death, you act like I'm a stray off the street that you were burdened with."

Stanley sighed. "If I have treated you different

from Miles, it's only because I was trying to do what your mother would've wanted."

Confused, Sam asked, "What?"

"Beverly never wanted you to be part of the family business. She didn't want you to be swallowed up in all of this like I've always been. She knew Miles always wanted to be involved, so she didn't say too much about him. But you…" Stanley shook his head. "You were special. You were like an angel when you came to us. All that blond hair and those wide blue eyes. You were an image of your mother and I couldn't love you more."

The steel wall Sam had built up in defense before arriving here today suddenly crumbled. "But why were you so cruel to me after her death? Why did you always push me further and further away? Even now, you can hardly look at me."

He looked down, wiping both eyes with his forefinger and thumb. "It still hurts. Looking at you," he said softly. "I just see her. I know it's a poor excuse, but it's the truth."

Unsure of how to respond, Sam did the only thing she could think of. She came to her feet and went to her father. Wrapping her arms around his broad shoulders, she kissed the top of his head.

"I'm sorry," she whispered. "I'm so sorry you were grieving all that time and I was to blame."

He wrapped his hand around her arm. "No, Sam, you weren't to blame. I was. I tried placing blame everywhere but where it belonged. Had I been more of a husband, more active in my family's life, perhaps your mother wouldn't have been in a hurry that day. I know I should've been there for you, but I just couldn't. Looking at your face each day only added to the torment of knowing I'd never see her again. I devoted my life to my work, in the hopes of getting away from the pain."

Sam tightened her hold. "I see her face, too, each time I look in the mirror."

"I'm sorry if you thought I was pushing you away. The truth is, I'm proud of you. I'm proud of the woman you've become and I know your mother would be, as well."

Sam's heart swelled as a warm tear trickled down her cheek. This was the father she'd waited so many years to have. This was the moment she'd longed for, cried for.

"I've said some hurtful things to you," he went on. "If I could take them back, I would. You've accomplished so much in such a short time. Not only are you successful in business, but you take the time to enjoy life. I'm glad you didn't follow in my footsteps. I'm afraid Miles has, though."

Sam stepped back. "He has a stubborn streak, but he's a good man. You did just fine."

Stanley looked up with moist, red eyes. "Maybe, but I need him to know working himself to the bone won't make him happy. I want him to take time to enjoy life, too."

"Then talk to him," she suggested with a squeeze. "He probably longs for a one-on-one conversation about something other than business just like I did."

"I will. Can we have a new beginning?"

Sam smiled, with tears in her eyes and a hand on her belly. "Yes. I'd like that."

She couldn't tell her father yet. No one knew about the baby. She was ten weeks pregnant now and although some of the employees had noticed her getting sick on occasion, she'd always come up with a lie.

Sam didn't stay at her father's home long, but promised to visit often. The weighty burden of their strained relationship she'd carried in with her no longer existed when she left. At least now she knew. She knew her father had grieved all this time and that he hadn't hated her, he simply didn't know how to deal with his emotions.

As Sam made her way to the airport, she knew her next step should be to contact Brady about the baby. Even though he was a lying, coldhearted bastard, he was still going to be a father and Samantha didn't have the heart not to tell him.

After all, she'd essentially lost both parents. How could she deny her own child?

Brady paced in Samantha's suite at Lani Kaimana. Luckily he'd been let in by one of the maids who'd seen Brady and Sam together often enough that she knew they'd been seeing each other. Fortunately for him, the maid had no idea Samantha probably hated his guts right now.

Where the hell was she?

He was told she'd left yesterday for a personal reason, but was due back at the resort today. He was also told she had resigned and was only going to be manager for a few more days. So now he had to wait and find out what the hell she was doing. And why she was giving up on something she loved so much.

Tugging off his suit jacket, Brady draped it over the back of the sofa. He unbuttoned his sleeves, rolled them up and unfastened the top button of his shirt.

Might as well get comfortable, he thought as he seated himself on the couch.

A folder with the name of a local doctor stamped on the front drew Brady's attention to the squatty, glass coffee table.

When he opened the file, something fell into his lap.

A picture. Not just any picture, he thought as he studied it. A picture of an ultrasound.

Because he really couldn't tell what he was looking at, he glanced at the papers in the folder.

No. This couldn't be.

Samantha was ten weeks pregnant? *Pregnant?*

Brady did some quick figuring in his head. That meant she knew she was expecting his child when they'd seen each other last.

Brady dropped the file onto the table and came to his feet, still clutching the picture of his unborn baby.

Was she going to tell him? Did she plan on keeping up this preposterous job with a chaotic schedule while pregnant? Obviously that's why she was giving up the resort.

Did Miles know? Did anybody?

The idea of Samantha keeping this secret to herself, going through this alone, infuriated him.

At some point she'd have to shove her pride aside

and ask for help. And, dammit, he'd be the one to give it to her.

The buzz from a key card at the suite door had him jerking around.

Samantha stepped in and jumped. "Brady! What are you doing here?"

For a moment, he could do nothing but stare. He didn't know what he expected. A big belly? No, that didn't come until later. But she did look beautiful. Her skin had a healthy, tanned tone, indicating she'd probably taken advantage of the sandy beach only steps away.

She looked sexy in the simple white sundress that stopped just above her knees. Her hair was down, the way he liked it, spilling over her shoulders, giving her an innocent look.

And wasn't that what killed him the most? She had been innocent in this whole thing.

"You look good," he said, once he got passed the lump in his throat.

"You have two minutes to say whatever it is you came for. I have to meet my father in San Francisco." She sat down her overnight bag and purse and crossed her arms. "Go."

"Can we have a seat and talk?"

"No."

Brady held up the picture. "Fine. When were you going to tell me about this?"

He had to give her credit, she didn't even bat an eye before she responded.

"The same day I found out the father of my baby was a conniving jerk. Funny, I didn't get around to it."

She moved from the doorway, shoving her bags aside with her foot and letting the door slam behind her. Striding across the room, she didn't even look at him as she went into her bedroom.

Brady followed.

"Were you ever going to tell me?" he asked.

Samantha reached into her drawers and started pulling clothes out and piling them on the bed. "Yes."

"You're sure?"

She stopped, a pile of silky bras dangling from her hands. "I'm not a liar. And I wouldn't deprive my child from knowing its parents."

At least that was something.

"I came back because you need to listen to me," he told her.

She rounded on him, hands on her hips. "I don't have to do anything. What I need to do right now is pack because I'm currently unemployed."

"Then come work for me."

He wasn't surprised at her outburst of laughter, but that didn't negate the fact that her dismissal hurt.

"You're kidding, right? I wouldn't work for you for any amount of money you offered."

"Then do it for the baby." He searched her face, hoping she'd see the love in his eyes. "Don't shut me out, not now. Not when I've fallen in love with you."

She stepped back, placed a hand out to the bed and eased down. "Don't. Don't throw that word out like you mean it. I won't be fooled again."

Putting everything he had on the line, his pride, his heart, Brady squatted down in front of her and took her hands.

"Do you think I'd come back if I didn't care for you?" he asked. "I'm not here for the baby, I didn't even know until I saw the file. I'm here because I realized you were more important than any resort, any business deal."

She tugged her hands free and wiped her damp eyes. "That may be true, but I can't trust what you say anymore. I won't be misled or used again."

She came to her feet, causing him to take a step back.

"Now," she said with her chin high, "I need to be alone. Please don't call me. I'll let you know all about the baby's doctor's appointments and keep you up-to-date, but other than that, I don't want any contact with you."

Brady fisted his hands at his side and swallowed. He wouldn't push, not when her condition was so delicate, but he wouldn't give up. Ever.

"You'll see how much I love you," he promised as he kissed her lightly on the cheek.

Without another word, and with a heavy heart, Brady left.

Sixteen

Without Sam's bright, sunny smile to fill the building, fill his life, Brady's days were lifeless.

Just as they'd been before she'd entered his life.

Of course, he hadn't known how boring and empty his life had been, but now that he'd experienced love, well, nothing mattered if he had to live without.

He'd caused the damage by getting the ball rolling the second he decided to get closer to Sam. And now he had to do some major work to undo what he'd done.

A week had come and gone since he'd seen her in Kauai. Brady didn't recall a longer seven days in his life.

As he shut down his computer and grabbed his suit jacket from the back of his leather chair, his desk line rang.

"Brady Stone."

"Brady, this is Stanley Donovan." The elderly man cleared his throat. "I'm with Sam at St. Mary's Hospital. I stopped by her house and she was having some stomach pains. We're waiting to see the doctor. I don't know what the personal nature of your relationship is now, but I thought you'd want to know."

Before Brady could process what the old man had said, much less ask questions, Stanley had hung up.

Fear, guilt and just plain terror ripped through him as he made a mad dash down the stairs and out to his SUV. He didn't bother saying anything to Abby or Cade—there was no time.

Was the baby okay? Was Sam? She had to be so scared. Brady was grateful Stanley had thought to call.

God, she couldn't lose the baby. Brady's hands tightened on the steering wheel as he cursed the weekend rush-hour traffic.

Arguments, betrayals, secrets, none of it mattered now. All that mattered was Sam and the baby. They had to be all right. They *had* to.

The usual twenty-minute drive to the hospital ended up taking nearly an hour. After handing his keys over to the valet driving attendant, Brady raced inside the main glass doors and up to the information desk.

"Samantha Donovan," he said breathlessly. "She was brought in a little over an hour ago. Probably in maternity."

The young receptionist glanced to her computer, typed in the name and drew her brows together. "She's in triage—third floor."

Brady took the elevator and prayed everything would be fine. Damn, he couldn't lose his future.

"Brady."

As he stepped off the elevator, he turned to the sound of his name. Brady nearly wept with relief when he saw Stanley strutting toward him.

"Where is she?" he demanded.

Stanley nodded with his head. "Follow me."

Allowing Sam's father to lead the way, Brady sent up another prayer that everything was all right. But he braced himself for the worst.

"How is she?" Brady asked as they walked back through the sterile hall.

"She's says she's fine."

"What are the doctors saying?"

Stanley stopped in front of the sliding-glass door. "She spoke with them alone and she won't tell me what's wrong. She did reassure me that she was indeed fine and she got teary when I told her you were on your way."

Brady didn't know what to make of that other than the fact Stanley obviously didn't know about the baby. But he did know being in a hospital was not helping his nerves any.

The antiseptic scent made him want to gag, to run away and avoid the hurt of losing someone else he loved with every fiber of his being. He hadn't been here since his father's illness.

Thankfully before he got even more carried away with his thoughts, he slid the door open, stepped into her room and shoved the pale blue curtain aside.

Brady's heart nearly stopped when she turned to look at him. Her eyes were red, puffy, her color was off. The oversize hospital gown swallowed up her petite frame.

She was still the most beautiful sight he'd ever laid eyes on.

And wasn't this ironic? The very man he'd set

out to destroy was now the crutch he may very well have to lean on during this time.

Brady moved to one side of the bed and took her hand. "Sam, are you all right?"

Her misty eyes darted over his shoulder. "Dad, would you give us a minute?"

"I'll give you five," Stanley said. "But after that, I want to know what is going on."

A smile played at the corners of her mouth. "I promise."

The sliding door opened, then closed, once again silencing the chaos on the other side.

Brady bent, kissed her head and inhaled her sweet aroma. "God, Sam, please tell me…"

"Shh, it's all right," she assured him. "I'm sorry my father scared you. The baby is fine and so am I."

"May I sit here?" he asked as his hip rested on the edge of the bed.

"Please."

Brady waited for her to say something. He couldn't imagine why she told her father she was fine when clearly she wasn't. What had caused her to cry so much the tip of her little nose was red?

He couldn't take the silence. "Your father said you got upset when he told you he called me."

She glanced down to her hands as they toyed with the hem of the bleached-white blanket. "Yes."

"Do you want me to go?"

"No." She continued to work her shaky hands. "I just… I don't know how to tell you this. Not with the tension between us and the harsh words."

Brady's chest tightened as he lifted her chin with his index finger. "Forget about that for now. I'm going crazy here. What's wrong?"

"Twins," she blurted out before shielding her face with her hands and bursting into tears.

Twins? The word registered in Brady's head. *Two* babies.

A grin split across his face as a chuckle bubbled its way up. "Sam," he said, easing her hands down. "Why are you so upset?"

She looked up, sniffed. "Are you laughing?"

Squeezing her delicate, wet hands between his own, he kissed her loudly on the mouth. "God, you have no idea what had been going through my mind. But, two babies? How could I not be happy?"

Brady covered her mouth with his hand, then slid his fingers around to caress her cheek. "Sam, I love you."

"I know. I saw your face when you came in." She

smiled through teary eyes. "You were frightened and I know you wouldn't have been if you didn't care. I guess I should've listened to my heart days ago."

Relief swept through him. "I'm glad your heart knew the right answer."

"I spoke with Miles today," she told him. "He told me the two of you are considering joining forces with the resort."

Brady shrugged. "I wanted to do something to ease your pain, to make sure you didn't have to choose sides and you could have control over the dealings with Lani Kaimana."

"That's another reason I knew you loved me," she confessed.

Brady squeezed her hands. "So why did you have pain? Did the doctors say?"

"Because with two babies, my uterus is stretching faster, so I was cramping a lot."

"I still can't believe it," he muttered. "Why didn't you tell your father?"

"We're just getting back to a father-daughter relationship, so I haven't filled him in on too much of my personal life."

"I noticed the tension that normally surrounded the two of you wasn't there." Brady moved his hand from her cheek back to her hand. "I know I don't deserve a second chance, but I want to be a part of my babies' lives."

"Are you saying you only want to be in their lives?"

His heart nearly leaped through his chest. "No. I'd love to be in your life again, Sam. I want so much from you, it scares me. I want you to be my wife. Say yes."

Sam sat up straighter, reached to touch his cheek. "Brady, I love you. Yes, I'll be your wife."

Epilogue

One month later, subtle waves rippled onto the beach as the vibrant orange sun set beyond the water.

Sam couldn't believe she was marrying Brady on the beach in front of their resort. He looked so handsome barefoot in his khaki linen pants and white button-up shirt. She'd wanted a simple wedding and when he'd suggested the location, she knew they couldn't begin their life together at a better spot.

"I now pronounce you husband and wife,"

the priest said. "You may kiss your bride, Mr. Stone."

Brady's eyes focused on her lips as his mouth spread into a grin. "My pleasure."

He kissed her slowly, passionately. Their first kiss as Mr. and Mrs. Stone.

Brady eased back, then whispered in her ear, "You look beautiful."

Sam had chosen a pale pink strapless chiffon dress that stopped just below her knees. She wore her mother's diamond earrings and necklace, a present from her father.

Rising on her tiptoes, she whispered, "Let's break the news."

"Okay."

The priest announced the new couple and Cade and Sam's father applauded. Sam hugged her dad and kissed him on the cheek.

"I have an announcement to make," she said, clasping her husband's hand. All eyes were on her as the quivering in her belly took control. "You know how we Donovans and Stones don't do anything halfway."

She smiled at their nods. "Well, there will be two babies in the spring, not just one."

Stanley slapped Brady on the back, hugged Samantha. "A new legacy with two of the strongest families. I'd say that's a great way to start a life together."

"I couldn't have said it better myself," Brady announced as he looked into the eyes of his bride.

* * * * *

Don't miss Cade's story,
For Business…Or Marriage?
available March 2011
from Mills & Boon® Desire™.

2 *in* **1**
GREAT
VALUE

THE DESERT PRINCE by Jennifer Lewis

Yes, Salim had once rejected Celia Davidson as a suitable bride, but now it's proving difficult to keep their relationship strictly business…

THE PLAYBOY'S PROPOSITION by Leanne Banks

When Michael Medici spotted the beautiful cocktail waitress, he made his move. One extraordinary night later, he knew he wanted more from Bella St Clair…

BILLIONAIRE'S CONTRACT ENGAGEMENT by Maya Banks

Evan is falling for stunning career woman Celia and he can tell the stunning ad exec desires him too. But will she play the role of his fake fiancée…?

MONEY MAN'S FIANCÉE NEGOTIATION by Michelle Celmer

Ash is devastated when his girlfriend leaves him but when he hears she has been in an accident he rushes to her. Why did she leave?

AFFAIR WITH THE REBEL HEIRESS by Emily McKay

CEO Ford Langley is known for his boardroom—and bedroom—conquests, but Kitty Biedermann isn't about to let Ford get his own way, in the boardroom *or* bedroom!

THE MAGNATE'S PREGNANCY PROPOSAL by Sandra Hyatt

She came to tell him the IVF has worked, Chastity is carrying Gabe's late brother's baby. Then Gabe drops the bombshell—the baby is actually his!

On sale from 21st January 2011
Don't miss out!

*Available at WHSmith, Tesco, ASDA, Eason
and all good bookshops*

www.millsandboon.co.uk

0111/5

2 FREE BOOKS
AND A SURPRISE GIFT

We would like to take this opportunity to thank you for reading this Mills & Boon® book by offering you the chance to take TWO more specially selected books from the Desire™ 2-in-1 series absolutely FREE! We're also making this offer to introduce you to the benefits of the Mills & Boon® Book Club™—

- **FREE home delivery**
- **FREE gifts and competitions**
- **FREE monthly Newsletter**
- **Exclusive Mills & Boon Book Club offers**
- **Books available before they're in the shops**

Accepting these FREE books and gift places you under no obligation to buy, you may cancel at any time, even after receiving your free books. Simply complete your details below and return the entire page to the address below. You don't even need a stamp!

YES Please send me 2 free Desire stories in a 2-in-1 volume and a surprise gift. I understand that unless you hear from me, I will receive 2 superb new 2-in-1 books every month for just £5.30 each, postage and packing free. I am under no obligation to purchase any books and may cancel my subscription at any time. The free books and gift will be mine to keep in any case.

Ms/Mrs/Miss/Mr _____ Initials _____

Surname _____

Address _____

_____

_____ Postcode _____

E-mail_____

Send this whole page to: Mills & Boon Book Club, Free Book Offer, FREEPOST NAT 10298, Richmond, TW9 1BR